DREAMING THE GOD

An Anthology

Edited by

Karen Dales

Dreaming the God

Dark Dragon Publishing
88 Charleswood Drive
Toronto, Ontario
M3H 1X6
CANADA
www.darkdragonpublishing.com

Printed in the United States of America.

An Anthology

Edited by

Karen Dales

Dark Dragon Publishing
Toronto, Ontario, Canada

Contents

Introduction

TWO YEARS AGO, DREAMING THE GODDDESS was published. When I was working on Dreaming The Goddess, I had planned on doing a companion anthology, which you are now holding: Dreaming The God.

It took a little longer than I expected to get this anthology out. That's what happens when life and responsibilities can get in the way. The other aspect as to why it took two years to publish Dreaming The God is that, despite the very clear expression of intent of this anthology being a representation of many different gods from around the world, I received many stories that were rooted in Christianity and Jesus. Though those stories were interesting, they did not fit with the paradigm that had been set up with Dreaming The Goddess, which was to showcase stories of non-Abrahamic masculine deities found throughout the world. Despite having to issue rejection emails to those who sent me Christian/Jesus/Abrahamic faith based stories, I did receive some exceptional stories, which you will find within the pages of this book.

I am also pleased to have several of our authors from

Dreaming The Goddess return to write stories for this anthology. Moira Scott has written a wonderful piece, steeped in legend and history; Stephen B. Pearl has given an introspective look into one's experience with moving from one life to the next; Ira Nayman's amazing humour in revealing the archetype of The Trickster; James Dick's exploration of two Slavic Gods and their relationship with one another; and of course, the brilliant Rosemary Edghill whose story was initially published in *Young Warriors: Stories of Strength* by Tamora Pierce and Josepha Sherman.

We are also happy to have seasoned authors bringing their stories to you; Glen Bresciani brings a new version Hades; Seth Augenstein's story will titillate you with an Indigenous inspired story; LA Selby lends her expertise and asks the question, *What does a God of War do when there is no more war?*; and Jeff Provine introduces a Maori God to those who would never have heard of Him.

We welcome new writers as well: Ross Carter mingles mythology, legend, history and dream to reveal the origins of a God many of heard of but do not truly know, and Ralph Mack whose story is about how a God truly manifests within a Priest.

Last, but not least, I have dusted off a short story that is part of my book series, *The Chosen Chronicles.*

I hope that this anthology opens your eyes and your imagination to the many different Gods found around the world, and if you're truly lucky, you'll have learned something new.

Karen Dales
Toronto, Ontario, Canada
Samhain 2023.

For all the Hidden Children of the God.

By Glenn Bresciani

"TRUST MOTHER EARTH, GAIA, TO have stretch marks of pure silver," said Melina, hurrying along the cave tunnel, glittering veins in the rock above her head reflecting the light from her flaming torch.

Melina stopped in front of a bronze door, studded with rubies, and sighed. The bedchamber of the maiden whom she served stood on the other side. How unfair. She had been a maid servant when she lived, and now she must do it all again while dead.

She raised a fist to announce herself with a knock, but instead pressed an index finger against her cheek. Why, look at that. The door was ajar, allowing Melina to sneak a quick peek into the chamber. The maiden on the other side of the door need never know that she was being observed.

Melina spied with her little eye, something beginning with "S." As in seeds. A clay bowl full of seeds to be precise. The maiden sat cross-legged on her plush bed, scooped a handful of seeds from the bowl, and raised them to her full lips.

Melina held her breath. Was the maiden going to eat them?

No. Stranger than that. She whispered to them. Whether it was words of encouragement or words of warning, Melina would never know.

The maiden flung seeds at the rock wall above her night stand. The wall absorbed the seeds, that would begin their ascent to the world of the living. Once they had transcended solid rock and entered the realm of damp, worm-nourished soil, the seeds would crack and seedlings would sprout. Caressed by rain, wind, and sunshine, the seedlings would flourish and Narcissus flowers would bloom.

With a gasp, Melina backed away from the door. How dare she spy upon this maiden. The poor dear was the only living resident in the Underworld, and an unwilling one at that. Melina adjusted her cloth girdle, finding comfort in her fidgeting. At last, she knocked on the door.

"Go away," shouted the maiden.

Melina entered the bedchamber anyway, stood in front of the bed with a scene of dryads dancing in a forest carved into a wooden ornamental headboard. The violet linen sheets were disheveled, the messy folds having followed the movements of the maiden as she lounged on the bed. Rosemary scented candles conjured memories of evenings spent in her herb garden when she had been alive.

The maiden swept her dark wavy hair away from her heart shaped face, tucking it behind her ear. The daughter of a goddess, which would explain why she was so stunning, an orchid among daffodils. No doubt, the men would have been buzzing around her in the living world, eager to dip themselves into her pollen.

"My Lady," said Melina, giving a lackluster curtsey. "Hades has requested your presence in his throne room."

At the mention of Hades, the young maiden flinched. "Why, I would be delighted," she said with a sneer.

Melina nodded, and wondered when this exquisite beauty, with the odd name of Persephone, would attempt to escape from the god who held her prisoner in his palace.

*

The purpose of the blockish, polished obsidian throne was to diminish the confidence of all who looked upon it. The throne would have done just that had Alexis, the courtier, been looking at Hades who sat upon it. Instead, Alexis gaped at the right side of Hades where Persephone sat on a slender throne carved from a block of rose quartz.

Hades spun his two-pronged bident in his hand as he gazed at Persephone, his smile a crescent moon in the darkness of his shaggy black beard. "She is a beauty."

The himation, that Alexis wore over his knee length chiton and draped over one shoulder, fanned out around him as he dropped to one knee. "I apologize, my Lord. I didn't mean to stare."

Hades dismissed his courtier's apology with a half-hearted wave of his hand. "I understand Alexis. I am as dazzled as you are."

Persephone sniffled. She stared, with swollen eyes, into the orange glow from hundreds of candle flames that lined the throne room and circled the base of each column. When she blinked, a tear rolled down her soft cheek.

Alexis gasped. A real tear! Down here among the dead. He had not seen a tear since—well, since he was alive.

Reaching out to the throne next to him, the Lord of the Underworld grasped Persephone's delicate fingers in his own. "You see, my dear? Everyone is enchanted by your beauty. You are as radiant as the morning light glinting off the icicles that hang from a frozen corpse."

Gagging, Persephone snatched her hand away from Hades' touch.

Alexis sighed. "Actually, my Lord, I was reminded of the flowers in the Elysian Fields whose petals of gold blaze when they catch the rays of the setting sun."

Hades sniffed; his face expressionless. "Your metaphor makes no sense to me."

Persephone's wavy long hair swished over her shoulder as she turned to face Hades. "You will regret bringing me here against my will."

"Forget your mother," shouted Hades, pounding his fist on the armrest of his throne. "She would never have agreed to our wedding. That's why she doesn't know you're here."

"I wasn't referring to my mother," Persephone said with pouting ruby lips, crossing her arms over an ample bosom.

"What news concerning my kingdom, Alexis?" Hades struck the end of his bident against the floor. The loud thud made his announcement feel more official.

Alexis coughed to clear his throat. "These past few days, no new souls have increased the population of your kingdom, my lord."

Raising her feet and clasping her shins, Persephone pressed her face against her knees to hide her smirk.

"Impossible," Hades' grip on his bident tightened. "Every day that goes by, a mortal will die."

Swallowing, Alexis considered his words carefully. "I can assure you my lord, death is still an everyday occurrence up above. The dead are still arriving. They're just refusing to cross the River Styx."

"They know the rules. Where are their coins?"

"Coins aren't the issue, my lord. They refuse to enter,"

Hades rose from his throne and stood with his legs apart to make room for his angry posture. Twice, he struck the floor with his bident. "Bring me my Helmet of Invisibility."

The sound of bare feet slapping against the stone floor could be heard before the servant could be seen running towards the blockish throne. The servant dropped to his knees, lowered his head, and raised his arms to offer the helmet to his master. A pair of goat horns curved upwards from the crown of the helmet.

The Lord of the Underworld tucked his helmet in the crook of his arm, and bowed to Persephone, the edge of his black cloak swept the stone floor. "I shan't be long, my beloved."

Many tiny flames were extinguished as Hades strode between the rows of columns. The death of each flame cut a dark path through the candle glow, the darkness following Hades to the throne room entrance.

*

No living could enter; no dead could leave. That was the rule. No mortal, dead or alive, would dare break this rule, for fear of being devoured by the three heads of Cerberus. Only immortals were an exception to this rule.

Cerberus sat under the portico that sheltered the only entrance to Hades' domain. His multiple ears swiveled as he simultaneously looked left, straight up, and at the opposite bank of the River Styx.

A halo of polished gems, circling the symbol of a cypress tree, decorated the double doors that silently swung inwards.

Cerberus spun around, jaws snapping, saliva spraying. His triple bark shook the columns supporting the roof of the portico.

"It's only me, Spot," said Hades, striding through the doorway, his black cloak billowing.

At the sight of his master, Cerberus switched from ferocious guard dog to jolly playful pet, his heads jostling one another to be the first to lick the god.

Hades donned his horned helmet, adjusting the straps until they were tight under his chin.

Cerberus wagged his tail; his tongues flopped out of panting mouths. When his master wore his helmet was when the fun began, when Cerberus could show off his finest hallmark—his noses. With a sniff here, and a sniff there, Cerberus nostrils flared until he locked onto his master's scent, following him down the stairs that ended in the River Styx.

Hades stepped onto the river, walking on water as if it were land. Further up river, the black water flowed between massive stalagmites, silhouetted by the reddish glow from a lava flow somewhere in the distance.

A fog, tumbling over the water, was the only movement. Everything else was as still and silent as a corpse on a table awaiting an autopsy. Even the skiff in the middle of the river was motionless.

Hades strode towards the skiff, eyes narrowed. Ever since the first mortal souls had arrived in the Underworld, that vessel had always ferried them across the river to their new home.

Standing over the skiff, Hades scowled at Charon, who lay on his back, legs dangling over the gunwale. A long wooden pole rested on his narrow torso. The cloak that hung over his left shoulder was as greasy as his uncombed grey beard and hair.

Bastard! Miscreant! Hades' fingers yanked the straps of his helmet through the brass clasp. Slamming Charon with the full blast of his fury required him to be visible, thus the helmet had to go.

Plop. Ripples circled the spot were something had disturbed the water. Hades spun around; his head still encased in his helmet. What was that? It couldn't be a fish. Animals have no soul. He glanced over the water.

Plop. A tiny splash followed by more ripples. Something had dropped into the water. Gazing upon the river bank, Hades clenched his teeth. Dozens of the dead had congregated along the water's edge. Some of them were shouting at one another. A woman shoved an elderly man into the water. A boy threw something tiny and sparkling into the river.

A coin flipped head over tails through the air, and struck the water.

"What the—" was all Hades had to say about the situation before his mind collided into a solid wall of disbelief.

Charon sat up, pulled his tattered cloak over his shoulder, strands of his long wispy beard and hair swayed as he looked in every direction. "You there boss?"

Hades didn't answer. Hades was gone. He marched towards the river bank where the dead had gathered. Another coin struck the water. The god of the Underworld stepped over the circling ripples.

"Don't do it," shouted a pot-bellied man.

Another man nodded in agreement. "Don't pay the ferry man."

"Don't even fix a price," said an old lady, spitting a coin out of her mouth and throwing it away.

Hades stood so close to the dead that he could have reached out and poked them with his bident. The dead would never see him, there was nothing to see while he wore his helmet.

"There's nothing here," an exasperated woman shouted, her coin imprisoned inside her clenched fist. "We have to keep moving. We should be crossing that river."

A skinny man pointed at Hades' palace on the opposite side

of the Styx. "I'd rather stay here than burn for eternity over there."

Burn? Hades glanced over his shoulder, expecting to see his palace on fire. A few windows glowed orange from candle light from within, that was about it.

"The eternal lake of fire. It's all the priestess in my village ever talks about," said a woman with missing fingers.

A scruffy man beside her scoffed. "The priestess from my village wouldn't shut up about it."

A Spartan, no doubt killed in battle, puffed out his chest. "I ain't burning forever. No way. Not even the gods could make me cross that river."

Hades could have easily grabbed the Spartan and hurled him across the river. Instead, his brow wrinkled while he wondered where one would find an eternal supply of fuel for an eternity of fire. Not even the Titans could have achieved that, and they were the creators of the universe.

"Whagh," wailed a new born baby, cradled in their mother's arm. "I don't want to burn for eternity. Whagh. I don't want to burn at all. What's the point of living if our death is punishment? I never asked to be born."

"There, there. Hush dear," said the mother, kissing her baby's forehead. "The gods are cruel."

What psycho-sicko would burn souls forever as if they were chopped wood in a stove? Hades would never do that. He prided himself in giving humanity hope, life after death, here in his domain. It was more than Zeus could ever achieve.

What was going on up there under the Mycenean sun? Who was feeding humanity such a scandalous lie? Hades must know. His reputation, as an afterlife service provider, depended on it.

Hades snapped his fingers. He didn't have long to wait, thirty-nine seconds to be precise. The splashing of hooves striking water announced the arrival of his two black mares pulling his chariot. The chariot rolled across the river as if it were ice.

All the dead gasped in unison at the approaching chariot. Had Hades come to personally apologize for the delays? Many waved their arms and shouted, then froze when they realized that the chariot was empty.

Hades lips were tightly pressed, air blasting out of his nostrils while he glowered at his palace. Right about now, Persephone would be having her bath, dried herbs and petals floating in the steaming water. Her shoulders and arms, resting on the rim of the bath, as smooth and fair as bleached bones baking in the hot sun.

He growled, dreading this bullshit mission he'd been forced to undertake. His beloved Persephone would suffer heartache and loneliness while he was gone, and much worse should Zeus discover her whereabouts and claim her for his own. Should that happen, there was nothing Hades could do about it as he will be on the wrong side of a barrier that separated the living from the dead.

Jumping into his chariot, Hades clawed the air with one hand as he raged. "Bastard! Dead flesh burrowing maggot! Whoever started this rumor of my realm being a lake of fire, I will find you, and I will hurl you into Hephaestus' furnace to watch you burn."

Hearing Hades' voice, the dead shouted in unison. The meek begged for mercy, while the assholes demanded to speak to Hades' manager. When no god could be seen, the shouting diminished into grunts of bewilderment.

Sensing their master's foul mood, the mares launched into a gallop, the rumbling wheels of the chariot spraying a wall of mist into the air behind Hades.

The mares charged into the space above the river at an angle similar to the slope of a hill. They galloped towards the cavern ceiling that dripped with stalactites, sharper than the fangs of the Lernean Hydra.

Teeth clamped on the bronze bits, the mares converted their will power to horse power. A collision with the roof of the cavern would commence in five blinks of an eye. They needn't have worried. They were in good hands. After all, it was a god who steered the chariot.

Hades waved his bident in a wide arc. Stalactites shuddered and snapped, rock rumbled and broke apart. Bright sunlight burst through a yawning cavity and pierced the dark depths of the River Styx. The two mares and the chariot leapt through the rift that shrunk, rock grinding against rock, once they had passed. The intruding light vanquished; darkness prevailed.

*

"Huh, that's odd," said the woodcutter, removing his straw hat and wiping sweat off his brow. He watched two black mares pull a driverless chariot along the dusty road. Beside the woodcutter, his mule raised its head to sniff at the chariot. There was no fooling the mule. It may be unable to see the driver, but it sure could smell them. Whoever they were, they smelled like licorice.

The mule snorted to rid the offensive sweet stench from its nostrils.

With his bident in one hand and reins in the other, Hades surveyed his surroundings. Behind him, the rattling chariot wheels had churned up dust clouds.

To the left of Hades, dead grass clung to the hills, a paler shade of scorched yellow. Up and up the hills climbed, ending where the mountains began. To the right of Hades, the cool turquoise of the Mediterranean Sea mocked the dry, thirsty land and islands that hadn't seen a drop of rain since—well, since Persephone had arrived in the Underworld.

Above it all, the sun burnt a white hole in the cloudless sky, rays so intense that they bleached the blue out of the Big Blue.

Hades whistled, impressed by the severity of the drought that plagued the land of the living. No doubt, the goddess Demeter had postponed her divine duties so she could focus on her search for her missing daughter.

In the distance, an unnatural row of olive trees contradicted the natural landscape. Hades slowed his chariot, examined the trees to confirm what he suspected. Sure enough, beyond the olive trees were the thatched rooftops of a dozen huts.

Hades nodded. Good. Where there was a village, there were mortals. Tugging on the reins, he signaled the mares to stop. They and the chariot did just that, with dust clouds sailing by.

Stepping out of the chariot, Hades gave each mare a rub on the nose. "I shan't be long."

Dead grass crackled under his feet as he marched towards the village. Only a few leaves clung to the skeletal branches of the surrounding shrubs. He stepped over a dead rabbit, its thin dehydrated skin stretched tight over its ribs. Flies buzzed in and out of the gaps in its skull.

Ten yards out from the border of the village, three maidens strolled through a patch of white Narcissus flowers. Shawls, draped over their heads and shoulders, shielded them from the rays of the sweltering sun. They each plucked a Narcissus from the dry soil, adding it to the bundles of flowers cradled in their arms. Each Narcissus was plump with moisture and vigor. At the center of their star shaped petals was a yellow crown of pollen.

"We've got enough flowers here for two funerals," said one of the maidens. "Why are we still picking more?"

"Nonsense," said another maiden. "Zorba deserves to have all the flowers we can carry placed on his grave."

With his bearded chin raised high, Hades spread his legs, thrust his pelvis in the direction of the Narcissus. What a fine specimen it was. Hades' finest creation yet. The Narcissus was his gift to the living so they could adorn their dead the same way a chef used parsley to decorate a meat dish. It began as a seed in the darkness of the Underworld, burrowing through rock until it reached the living world to bloom in the soil and sunlight.

"Why couldn't dead be dead? Why do we have to have an afterlife?" said a maiden, her tunic pulled tight around her crouching body. She uprooted a flower, stalk and all.

Hades' pride deflated. The maidens' statement struck him like a Spartan shield in the crotch.

The shortest maiden with the widest hips nodded in agreement. "I wish Zorba was forever dead."

"Me too," said a thin willowy maiden, her face hidden in shadow by her shawl. "I'd rather be forever dead than have my soul burn forever."

Hades' jaw clenched, teeth grinding as he scowled at the maidens. *Death being reviled? It's outrageous. Death is beautiful. I made it so. That is why Persephone chose me over all the other gods. Not even Zeus could have accomplished what I have achieved: the continuation of life after death in my underground kingdom.*

"No one should have to burn for eternity," said the one

with wide hips, peeling a strand of sweat soaked hair from her face. "The gods are cruel."

Willowy maiden shook her shawl covered head. "No, not the gods. The Devil. He rules the Underworld now."

"Devil?" blurted Hades, stumbling backwards, unbalanced by his shock.

The maidens spun around, glanced every which way to see who had spoken.

"W-was that the Devil?" the youngest maiden said between rapid breaths. "Can it hear us?"

"Better not mention its name again," said willowy maiden, clutching the bundle of Narcissus close to her body. "Just in case."

The maidens hurried back to their village. They didn't even stop to pick up the flowers that had fallen out of their bundles.

Devil? Who was this Devil? What beast would spread lies about the Afterlife? What monstrosity would terrify mortals by spreading rumors about dead souls burning in a lake of fire?

For the sake of humanity, for the sake of Persephone, sitting all alone somewhere in his palace, Hades hoped that by attending this funeral, all his questions would be answered.

*

The funeral procession had already begun by the time Hades had arrived at the wooden boundary fence of the village. Men, women and children walked single file, their frowns so severe, the creases of their brows could have clasped a coin. They shuffled along a path that ended at a lone cypress tree on a small hill.

Leading the procession, the village priestess marched barefoot, the hem of her black chiton tunic sweeping her ankles. Not even the pebbles, stabbing the soles of her feet, could bring her out of her trance. Her narrow nose and sunken cheeks were as sharp as the blade of her dagger stashed into the rope belt tied around her thin waist.

A shaggy goat on a leash trotted beside the priestess. The gaudy garlands and ribbons, draped over its back and horns, were loud enough to be seen from as far away as the top of

Mount Olympus. But isn't that the whole point of a sacrificial goat?

Behind the priestess and the goat, a donkey, its knees trembling, pulled a creaky cart, the beast's long ears flat against its neck. The poor donkey's fatigue was as plain to see as its exposed ribs. Zorba, the deceased, wrapped head to toe in linen, rode in the back of the cart.

Still invisible, Hades added himself to the end of the procession. He removed his horned helmet, ran his fingers through his short dark hair turning it long and grey. His bushy beard shriveled until all that remained were a few grey curls on his wrinkled chin. The horns on his helmet shrunk while the helmet itself converted into a clay pot. The bident was the last to be transmuted, becoming a humble wooden staff held by feminine fingers with joints disfigured by arthritis. If any of the villagers, at the rear of the procession, glanced over their shoulder, they would have spot, not a god, but an old woman, her back hunched, with a grin all gum and no teeth.

The priestess called a halt to the procession at the bottom of the hill. Beating a tambourine with the palm of her hand, she made a ritual out of instructing four young men to remove Zorba from the cart. The men hefted the corpse onto their shoulders and carried it up the slope of the hill. Two musicians swayed as they played double-flutes, a haunting melody that complemented the moans and sniffles from the weeping villagers.

On top of the hill, the crowd gathered in front of the cypress tree. Hades remained at the rear, leaning forward, old woman eyes gleaming with anticipation. His grip tightened on his wooden staff, his arthritis bloated joints resembling a miniscule mountain range. The funeral rites were about to begin. Talk about this Devil should reveal its identity—whoever it may be.

The priestess hitched up her tunic so she could kneel on the ground facing the tree. Lying prone in the dirt, she spread her arms wide. "I call upon thee, O great Devil, Lord of the world beneath our feet. He who gathers dead souls like sheep, to roast for eternity in a lake of fire."

All the villagers recoiled at the thought of burning alive,

while the goat pulled a garland off its back with its teeth, nibbled a chain of flowers one by one until there were none.

Nothing cries out grief more than a shaved head, and Zorba's wife had her scalp as smooth as a river stone. She separated herself from the crowd, carrying a statue of Hades that she placed into an alcove cut into the trunk of the Cypress tree.

Hades looked at the statue of himself and his eyes bulged, the loose skin, hanging off his jowls, wobbled when his mouth opened wide then snapped shut. The head of the alabaster statue had been lopped off and replaced by a goat head with curved horns.

I-I don't have horns, thought Hades, pouting. The horns on his helmet made him look intimidating, or so he believed. But now he wondered if they just made him look silly.

The god's breathing quickened, the longer he gazed at the statue. Its skin had been painted red, the same shade of red as Aphrodite's love heart symbol: The color of passion. Pinned to the rear end of this goat headed horror was a red ribbon for a tail. More stone had been carved to replace the statue's feet with hooves.

But the most offensive alteration to this statue, the one that really got his goat—as the mortals would say—was his bident replaced by a pitchfork. A pitchfork! Not even Demeter, every farmer's go-to-goddess when the crops failed, had such a lowly tool for a symbol.

"Great," shouted Hades. "Just great. I'm the Devil."

"Quiet old woman," said a thin man, his scowl as tight as his fists. "You should know better."

A burly man, with burn scars on his beefy forearms, spun around to showcase his snarl. "If you don't both shut up," he stabbed a finger at the thin man's chest. "I'll punch your lights out."

"Me?" blurted the thin man in a squeaky voice. He pointed at Hades. "She started it."

Burly man laughed once. "Well, I'm not gonna hit an old woman now, am I?"

A wife, next to Hades, leaned closer to her husband. "Oh, I didn't catch what the priestess said," she glowered at Hades, "too many rude people are talking when they should be listening."

The priestess raised a bronze chalice, thrust it at arm's-length to the East, then to the West. Tilting the chalice, she poured wine onto the ground.

The wife's husband provided an explanation, his arms folded across his chest as he spoke."The priestess just prayed to all the gods on Olympus, asking them to hide Zorba's soul so the Devil can't punish him in the Afterlife."

The wife clucked, nodded her approval."Oh, that's nice."

"Right. That's it," shouted Hades, pointing a crooked finger at the statue behind the priestess. The statue toppled out of the alcove, struck a tree root and shattered. Broken pieces skipped across the ground, and disappeared into the freshly dug grave.

The priestess froze, mid-sacrifice, with one hand raising the goat's head by its horn, the other clutching a knife over the beast's exposed throat, ready to slice. Instead, she pushed the animal aside, glowering at the villagers."Who did that? Who threw that rock?"

Those closest to Hades backed away, puffs of dirt swirling around their shuffling feet.

"She did it," shouted the villagers in unison. They raised their arms, placing Hades at the center of a ring of pointing fingers.

The priestess bared her teeth before she raged. "How dare you disrespect a sacred ritual? The gods will be offended. I should call upon Zeus to strike you down with a lightning bolt."

Everyone backed further away from Hades at the mention of lightening.

"Zeus," said Hades with a chortle. "I'd like to see my brother try that."

Blinking, the priestess gawked. "Huh?"

"You had one job," said Hades, raising a finger. "One job. To give these people hope by preaching to them that their lives would continue after death in Elysium—"

"Elysium doesn't exist," snapped the priestess. "It's a lie. A trick."

Hades threw his head back and groaned. "Why would I lie about something as important as Elysium?"

"You?"

"Eh? I mean Hades."

"You mean the Devil?"

"No." Hades straightened his back so his old woman disguise stood as erect as a warrior facing off against their enemy. "There is no Devil. Shut-up about the Devil."

Having returned from their flower hunt, the three maidens took one look at the hostility between the priestess and the old crone and squealed, dropping their bundle of Narcissus that they trampled in their haste to hide behind the tree.

Hades raised his hand to indicate he had had enough. "Hades. Devil. It doesn't matter. It's all the same to you, isn't it? No doubt, your head is full of bullshit. Tell me, why would the Lord of the Underworld lie about Elysium?"

"Think about it, old crone," said the priestess, raising her chin. "Would you give a coin to Charon to cross the River Styx if you knew you would burn forever in a lake of fire?"

Hades bashed the tip of his staff against the ground. "There is no lake of fire!"

"There is no Elysium!" shouted the priestess, waving her dagger at Hades. "The Devil told us so. He speaks the truth. Hades was the one who lied to us."

Hades took a few steps towards the priestess; the crowd took several steps away from the old crone, almost tripping over one another in their haste. A faint noise bounced off Hades' eardrums. Why, it sounded like—

He glanced over the villagers, glanced at the tree branches above their heads. "Someone is whispering. Who is that?"

His shuffling feet kicked up dust, villagers in a panic to clear a path for him, which proved difficult as he changed direction every few steps in his search for the whisperer.

The priestess rubbed the back of her head. "You can hear it?"

"Of course, I can. I have ears, haven't I? Why wouldn't I be able to hear it?"

The villagers gasped, horrified by this impudent old crone. Some of them looked to the sky for an incoming lightning strike.

Eyes narrowing to slits, the priestess glared at the god.

"Who are you?"

"There it is again," said Hades, staring at Zorba, the deceased, beside the freshly dug grave. "The whisper is coming from there."

The closer Hades was to the linen wrapped corpse, the clearer the whispering, making it possible to distinguish a few words.

"…The Devil…punished souls…sacred pomegranate…"

Hades' old woman disguise frowned, giving him more wrinkles than a bed sheet after a restless sleep. "Is that…that's Zeus, isn't it?"

The villagers chattered among themselves. What whispering were the crone and priestess talking about? No one else could hear it.

"Why would it be Zeus?" The priestess glared at Hades as if he were a child asking childish questions. "He's the sky father. He rules over everything. He's a very busy god."

"Busy," Hades snorted. "Yeah, busy soaring through the sky, looking for his next young beauty to ravish—"Air burst out of his lungs in one long gasp. He pressed his palms to the side of his head, as if holding his skull together. "Oh, fuck no!"

The villagers whimpered. Some of them wet themselves. The priestess squeezed her eyes shut.

By the time Hades transitioned himself from the world of the living to the Underworld, Zeus would have already stormed Hades' palace, had his way with Persephone and still have time to celebrate with a jug of wine. Had this been Zeus' plan all along?

"Bastard!" Hades roared, doubled over, waving his fists. The mere thought of Zeus touching his beloved made him want to rush to Mount Olympus, rip Zeus throne from its foundation, find the horny lightning god, and crack his head open with his own throne. How dare Zeus ruin Hades' reputation, make a mockery out of the Afterlife. And for what? So, Zeus could taste the nectar of Persephone's rose?

His body quivering, teeth grinding, too infuriated to focus on what he was doing, Hades stumbled closer to the corpse decorated in white Narcissus. The whispering voice was clearer. He could hear every word being whispered.

"The pomegranate is sacred," said the whispering voice, "It is the holiest of holy symbols. In the beginning, before the light, before life, before the gods, there was only the pomegranate and it was good. For from this fruit's seed sprouted the universe and everything in it."

"Huh?" blurted Hades, his red-faced anger replaced by a goofy expression. The holy pomegranate? A yummy fruit every Athenian enjoyed for dessert? What nonsense was this? Not even Zeus would come up with something so childish and stupid. But if not Zeus, then who? Hades leaned closer to a Narcissus, the petals brushing his cheek. Oh wow, it was like someone whispered into his ear. He could feel their breath. Spooky.

"Burn, you will forever burn," whispered the voice, a female voice. Definitely not Zeus. "Suffer never ending pain, and yet such a punishment is too lenient for such a blasphemous sin as choosing to eat the holiest of holy fruit. How dare you treat the sacred pomegranate with such contempt? You will burn in eternal flames for your sin. Thus I, the Devil, has spoken."

Hades looked up at the priestess. "Is your Devil a woman?"

The priestess swallowed, her body tense, ready to flee. "You're not mortal."

Hades froze, eyes wide, mouth shrunken from lips clamped together tighter than his anus. He recognized the voice. The same voice that spoke to him in the dining room while eating breakfast, even though she refused to eat. The same female voice from the beauty who sat upon her throne next to his.

Betrayed, jilted, and made a fool. These emotions in a god contain more energy than a splitting atom. All the bodily fluids inside Hades old woman disguise reached boiling point, the veins in his neck straining against his paper-thin, wrinkled skin. Steam blasted out of his ears, shocking the villagers on either side of him.

Too angry to concentrate on his human form, Hades slipped back into his true form. He was divine energy, fierce and radiant as a star—no! A galaxy of stars.

The priestess, the villagers, the cypress tree, heck, even the sacrificial goat were all incinerated. One heartbeat, they were all attending Zorba's funeral, the next heartbeat, they had no heart, their naked souls stood on the crowded shores of the River Styx.

Recognizing his friends and family, Zorba jostled through the crowd to reach the new arrivals.

"Don't pay the ferry man," he shouted at the disorientated villagers.

*

Melina hurried along the cave tunnel, the light from her torch reflected off the silver veins that streaked the ceiling. She stopped at a bronze door studded with rubies. Persephone's bedchamber on the other side. Melina huffed, blew a strand of hair off her face. How unfair. She had been a maid servant when she lived and now, she must do it all again while dead.

Melina raised a fist to knock upon the door.

"Move," shouted Hades, grabbing Melina by the back of her chiton, yanking her away from the door. With a scream, Melina slammed into the wall on the opposite side of the corridor.

Raising his foot, Hades kicked the door off its hinges. The bronze panel struck the rock floor with a thunderous clang.

Persephone sat on her bed; the clay bowl filled with seeds beside her. She held a handful of seeds close enough to her lips that she could breathe on them or whisper.

"About time," she said after a long sigh, gazing with contempt at the wreckage that had been her door.

"You!" shouted Hades, yanking off his helmet, making himself visible. He threw the metal thing at the floor, snapping off a horn. "Feeling proud of yourself, I suppose? Hmm? Convincing everyone to fear my domain. You must be chuffed to have achieved all that."

Sliding off her bed, Persephone lowered her head to gaze at her feet. "I don't blame you for wanting to banish me from your realm. I went too far with my mischief, besmirched your reputation and your honor."

"Besmirched?" Hades turned his head sideways to loosen the knotted muscles in his neck. "You haven't besmirched my reputation. You've obliterated it. Not even a puff of smoke remains. I provided comfort and solace in death for all mortals, and your 'mischief' has stripped all that away."

Persephone clasped her hands tightly together, faked the trembling of her knees. "I go willingly to my banishment. I won't even waste time gathering my belongings."

Hades paced the chamber, and shattered a chair with one strike of his bident. "Devil? Why did you compare me to a Devil? What exactly is a Devil? Hmm?"

Persephone shrugged. "I don't know. It's all I could think of that rhymed with peril. You're going to banish me, right? You look angry enough to banish me."

"Peril? Peril? You think of me as a peril?" Hades snatched up a vase, hurled it at the wall to explode.

Persephone rolled her eyes. "You're not even listening."

His shoulders quivering, Hades grabbed the bedpost that was part of the frame supporting the bed curtains. He turned his back so Persephone couldn't see him sobbing, only hear him.

"Are…are you crying?"

The god sat his rear end onto the bed, a miniature River Styx of tears flowing down his cheeks. "You hurt me. Why would you do that?"

Scowling, Persephone waved a finger at Hades. "No. no. no. You don't get to make this about you. I was abducted. I was forced to live among the dead. I'm the one who should be crying."

Hades howled, slid off the bed onto the floor. "I—I love you."

"You kidnapped me!" Persephone shouted at Hades.

Tears versus mucus. It was a competition between Hade's eyes and nose to see which one could produce the most fluid. "Why? Why did you betray me? I would've made you a queen."

Persephone folded her arms, glared at the god on the floor. "Are you going to banish me or not?"

Hades, pointed a finger at Persephone. "You're the Devil. The living should be knocking the head off your statue and replace it with a goat's head." His leg jerked, kicking over the night stand. All that wailing, and sobbing, and spluttering. To see it, one would be forgiven for mistaking the God of the Dead for the God of Grief. "This never happens to Zeus! Why does it have to happen to me? Why?"

"Fine then. I'll banish myself."Persephone marched out of her bedchamber.

Hades lay on his back on the bed, his ugly crying more dramatic than the sobs of a princess abandoned on her wedding day. His breathing was jagged and too rapid to be of any use.

Persephone returned to the bedchamber, lifting the hem of her chiton so she could step over the warped and dented bronze door lying on the floor.

At the sight of his beloved, Hades inhaled noisily, an exhale of air blasting out of his gaping mouth. He sat up, arms out stretched, fingers wriggling as he reached out for the exquisite goddess. "I knew you'd come back. I knew it. Like a vulture circling a dying antelope, we were meant to be."

Persephone grabbed Hades' helmet by one horn, lifted it off the floor, "I'll be needing this," she said, raising it above her head.

"No," whimpered Hades, shaking his head in disbelief. "No."

Persephone donned the helmet and vanished. The sound of her bare feet slapping against the floor could be heard outside the bedchamber as she made a run for freedom.

Glenn works as a support worker in community aged care. Fantasy and Sci-Fi are his favourite genres that he enjoys reading and wants to write about. Glenn could spend hours reading about mythology, and would like to see ancient Persia become as common as medieval Europe in fantasy novels. Glenn wishes that the process of writing a short story was the same as eating a bowl of ice cream—every spoonful is a pleasant experience, and it's all over in about five minutes. His writing has appeared in Valor anthology by Dragon Soul Press and The Best of Metastellar Year One. Glenn is on the lookout for a breed of cat that doesn't take cat naps on paper.

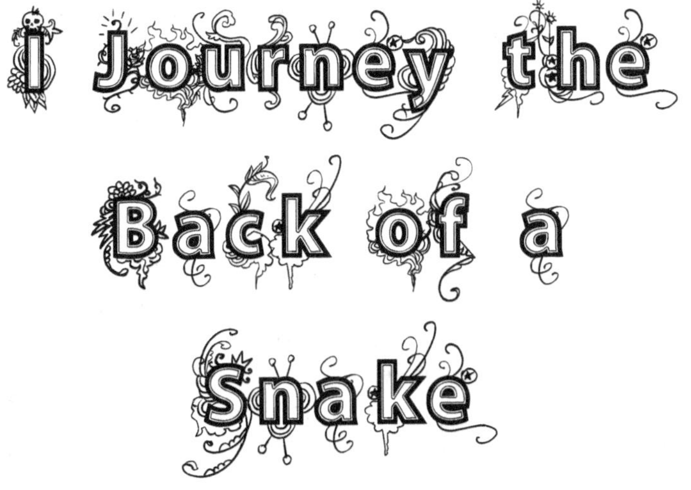

By Stephen B Pearl

I COME TO A STONY DESERT circled by mountains, grown apart from the green land I knew, but in the shape of its memory. I round a corner, and the view revealed reminds me of a day I passed fifty-two years ago in my grandfather's orchard. Soon I will be with the old man, my father and my family. The smell of the garden already beguiles me.

But no, there is only a crumbling stone wall dividing the man from the boy he was. The dirt road behind me changes, twisting and winding like the back of a snake under a night without stars. Hills rise, blocking my vision forward and back. I am frozen in time, frightened to move, helpless and afraid.

"All roads lead someplace. If you undertake the journey. None see ahead, and behind is dead and frozen."

The soothing, baritone voice comes from the air. If I look

towards it, there is a deeper shadow against the shadows surrounding me.

I step forward. A stone gate appears before me. One support pillar is in the shape of a crocodile, the other a stalk of wheat, and the lintel is carved as a serpent.

"Let me pass, let me pass, let the memory of an old man pass." I speak the words and step forward.

It is a sunny day. I watch the Nile like the falcon-eyed Ra himself. A large reed barge pulls up to the dock. A familiar man steps ashore. I run to him. It has been so long. His shenti-kilt is torn and dusty, and he looks thinner than I remember.

"Father!" I cry out.

He smiles at me, wrinkles forming at the corners of his eyes. "Son."

"So much has happened. I must tell you it all."

Father raises his hand and speaks with command. "Later. I wish to inspect the fields. The flood has been and gone. We must seed them immediately."

Pain courses through me. Months away, and all my father can think of is the crops. I matter less than wheat. Resentment grows.

"Come," the shadow beside me speaks. It seems more solid now, vaguely man-shaped.

*

It is thirty years later. Every muscle aches from the effort of moving stone. Being free of Pharaoh's tithing of the third means that there will be enough food for my family this year. The survival of the family is up to me. It all rests on me. My daughter runs to me as I step off the barge, my cloth carry bag over my shoulder. She has gotten so big. They change so much around seven summers. The twinge in my back warns me not to pick her up as I once would have.

"Father, you're home. So much has happened. I must tell you everything."

The little girl sounds so fresh, so young. She doesn't worry about what will happen if the crops fail.

I kneel and hug her, but I don't pick her up when she

reaches for me. "You're too big for me to do that now, my little love."

I scan the fields around me. The soil is already drying under Ra's gaze.

"I have to plant the grain before the soil is baked hard. Tell your mother I will be home when Ra enters the duat. Take my bag." I push the bag with my only change of clothes and some meagre things I picked up as I served Pharaoh into my daughter's hands and walk off to see that she will have enough to eat come harvest.

The memories share space in my heart, tearing at me in different ways. I had been so angry with my father, but, as a man, what else could he have done? I'd hated not giving my daughter those minutes, but, as a man, what else could I have done? I let go of resentment and guilt.

The shadow beside me becomes more distinct. It is shaped like a man, but not quite.

*

I step forward. Another stone gate appears. Two carved armed men form the pillars, and a lion is carved on the lintel. I step through.

My father lies on his sleeping mat. His joints are gnarled, and most of his teeth are missing. My wife scowls as she spoons gruel into the withered mouth.

I am back from working the fields, exhausted, but there is no time for me. Father has taken it. I can remember when he was strong. When he would work the shaduf to irrigate the ground. That man is gone. I don't see the father I knew, and I am forgetting the memory of him as he was against the onslaught of the demanding, complaining, wizened shell that lays on my floor. I do not want to feel this way, but it is hard not to. I fear I will forget the man who carried me in my youth.

"See," speaks the shadowy form beside me.

I look closer. It isn't my father. It is me on the mat. The woman is not my wife but my daughter. I remember how the pain in my joints made me quarrelsome, how not seeing clearly, I tried to hold all things as I remembered them. I was the old man my father had been. Still, even as I had done my duty to my father, my daughter did her duty to me.

I lay on the mat and look at the face of my daughter. I reach up and touch her cheek. "Thank you, I have always loved you and always will, my little one."

The words are small reward, but they are spoken. I can only hope she hears them.

"The wheel turns for all mortal kind," observes the shadowy form that now resembles a man with a black cloud for a head. He is holding a Was sceptre in one hand.

*

I step up to a third gate. Two jackal-headed forms, carved as dancers, form the pillars. A serpent entwining a stalk of corn forms the lintel.

I am young once more. I step through and hear the inner thoughts I fear. I see myself with my neighbour's wife, our arms entwined as they never were, but at times as I wanted it to be. I walk away from my family and farm, leaving them to starve as I'd been tempted to do. The shadow of a thousand temptations denied reminds me that I was never a perfect man. I see myself slitting my neighbour's throat so I can take his land.

"It is a lie. I never did!" I scream.

"You thought," the shadow form beside me responds.

"But I didn't!" There is heat in my voice.

"It is a start."

The shadow's face grows clear. My companion wears the head of a jackal. Lord Anubis walks with me along the back of a snake.

"Come." Anubis gestures ahead. Another gate appears.

*

One pillar is a man with a lion's head. The other is a lion with a man's head and a golden Hawk sores above on the lintel.

I step forward and hear a sound as if someone were beating a giant drum. A moment passes. I realise it is the sound of my own heart. It drifts in front of me a thing of gold with scars of black and red running across it.

"In perfect love, you were cast on Khnum's wheel. Your heart was purest gold. What have you made of this gift?" demands Anubis.

I look at the shining heart. The blemishes of hate, envy, and cruelty. Not consequences of a harsh world but seeds sown and carefully nurtured by my choice and will.

Anubis passes me a khopesh. The sword's curved blade is deadly sharp. The jackal-headed guide to all nods.

Bracing against a pain that sears through me, I cut away at my golden heart. Hatred is sliced from me. Injustice, cruelty, envy. I am reduced and purified by the harsh blade of truth.

The golden heart still beats. Its defects sink into the back of the serpent beneath my feet. I embrace what is left of my beating heart. It is enough. I fill with the purity of its love. A gift from the Gods, now uncorrupted.

Anubis nods his head and beckons. I continue along the twisting, snake road.

*

I step to the next gate. The pillar to my right is a hawk-headed God, the one to my left a Godly form with the heads of seven serpents. The gate is guarded by a hippopotamus, the deadliest of creatures.

"Speak thy name, and you may pass," commands the hippopotamus.

I open my mouth, but I cannot remember. I look to Anubis, whose jackal eyes regard me as one would a curiosity.

The hippopotamus regards me with infinite patience.

"What is in a name, friend?" Anubis speaks gently. "A label. A cat may have a name, but does the name define the cat? What is your name?" He who is the great guide seems bereft of terror. He is each road walked; each camp made on a journey.

I know a part of the answer. "I am he who was born of his mother and nurtured by his father. I am son, husband, father, grandfather. I am architect, farmer, priest, lover, friend and foe. I am all I have willed myself to be. The summation of a life lived and a soul that stretches to the first sparks of light when

I JOURNEY THE BACK OF A SNAKE

Atum fought free of the folds of Nun. I am I, and I am unique among a multitude who, in the end, are all Atum, an experiment as the divine seeks to know itself. A meditation on the self that is all things. I am me."

The hippo steps aside.

Anubis nods. "It is not much farther, or perhaps it is farther than the stars. The journey is all."

I step past the hippo to the next gate.

*

The stone columns are plain. In the gateway lay three sleeping dogs. Terrible in size and fearsome of tooth and claw. One lifts its head and growls as I approach.

I try to retreat from the fearsome visage, to deny it. I know I am unworthy to pass. I am not a God to face such beasts, and they block the black road where I must place my feet.

"Is it so long since you were among your brethren that you have forgotten? You are a child of Atum, as are we all. A seed born of him/her. A part of him/her. Be what you are, and the guardians will hold no power." Anubis's words stir something deep in me.

"I am of Atum. I travel as freely as Anubis. I am Ba." As I speak the words, I feel my body reform. Arms become wings. Talons grow where feet once were. I am the Ba, the essence of spirit. I have shed the limitations of Earth and echo the creation of Atum. My head is formed as the man I was, but I am more. I take wing and soar over the sleeping dogs with the power of Atum manifest in me. The spark of the great one that brought me into being at the dawn of time.

I land past the gate and am once more the man I knew, but different. Other lives touch my thoughts, informing me, adding to my store of wisdom. They show me a transformation that began when Atum first shed tears at the return of his beloved children, Shu and Tefnut.

"Very good, brother." Anubis stands beside me.

I step forward without fear, knowing what is to come. I have walked the back of this snake many times, ever twisting, ever-changing, but ever the same. The guide has brought me

26

this way, steered me around the dangers. Led me to grow in the maze of a transient world.

I step forward. I can smell the scents of my grandfather's garden as the next gate comes into view. Above me, the sky is resplendent with stars, and the darkness retreats against a light that comes from my flesh.

*

The gateposts are a lion and a hare armed with lances. They seek to bar my way. Between them, is an old man holding ears of corn. He resembles me.

I speak the words, though now I know them to be nothing more than artifice.

"Let me pass, Let me pass, let the marrow of an old man pass."

I smile back at the old man who is me. I reach out and am on the other side of the gate. I am all. I am from lives un-counted. I remember moving through the kingdom of Earth so, so long ago, of growing and travelling the spiral road of experience. I remember lives as a fish swimming in the sea and a lizard warming myself on a rock. I have been man, beast, husband, wife, king and slave, and I have been Atum, learning of him/herself travelling spirals within spirals to understanding. I recall the feel of my daughter's downy cheek, the embrace of my wife. The warmth of friends, and more, so much more.

"The journey never ends. To live is to walk the back of a snake, for life is ever-changing, yet ever the same." Anubis stands beside me. "But, for the moment, you should make camp. There are those who wish to see you."

I am in my grandfather's garden. My father embraces me. My family and friends welcome me. My wife calls from the clay brick house in the field's corner. I can smell the bread she is baking for me. I am home. The journey will continue. I look where I have come from. The snake is now a road running through a rich land. Experience, education, testing. The great teacher stands upon it, his jackal head smiling. There is a gate on the far side of the garden. I know in time, I will step through it and journey the back of the snake again, but for now, my father's embrace is comfort. The sound of my wife's voice bliss. I have earned a time of rest before I once more embark on the journey of discovery.

*

Anubis watched the family reunite and remembered ages past when he had been the one guided. Remembered so many lives ascending and growing. He looked forward and knew only that the journey continued even for him. Climbing spirals within spirals to Atum and the lessons to be learned.

Continuation.

☿ ☿ ☿

Stephen B. Pearl is an author of several novels, including *Nukekubi* and *Worlds' Apart*, and has numerous short stories published in anthologies, such as *Canadian Dreadful*. His works range from romance to dark urban fantasy to dystopian genres. He has been an author guest at a multitude of literary and media conventions. When he is not writing, he spends time with his wife and plays servant to his beloved cats. For more information on his works, www.stephenpearl.com

By Ross W. Carter

MANY CENTURIES AGO, THERE WAS an Irish fisherman who stared out over the ocean from his home in An Cladachon. He was intrigued by the ocean, by its endlessness and so he decided to go on a journey to find the ocean's end. He built a new sailing vessel, loaded it with provisions, and set sail at dawn on what would prove to be a lovely summer's morning.

The water before the bow of his ship appeared to be even more endless than he had dreamt, once the land that he had left was out of view behind him. As endless, he thought, as was the sky above.

*

Days passed and still the man could find nothing ahead but

more ocean. The sun burned bright from dawn until dusk, giving a reddish hue to his skin. His blond hair and beard grew longer, and as he watched the ocean before him expand into little more than more ocean, he became increasingly aware of the sun's great strength. He fashioned a barrier from some extra hides that he had brought with him to keep warm and dry in a storm to block the direct sunlight. He tried as hard as he could to keep the bright sunlight off of his skin, but it seemed that no matter where he sat in his tiny vessel, the sun would find him. Soon he ran out of fresh water and his food supply dwindled. The ocean simply continued to grow larger and larger.

His clothing became hot and heavy, and so, being alone, he decided to remove it and incorporate the material into the barrier to extend it for more protection from the sun. He learned that if he filtered the seawater through a piece of deer hide, which he had taken from one side of the canopy, much of the salt would remain within the hide and the water would be more palatable.

Days became weeks and weeks became too many to count until finally the sun and the salt water began to take their toll on the man. A fever fell over him as he lay naked in his tiny vessel. The water and the food were gone and yet the ocean continued to expand before him. Ill, he began to fear that death would take him before the ocean would end in an expanse of land. He slipped into a trance to conserve his energy and to slow his body down, for he felt sure that the end of the ocean must be near.

As he lay on his back in this waking sleep, he studied what he could see of the sky around his vessel. Moving the barrier from place to place as the sun crossed the sky on its daily voyage, he watched the way that the sun would appear in the east at each new dawn and ride above the clouds each day to set in the west. It was the most common of occurrences in his day-to-day life in the middle of the ocean where there was very little else to distract him. The sun's journey became surreal.

He watched as the pending darkness rose from the sky behind him and chased the sun toward the west. Then, the stars would rise to fill the darkness. He watched the moon as it appeared, full and round, and then hardly at all, and then full again. He marvelled at the way that the stars would be fewer as the moon became full, and many more stars would light the sky when the moon became dark. He thought that it was almost as if the moon kept the stars at bay, somehow protecting the sun from the stars.

Night after night he lay on his back and watched the cosmic mystery unfold, and he learned to understand the language of the sky. He became aware that the sun and the moon were lovers engaged in a cosmic chase; the Sun ever soaring above the ocean, sleeping and then rising renewed each dawn, and the moon chasing him while protecting him from the fury of the stars, which in turn chased him. She would become weaker and would ultimately have to rest before continuing the chase. To the sun and moon, it seemed to be a game, yet to the stars, it appeared as an act of survival.

One morning as the sky began to brighten, the man heard the sound of many seagulls. This piqued his curiosity. He decided to come out of his trance so that he might better see what part these birds would play in the language of the sky. As he started to rise, he realized that the cries of the gulls were followed by echoes. He rose to discover that his vessel was approaching land..

How many days had it been? He'd not been able to keep track, but he believed that he had seen the moon in its fullness twice. He couldn't be sure.

As he stood naked in the vessel, the dawning sun behind him, he saw in its rays that people stood upon a sandy shore which stretched out before him. The people appeared to have dark hair and red skin, unlike the traveller's own sun-reddened, white flesh, and blond hair and beard. They too were naked.

As the vessel drew closer to the shore, the people began to drop to their knees.

The traveller stepped off the vessel and onto the sand for the first time in a very long time. He wanted to bid them hello and ask if there was any fresh water, but his voice failed him. He had lost it to the salt water. He motioned with his hands and his eyes as best he could. He was parched and barely alive. They responded to him in a tongue that he could not understand, yet women and children soon appeared from behind the crowd with bowls of fruit and flasks of water as if they had understood.

A tall man appeared from out of the crowd that had gathered. He was adorned with a band of brightly coloured feathers draped around his neck, a head-dress of colourful green and red quetzal feathers. The traveller looked upon this man and wondered if these people were the Gods of his people? How else do they appear out of nowhere, at dawn, speaking in an inhuman tongue, yet understanding his wordless requests?

The tall, red-skinned man looked upon the traveller and thought, *Is this man a god? How else does one rise out of the sun's first light and cross the water as the dawn breaks upon the land of our people? His skin and his hair, they are the colours of the rising sun!*

The people then led the traveller back to a small village populated with several adobe huts. They fed him and bathed him and treated him as though he were indeed a god. Each day as the sun rose, two women would appear with a cup filled with dark, warm chocolate, something that the traveller had never known of before. He supposed that this must surely be the sacred drink of the gods.

The tall man with the feathers had a similar thought upon seeing the traveller's expression after taking his very first sip. Believing that his offering had pleased this new god, he then directed the two women to bring the stranger the warm drink each day at dawn.

As the traveller regained his health, he was able to learn their language, just as he had come to learn the language of the sky. His voice returned, gradually, and he began to teach the two women his language. The women seemed to learn as quickly as did he, and soon, the three became conversant in both tongues.

The traveller told the women of his travels, of the village that had been his home, and of his curiosity to find the ocean's end. The women told the man of a great city, many days away where there were monuments to their Gods that were so tall that a man could climb up to the clouds to talk with them. The women spoke at length of the Gods of their people, and the traveller soon became aware that these people were not gods at all.

He began to teach them the ways of his people, to teach them skills not previously known to them, new ways of hunting and fishing, new tools, and new ways to dance and sing. And he taught them how to speak the language of the skies.

Many moons later, the two women approached the traveller and told him that it was time for him to go to the great city. They said that it was the place where their old gods had gathered many long years ago to create the earth and sky, and the people. They told him legends of their gods and he began to understand that they thought that he was a god, just as he had once thought that the red people were his gods.

It took many days to travel to the city, almost as long by land, he thought, as his journey upon the ocean had been. When they arrived at the great city of Teotihuacan, the traveller was once again greeted with the same reverence and respect as the people on the shore had shown him when he first appeared.

The people, who called themselves Tolteca, welcomed him into their city with a great celebration, for to the Tolteca, it seemed that their God had come to live among them. They named him Quetzalcoatl, which means feathered serpent, after the image of his long, blonde hair, the like of which they had never seen before, blowing in the wind like feathers of a head-dress, and the scaling patches on his arms from the burning sun.

Soon, they made him their leader and they built a temple to honour him, and within it, he lived for many years. The two women from the coastal village stayed with him throughout all of his days in the great city.

He became known to the Tolteca as the god of learning, for he brought them new knowledge and new skills. He was the god of civilization, for he helped them to create new laws and manners. And he taught them the language of the sky. Most importantly, he was the god who rose from out of the rising sun to walk the earth and to live among the people.

*

One day, the traveller decided that it was time to leave, perhaps to find his home again or perhaps on a new adventure. He had found the end of the ocean, and now he stood facing yet another ocean. On this journey, he would sail to the west. Older and much wiser than before, he built a larger vessel with a great canopy and more room for provisions. On the day that he was to leave, the Tolteca came from the great city to bid him farewell and to wish him well. Together, the Tolteca and the white-skinned, bearded man with hair the colour of maize silk, shared one last cup of chocolate.

It was late in the day by the time he was able to get underway. To the two women who had been by his side for many years and who were now also no longer young, he gave his eternal gratitude. He sailed away again, on a golden ship with a canopy and a sail made of quetzal feathers, and an ample supply of chocolate.

From the coastline, the Tolteca watched as the vessel sailed its way across the sea, and to the horizon beyond where they watched as the setting sun seemingly descended into the ocean directly into the path of the traveller and his vessel. The traveller and the vessel appeared to become one with the sun as it slipped below the horizon, disappearing into the endless ocean in a vibrant display of yellow and crimson wonder.

The Tolteca would remember the story of the white-skinned, bearded man who sailed into the world of man from out of the rising sun, lived among them as a god among men, and then sailed out once again, this time into the setting sun, to live once more among their Gods. They believed that the traveller sailed his vessel directly into the setting Sun and that as the traveller, the vessel, and the Sun became one, many thousands of bright sparks of divinity were spread throughout the darkening sky, creating new stars and adding yet another story to the language of the sky.

Many of these sparks were spread out across the land to remain forever so that one day, the wind might find one of those sparks and bring it into the life of some curious being to spark within them the curiosity to become a traveller themselves, that the world shall never forget the story of the traveller, or of the language of the sky.

Ross W. Carter is a Wiccan High Priest and has been involved with the Wiccan Church of Canada (WCC) since 1981. He has been the Leading High Priest of the WCC since 2018. In addition to his work with the WCC, Ross

Ross W. Carter

has been employed as a Wiccan Chaplain in the Canadian Corrections system for nearly a decade. During his time with the WCC, he developed an interest in Aztec culture and the practice of sacrifice which would eventually become the inspiration for this story which came to him in a dream.

Ross lives a quiet life in Toronto with his amazing wife, Tamara. He is a drummer, an avid traveller and a grandfather. He has been a hobby writer since he first learned his ABC's and he is sure that someday he will finish that book he's been working on.

By Moira Scott

I SAT ALONE IN MY hotel room with a pile of history books strewn haphazardly upon the double bed. Jet lag still ate away at my energy which annoyed me to no end. I had things to do while visiting Merry Olde England and was not happy about not being able to do them without feeling tapped out too soon.

I glanced at the books again. One well-worn leather-bound tome in particular had more than its fair share of post-it notes marking what purported to be interesting pages. All I knew was that *I* didn't mark them. I'm not sure who did to be perfectly honest, but it should be a good read. Judging from its well bent spine and its cover, the original red leather had faded to a patchy russet and brown. I glanced at its worn cover again, *Myths and Folkloric Tales of Pagan Britain*. Or at least that's what my brain thought it said. No matter, I would get around to reading it, eventually.

For a split second, I turned my attention back to the book's cover. The title's embossing appeared to darken then returned to its faded russet colour. Shaking my head as if to dislodge what I'd just seen, I continued to go about my business, gathering my things before heading out. Best I stuff it in my backpack before I forget.

Mum and Dad were bustling around in the adjoining suite. I couldn't quite hear what they were saying, but it sounded like one juicy argument. Whatever, I would be free of them soon. Mum could wander around the shops for a while before meeting up with Dad again to attend his lecture. What was it on again? Oh, yeah, something about myths and legends in Roman England, or some such. Sounds absolutely riveting—*Not.*

I had to gather my thoughts before heading out the door. With my backpack slung over one shoulder, I checked its pockets for my wallet. I had downloaded my route to my phone but being a bit old school, I decided to have a print version handy just in case my Canadian GPS went bonkers – which it often did. I decided to record my thoughts in my phone's memos app. Maybe it would be good for a laugh over a couple of pints later, who knows?

Dear Diary:

Honestly, I don't know what day it is today, but mother has decided to book me on a day trip tour around Windsor Castle and Windsor Great Park while we stay here in London. I'm to get on a train and haul myself up to Windsor. Of course, <u>they</u> aren't coming, and it's about an hour's trip. Good thing I have a bunch of books to read. Why did I ever agree to this – oh wait, I didn't - I was voluntold. More to come. Maybe.

I stopped the memo app and thrust my well-traveled phone with its slightly cracked screen into my handbag. Now was a good time to bid farewell to the parental units. Putting my hand to my ear, I listened for any more sounds emanating from their lair. Hearing none, I gingerly knocked on the door.

The door opened slightly. Mum's face appeared.

"Mum, I'm going now."

A thin veil of confusion clouded her face for a moment. "Where? Where are you going?"

THE MEMORY OF TREES

Oh, Lord, really? I guess the gin had kidnapped that memory and stomped on it—hard. I cleared my throat. "I'm going to Windsor, remember? Yesterday evening you said I was to go. You even booked me a ticket."

Mother blinked. My father pulled the door wide. Turning to his wife, he sighed, "Emma, do you not remember? You told Heather she was going. You thought it would be good for her English history research."

My eyes shot skyward, how convenient they had forgotten, *but whatever.* I turned on my heel, ignoring them as they bickered again. Mum had forgotten and Dad was just not willing to get into that discussion again. Closing the door, I went to the window and threw open the curtains for a quick eye-witness weather report before I headed for the lift.

The hall of the old hotel were dimly lit, yet the polished dark wainscoting gleamed in defiance. Somehow, the hallway not only appeared but also felt longer. Adjusting my eyes to the strange telescoping vision, I pressed on.

At the end of the hall, the lift with its semi-circular brass crown of ornate floor numbers and single floor indicator hand loomed larger than I recalled. The polished brass frame stood tall, beside it with two elaborate Deco sconces emitting a dim yellowish glow. Still, it was a lovely testament to a bygone era. Yup, they sure don't make 'em like that anymore. Hopefully, this time, my erratic attacks of claustrophobia will give me a hall pass and I can make my way down in peace.

Pressing the circular backlit down button, I waited for the distinct thud and the tell-tale hum of the lift's wakeup call as it shifted into gear. Hearing the hum grow louder, I waited for what I felt was longer than usual. When it finally arrived, I stepped into the car. Its overhead lights blinked a couple of times when I pushed the Ground floor button. *That's a bit odd… but no worries. Let's go, I have a train to catch.* Shuddering for a moment, the car began its descent. Again, the lights blinked then browned out for a few seconds. The car stopped, rattled on its creaking cables for a moment then lurched into action again.

Instinctively, I reached for the ornate brass railing that ran around the back and two sides of the car and white-knuckled it until we reached the bottom. *Get a grip. That lift is older than dirt, but it's still well maintained… fairly, I suppose…*

After what seemed like an eternity, I reached the ground floor. Straightening my shoulders, I exhaled loudly as I exited.

The beautiful lobby with its gleaming marble columns and stately tropical plants was oddly devoid of people. I blinked then rubbed my eyes. Where was everyone? Sighing, I checked my watch and noted that time was running short, so I'd better hoof it to the station. Exiting the great revolving doors, I stopped dead. The autumn weather seemed to be more unpredictable than usual my so-called eye-witness weather reported.

Sheets of pelting rain, augmented by gusts of wind, hit my head as I struggled to pull on my jacket and yank up its so-called waterproof jacket's hood. Achieving some sort of success, I realized I'd not make it on foot no matter how fast I ran. As the chill set in, I hailed a black cab.

A burly, meaty-faced cabbie rolled down the window and mumbled through one side of his mouth, "Where to?"

Straightening, "Waterloo Station, please."

Grunting, he blinked at me, "Y' know, i' tain't *that* far, Miss."

I gritted my teeth before answering, "Yes, I am aware of that, but I have a train to catch, and I'm sure I won't make it in this rain."

Hesitating for a moment, he let down his guard, grunting, "Gi' in, then."

"Thank you," I replied with a sigh. Throwing my backpack on to the seat behind the driver, I hauled myself in. With a lurch, Mr. Cabbie donned his Jackie Stewart persona and lead-footed it all the way. Strangely, he managed to avoid the stop signs and red lights as we careened through the narrow, bendy backstreets.

Damn him, he's really going to jack up the fare.

All sorts of segments of humanity milled about Waterloo Station, making it as crowded as one would expect. Some knew where they were going, others were glued to their phones or tablets, and a small group of those who were obviously so completely lost with their mouths hanging open as they glanced frantically between their handfuls of paperwork, phones, and directional signs.

Glancing at my phone, I searched for the ticket app to check my boarding pass. Yup, right on time—give or take ten minutes.

Picking up the pace, I found my platform and sighed with relief. With the train looming large before me, I felt a tingle of excitement knowing that venturing forth to unknown places—to *me* anyway—was pretty darned cool. I listened for the boarding call and moved toward the small line up. So far, so good, or 'tickety boo'. *I'm fairly certain no one says that anymore.* Finally, it was my turn to board.

Looking up, I noticed the distinct glower on the Conductor's face. His half-cocked eyebrow made me rather nervous. *Was there something wrong with my ticket? Is this the right day? Neurotic questions ad nauseam.* "Is there a problem with my ticket, sir?"

The conductor eyed me up and down and shook his head, before jamming his thumb in the direction of the door.

He knew I was a tourist. They can spot us a mile away. Checking my ticket, I found my assigned seat by the window and sat down. I felt tired. I could only gaze out my window for so long. Watching the Berkshire County landscape fly by was interesting, but after a while everything began to blend into a blur of sameness. The ventilation in this train's carriage was almost non-existent. Time to remove my still slightly sodden jacket and hang it on the old hook by the window. Sleepiness began to enfold me, but I knew the trip was short, so I needed to stay awake.

I turned my gaze away from the window and sighed. Remembering I had the old, worn pagan mythology book, I thrust my hand into my backpack and pulled it out, which, upon closer examination seemed to have aged slightly more. I dismissed that thought and casually leafed through it. Sure enough, there was a chapter on Windsor Great Park. *How could there not be?* Finding the chapter's start, I noted the title, *The Tale of Herne.*

I flipped the pages to its heading. On its facing page, a black and white photograph of a figure standing on a small hill within a clearing. With tall coniferous trees framing the shot, I looked closer. It was clearly a man backlit against a light cloud of fog. Upon his head I could make out a broad rack of a stag's antlers. Over his shoulder, there was what appeared to be a quiver loaded with arrows. In his left hand, he held a long bow with its string facing downward. The caption read: *"Herne the Hunter."*

As I scanned the image again, a sense of lightness engulfed me. I tried to look away from the photograph and turn my attention to the accompanying text—but not before being interrupted by the overhead announcement indicating the train's arrival at my stop.

Slamming the book shut, I threw it back into my backpack. Snatching my jacket without thinking, I nearly tore it off the hook and rose to my feet. I lost my balance as the train lurched and shuddered to a stop. Struggling to right myself, I caught a glimpse of antlers reflected in the window. Blinking, the image vanished.

Descending the train's stairs to the rain drenched concrete platform. '*Now what?* I reached into my pocket to pull out my phone. I needed direction in more ways than one. Choosing to ignore the electronic ticket Mum had purchased for this tour, I decided to make the best of it on my own. Of the many articles that discussed the history of both Windsor Castle and its magnificent surrounding grounds, they all seemed to reflect on its deep history, noting specifically that it remains the oldest inhabited castle, originally built by William the Conqueror in 1066. As the centuries passed, the castle and its legends also grew.

An elderly woman's voice came from behind. "Miss?"

I jerked my head around to see her standing beside me.

"Will you be joining the tour?" Slowly raising a gnarled, age-spotted hand, she gestured to her left where a small group of not quite elderly but certainly getting there mingled, making small talk as they neared the great gates. "They're gathering just over there."

"Thank you for letting me know, but I am keen to explore on my own." *Sorry, mum.*

The docent regarded me closely for a moment then nodded her head, "As you wish, my dear. But you'll need an umbrella, mind."

Nodding, I turned my attention back to the story on my phone for a short moment, but when I looked up again, she had vanished. The platform suddenly became quiet.

The daylight began to slide into twilight. My heart sank as I realized far too late that I had chosen a bad time for a visit. Kicking myself, I *knew* I should've joined that bloody tour. What the Hell, I am here now, so I'd better get going.

Consulting my phone's GPS, the screen showed only the terrain but no coordinates. Either the cell service was wonky, or I hadn't paid my bill. I hoped it was door number one. I kept walking. Before me, the shadow of Windsor Castle rose in the distance enshrouded in mist. Choosing to have the sunset behind me, lighting my path I set my sights on the castle. Until… until… *How in the HELL did the welcome gate manage to be in front of me? Idiot! You've been walking in circles.*

"Casting a Circle, you mean?"

I froze. I had no idea where the deeply resonating voice came from. My heart pounded in my chest. The light was almost gone and I thought I was completely alone. Evidently not, as I spun in circles trying to locate the source of the voice. Both the gates and the castle had vanished, yet the strange voice that apparently belonged to someone who was either following me, watching from a distance or both broke the silence of twilight.

A rustling of leaves and the breaking of small twigs stopped me in mid-twirl. A grand white stag emerged from the shadows. Its majestic sixteen-point antlers adorned its magnificent head. Bowing, it pawed the earth, snorting, with its breath showing white upon the air in a misty haze, swirling clockwise. For a split second, I saw my face, white and pale reflected in its eyes. A flicker of recognition burned for a moment in its dark eyes and vanished. I took a step back. The stag mirrored my movement, bellowed a mournful cry, before turning back into the shadows.

Darkness.

With my dry throat cracking, I attempted to summon the courage to inquire of the disembodied voice, "Who are you? W-what do you want?"

A hearty laugh followed, "Nay, madam, it is I who must ask *you* what do *you* want wandering around the castle's grounds before darkness falls?"

Breaking out in a cold sweat. I stood my ground as best I could. "Who are you? Show yourself!"

"Turn around." The voice seemed rather blasé.

I so wanted to ignore it but could not help myself. "I beg your pardon."

A heavy sigh rode the breeze as the voice answered, somewhat perturbed. "Turn. *Around!*"

I lifted my leaden feet that felt firmly affixed to the ground to turn to face whatever—or whomever—that spoke.

Out of the shadows, a crackling of leaves and twigs, accentuated his foot falls. Drawing in my breath, I almost forgot to exhale. My body shook with the damnable cold as the figure emerged from the mists. He stood before me. Larger than life. A long, braided dark brown beard hung from his chin. His wavy black hair fell well beneath his shoulders, framed a sallow skinned, chiselled face. His eyes – I couldn't take my own from them – were almost black, yet there was a tiny sparkle, defying the darkness.

As he emerged from the evening fog, he towered above me. Clad in dark cloak, covering his shoulders, clasped with a gleaming penannular pin, revealed a heavily tanned jerkin and dark leather leggings tucked into his boots. "You came here to find something. I imagine you came here to find *yourself.*"

I tried to answer him, yet no words came. Frustrated, my thoughts were scrambled. Nothing made sense here. Not. One. Damned. Thing.

He eyed me warily until a smile broke over his face. I could not tell if he was mocking me or if he was being kind. I straightened my shoulders and squared my stance before falling apart. What was I thinking? Who was I kidding? I had no idea who this… this—who *was* he? How could I stand up to—*Who the HELL was this?* I backed down from trying. Hanging my head in defeat, "Please, I just want to know who you are and why have you, for lack of a better term, engaged me, of all people?"

He threw his head back, roaring with laughter, "*Engaged* you? That is a *fascinating* turn of phrase, I daresay. Might I remind you, lady, that you are wandering—aimlessly, I might add—in my realm."

I blinked. "Realm? What on earth are you talking about?"

He blinked, shrugged his shoulders, and grinned, "You have no idea *where you are!*"

I smirked in spite of myself, "Where *I* am? I know damned

well where I—"

"*Oh no you don't…*"

I exhaled. My voice dropping to a croaking whisper replied, "No. I don't suppose I do."

The half smile returned to his face for but a moment, "At last, we are getting somewhere. So, I will ask you, *why are you here?*"

I had no answer. I had no idea to whom I was speaking. I felt tears welling in my eyes, stinging. What was I doing here? I didn't just come here on a whim. My mother just didn't buy me a ticket, which I *chose* not to use. All I knew was that I was here, alone in Windsor Great Park, under a rainy moonless sky, with wildlife all around me. I did not know. I simply, did *not* know. At a loss, I fell to my knees, burying my face in my hands, twisting in pain. Confusion ravaging my body.

A heavy sigh filled the air, "You came here for a reason. Nothing in this life should be dismissed as mere chance." I tore my hands away from my face, struggling to meet his gaze. Hesitating, he softened his tone, "Let me tell you my story. Mayhap you find comfort. So many times, throughout the centuries, *others* have told my tale, but do they really know who I am? I should think not. These tales are very like this:

"Hark! Hark! Do you hear the hounds baying and the thundering of hooves at night! Don't listen! Pay it no mind, lest you go mad! Snuff out your candles, keep the hearth fires low, lock your doors and close your curtains because He—

"—referring to myself of course, is leading some Otherworldly chase through Windsor Great Park. Nevertheless, there is more to this strange retelling; we apparently, according to them of course, are hunting for lost souls. *Lost Souls?* I ask you just what *is* a lost soul exactly? I do not know, for they are not of my faith. In my eyes, no soul is ever truly lost. Hesitant, perhaps, but abandoned or forgotten? *Never.*

"Spirit changes form. It regenerates. Truly for us to regain our sense of direction—if not our own moral compass—we must look to the natural world. Feel the changes riding the winds. From violent, raging tempests, where branches are loosed from tree trunks and are flung into the sky, only to come crashing down to the rain-soaked earth, to the gentle breezes that carry messages to the creatures that need to hear. From thundering storms upon the waters, sending waves crashing to the shore, destroying the ships that sail upon them, to the glassy waters of a stream-fed pond that slakes the thirst of animals and humans alike. And where, beneath its surface, lays the nearly hidden existence of the many fishes and frogs and emerald green plants.

"Amid this activity, there is the hint of chaos that could be the result of a lightning strike; a single flash of light that may ignite a fire, or perhaps it manifested as the striking iron to flint to light the cold hearth. These things may manifest in many ways, and they all happen when they are supposed to, whether their results appeal to us or not. That makes no never mind." Sighing heavily, his voice trailed off for a moment. Staring down at me, his eyes grew dark. "On your feet! There is much to be done!"

Wordlessly, I rose, my joints screaming as I hauled myself to stand, wondering how he had inexplicably become taller. I found myself stepping backwards, unable to take my eyes away from him.

Clearing his throat, he resumed, yet now his voice had dropped, leaden and dull, "For those who have succumbed to the myth that humans were given dominion over the Earth and thereby forsook it, we find ourselves barred from moving forward to true communion. The time was right for you to come to me. The time was right for you to immerse yourself in this place, laden with history… and *misinformation*, for who are *they* to know who *I* really am?" A smirk curled his lips, "Shall I go on?"

I nodded.

His eyes bore into me again, as he continued. "Here is a good yarn."

Dumbfounded, I nodded in agreement. I shifted my position on the muddy ground. Captured or captivated? I could not tell. The rain had seeped through my jeans and mac. I still had NO idea who he was, nor why on earth he was telling *me* his, yet I felt compelled to listen.

He squared his shoulders before beginning his tale. "Some stories about me speak of how in the fourteenth century, I was one of King Richard II's many huntsmen, the variations on this tale emphasize that I loved this job, which I most certainly did without question." I opened my mouth to speak, but with a simple wave of his hand, I thought better of it.

"Windsor was and remains my home. I knew every rock, tree, and rivulet of this land and all the creatures that inhabited them. Still, I did my duty and accompanied the King on his hunting expeditions. We had quite a few mouths to feed." Again, he fell silent as he collected his thoughts. "Probably one of the more oft-told tales about me. Hmmm... where to start?"

He drew in a deep breath, "Ah yes... just after sunrise we were gathered on a check. The hounds were trying to pick up the scent. Their low growls as they awaited the Hunt Master's command. The king raised his hand ordering us to gather in close and be silent. The hounds were impatient as they had not yet picked up a scent. The horses were slightly nervous as well, tossing their heads and stamping their hooves, but we paid them no mind. They were often excited when they knew they were going on a hunt." Glancing at me, his smile returned. "Within an instant, the hounds gave tongue and bolted off toward the woods in full cry! Our horses reared, champing at their bits as they plunged after the pack. The king's white steed bolted ahead and was almost upon the pack's heels. I urged my mount into a full gallop to keep up with His Majesty.

"I caught a glimpse of a strange look in his eye as he signalled to me by thrusting his gauntleted hand toward a thicket. Nodding, I fixed my gaze upon a flash of white as it vanished into the dark woods. "Before I continue, I need you to accompany me."

He grinned as the look of shock washed over my face "A-a-accompany you?"

"Yes. Come with me. T'would be better that I *show* you."

I struggled to move. My drenched clothing had chilled me through and through. *How was I to keep up with—who was he again?*

As we trudged through the muddy parkland, I had no idea how many minutes had passed before he held up his hand in silence, then pointed toward a small field surrounded by a copse of dense trees. "Do you see it?"

Other than the slight hills in the middle, I was unsure as to what he was trying to get me to see. "Let us move closer."

As we made our way to the centre of the field, he continued his tale. Gesturing over his shoulders from whence we came. "It was there that we first saw him, that fateful day. He was a splendid beast! As we moved closer, he pawed the ground and roared in defiance. The hounds bayed, the arrows flew, wounding him. Yet, he did not fall. Bounding through the woods, we caught glimpses of its brilliant, white coat flashing amid the dense forest leaves. It was here, within this clearing, that we had cornered him, forming a circle in front of the thicket so he could not escape. Our horses whinnied. The hounds howled, yet the great beast stood its ground, its rage flaming, burning in its eyes, tossing its head in defiance, challenging us.

"My king unsheathed his gleaming dagger. Spurring his mount forward, he tried to slash the stag's neck. It was not to be! The white stag thundered and reared on its haunches and plunged toward the king and gored his horse's throat. Screaming in pain, it writhed and kicked, throwing King Richard to the ground.

"Without a moment's notice, I sprang to his aid, throwing myself over his body. As the stag reared up again, bellowing in defiance and fury, I plunged my dagger deep into the beast's chest, but not before its great cloven hooves had slashed my neck. It screamed in anguish as blood from its veins sprayed upon us, convulsing in agony before falling dead.

"The hunters were dumbstruck. I turned my gaze to my king. Seeing his countenance change to one of shock to gratitude, I took him in his arms. 'Sire,' I whispered, 'I lay down my weapon before thee, as I took your kill. I await my punishment at your hands.'

"King Richard blinked in astonishment. 'Nay good sir, you have but saved my life, while risking yours.'

"After helping him to his feet, he stared at his own mount dead upon the ground, blood staining the stallion's neck. My king shed but a tear then wiped his face with his own bloodied gauntlet. With all the excitement I had forgotten that I too, was wounded! The men rushed to my aid, but no one among them was a chirurgeon."

"This is quite the tale, sir." It was too late for me to soften my response. I was frustrated and freezing. He still had not indicated who he was or *why* he was telling me all this. Perhaps he was plain mad and I was but a captive audience of one.

He held no torch and the moon was hidden, yet, in this blackness, he emitted a strange blue-white glow. His eyes looked down at me again, "Have you understood what I have said?"

I nodded but chose my words carefully before speaking, "I understand, but I do not know why you have told me all this. I'm having a really hard time trying to make sense of it."

"Then, I shall continue. Perhaps it will dawn on you then."

I felt a rush of indignation surge through my veins, "*Dawn on me?*"

Raising his chin and looking down his nose at me, he smirked at my annoyance, cleared his throat, and continued with his tale. "Indeed, I had lost a lot a blood. My head swam, and I felt that I should collapse at any moment. I do not remember the journey back to the castle. I was met by the Palace guard, who escorted me deep into the castle's vast array of rooms. I had not cast off the exhaustion, as such, I did not know where I was going. Next thing I knew, I was stood in one of the castle's many ornate gardens. King Richard stood before me. I acknowledged His Majesty with a deep bow.

"With a broad smile and clapping his hands together, he approached me, 'My good Herne, I am forever indebted to you for your act of courage during our last hunt.'

"'Sire', I replied cautiously, 'I thought nothing of it. I did what needed to be done.'

"The king's demeanour turned serious for a moment. 'I am well aware, but your good deed should not go unrewarded.'

"He then presented me with such wondrous gifts the likes of which I had not ever seen, including a key to an apartment within the castle. I was dumbstruck and thanked him.

"'Of course, with all these accolades comes one serious condition.'

"I blinked yet remained silent.

"'You are to accompany me upon all hunting expeditions.'

"I nodded my head in a reverent response. I am certain you will understand that a royal commission or patronage is quite the honour, yet there were two huntsmen whom I had called friends who did not share in this joy. Their jealousy spurred them on to create rumours about me. Try as they might, they could not sway the king's opinion that held me in such high regard, for I had indeed saved His Majesty's life. Yet these men persisted.

"They were in luck, as it came about, that my last hunt with the King proved fruitless and I returned, alone to the castle, in shame. I had failed. I had not lived up to the high esteem the king had placed upon me. I hung my head in shame. The tales about my life here at Windsor continue, saying that these men devised other plans to wrong me. They claimed that since I was unsuccessful with the hunt, I was not at all what the king had believed me to be. One even suggested that I had poached the kills—a grave offense indeed, but this was not proven.

"Heartbroken, King Richard, released me from his employ. It was then that my world collapsed." He stopped for a moment. Sighing heavily, he beckoned me to follow. The bluish glow that enveloped him was fading.

We returned to the vale where his tale began. Although I couldn't see them clearly, I heard the breeze picking up fallen leaves to swirl around us. He put his hand on my shoulder. I halted as the sound of angry thunder rolled in. Within moments, the sky lit up with lighting, tearing white streaks in the black sky. He paid it no mind and we kept walking.

I wanted to get to cover, *not* move toward a small dip in a meadow surrounded by tall trees. *Just what in the blazes was he doing?* This entire situation was absurd! Trudging through Windsor Great Park alongside a man whose identity I had yet to believe as a storm was rolling in was... Bloody HELL! Why was this happening to me? I had no idea what time it was, nor how many hours had passed.

As we moved down the slight incline leading to the clearing, I felt the winds shift yet again. His deep voice pierced the darkness. "It was here—"

I cut him off, "Where you butchered the white buck?"

He turned and faced me head on, his dark eyes hidden by his furrowed brow and deep sockets. His towering height caused me to flinch "Yes, it was. It was *here*." I squared my shoulders, trying to look bigger than my five-foot, two inches frame would allow. "And you have brought me to this spot. Why?" Saying nothing, he turned his back to me and took three steps forward. Raising his hands to the sky, he bellowed to the heavens as a blue-grey mist rose from the earth, swirling around his legs, torso, chest, and ultimately, his head. Tiny wisps of ice blue shot with white flickered and shone like stars. "Look. Cast your eyes before you at the grassy place at the bottom of the hill."

Confused, I looked to him for answers, but he ignored me. Drawing his sword, he raised it skyward and roared, "I shall *not* be forgotten! I *shall* be avenged!" Turning his sword down, he plunged the tip into the earth. Ripples of light, like lightning traveling ancient lines drawn in the earth, sparked to life then travelled at speed toward the base of the clearing, opening a dark, gaping chasm. The earth trembled beneath my feet.

Gasping, I caught my breath as thin branches emerged from the rent in the earth. Taking a step back, the thin branches grew thicker at their base, pushing the sodden soil further away. A fog enveloped the branches, I watched in stunned silence as he raised his hands in a circular motion then thrust them skyward with a cry. As the fog began to lift, a great oak stood before me. *He* had vanished from my side, yet the mists rising from the earth wove intricate patterns, rendering me transfixed for but a swift moment

Panicked, I ran down the hill. My lungs screamed in pain as I tried to catch my breath. The massive hole in the earth had disappeared yet traces of swirling smoky blue fog remained near the tree's roots. Overhead a raven's croak broke the silence. Spinning on my heels I turned back. It was then I saw him. It was as if the illustration in the old book had come to life.

Before me, on top of a small hillock, his body hung by the neck, swayed in the breeze from one of the lower branches.

I screamed.

This could not be happening! I rubbed my eyes and stared through tear-stung eyes before bolting up the hill to meet him face to face. Beneath his feet, upon the cold ground lay a crown of massive antlers. Falling to my knees, I cried out as I gazed upon his pale face. His lifeless eyes stared at the ground where his sheathed broadsword lay. I drew in a deep breath. The air rasped within my throat. My hands shook as I reached for his blade. Try as I might, I could not wield it without great effort.

Raising the sword from the ground, I pointed its tip toward him, *"You shall not be forgotten."*

As I uttered those words, a great thunderclap exploded over my head. My hands burned as the sword glowed red. The unkindness of six ravens shrieked as they circled overhead, distracting me for a moment. When I turned my gaze back toward him, the mists had vanished. He and the tree were no more, in their place lay the old book—the one I *should have read* before coming here.

Energies encircling this unearthly place held me fast for a moment. Blinking in astonishment, a small flash of light struck the earth, embossing *1863* upon the darkened spot where the tree once grew. As the skies overhead grew more threatening, I knew I had to take cover. Flashes of lightning ripped the darkness.

Without thinking I ran. I had no idea which direction to take. Before me, a short distance away, stood a small gardener's shed. It would have to do. Gathering all my strength I ran to it. Finding it locked I sank to the ground again under its small awning. My heart still pounding. I tried to catch my breath as I looked back at where the tree had once stood. What was that number? Flipping through the pages, my eyes scanned the text for any clue. I gasped when this passage seemed to jump out at me:

"During the reign of Her Majesty Queen Victoria, the mighty tree that had come to be known as Herne's Oak, was felled in storm. This tree was said to have stood on the same spot as one that was previously named 'Herne's Oak', felled in 1795."

I slammed the book shut. 1863 flashed in brilliant gold one by one in succession. I glanced down at its weather-beaten cover. Seeing it now with new eyes, it seemed it was far older. Realizing that it was entrusted to me to protect and cherish was a beautiful gift and yet, it struck me that it was not mine to keep. My hands white-knuckled the book as the storm died down. Rising to my feet, I stepped out from under the cover that had seemed to have protected me. Feeling the pull to return to the great oak—*his* oak, I hugged the book to my chest.

Birdsong rose among the trees as a faint orange glow began to crawl toward me. With my back to the dawning sun, my eyes scanned the spot where the great oak once stood, seeing nothing but my own shadow cast against the fertile soil, I smiled. Bending down, I placed the old, worn book down on the dew-covered grass. It sat still for a moment, before a faint rumbling heralded the surrounding grasses reaching skyward before arcing over and meeting in the middle, thickly intertwining themselves. I watched in awe as the earth slowly reclaimed it.

You have not been forgotten.

Moira H. Scott is a Gardnerian Witch living in Toronto, Canada and has been interested in Canadian Military History for many years. Active in the local Speculative and Science Fiction fandom community since the early 1990s, she has presented panels on Wicca, Witchcraft, folklore as well as popular culture.

Moira lives in Toronto and is currently working on a novella about Spiritualism and Technology at the turn of the twentieth century in Canada. When not hard at work doing research, Moira also reads Tarot professionally and continues with her studies in Heraldic history.

An Axe For Men

By Rosemary Edghill

THEY CARRIED SLEEPING TAR'ATHA BEFORE them, borne upon Her lions of gold and crystal. Ten kings followed Her—the Sacred Twins who had danced with the bulls within the walls of Saloe for Her fame and delight.

But Saloe was no more.

Since before the beginning of the world, the tricolored walls of Great Saloe had stood tall before the Reed Lake, beside the Blue River. Her pillars of red orichalcum called down Ut-ash-atha from heaven, all for the glory of Sleeping Tar'atha.

Saloe was changeless. But Saloe changed.

It was rain-time, the season that turned the plains dark and lush with pasturage for goats and horses. But that year there was more rain than Sais could remember ever having fallen before. Month after month, Tar'atha hid Ut-sin-atha in the sky by night and hid Ut-ash-atha in the sky by day. There was only darkness, and clouds, and rain.

One day, there was the sound of the world breaking.

Water rushed down into the valley in a great flood. It shattered villages. It drowned beasts in their pastures.

But Great Saloe was not destroyed.

Not then.

The people came to the city as the waters rose, begging for refuge, and the Lady of Saloe admitted them. Sais was only a very young Priestess of the Temple, but she cherished the way in which the Lady of Saloe spoke as the voice of the Sleeping Goddess. Perhaps someday, if she too bore twin kings to Tar'atha, she would stand where the Lady of Saloe stood now, and rule over the people with the same calm justice.

That had been three turns of the seasons ago.

Before the Reed Lake had turned entirely to salt.

Before it grew to cover the villages, the grazing lands, the fields. Before it grew to rise over the outer terraces of Great Saloe itself.

The rain had stopped, but the water kept rising.

And soon they had realized that they must leave Great Saloe… or starve.

The Lady of Saloe dreamed an oracle, and chose the most propitious day. They would leave at high summer and build a new city in the south. So Tar'atha ruled.

All the remaining people of the city gathered together their animals and their possessions. They built beautiful wheeled carts to carry them, and wove lovely clothes to wear.

On the first day, the Ten Kings led the sacred bulls through the great gilded gates of the city, garlanded in wreaths of beaten gold. They were followed by a glorious procession: the shadow-women of the Sleeping Goddess, dressed in their most ornate gowns, their most elaborate aprons, bearing the golden image of the Goddess on their muscular shoulders. Behind them walked the Lady of Saloe, with the gold crown of the City upon her head and the knotted belt of Sovereignty about her hips, and behind her, Sais and the rest of the Priestess-brides.

But the twenty sacred bulls had never been outside of the city in their lives. They balked as they were led down the long ramp outside the city gates, and when the feet of the first pair sank into the muddy ground outside the city, they panicked.

Bawling and shaking their heads in terror, the sacred bulls stood fast, and would not be moved.

It was a terrible omen. Sais could not see it, but she could hear the bellowing, and heard the whispered descriptions of the sight at the head of the column.

"Their throats are to be cut here," the Lady of Saloe said at last. "Tar'atha requires this sacrifice to bring us good fortune on our journey."

Sais felt a cold chill of dread creep over her. This was not the ancient ritual. Yes, the sacred bulls died for Tar'atha's favor, but the Twin Kings danced with them first, bringing them to the place of their death with stave and noose before slitting their throats with the stone knife, for no metal must ever touch their flesh. This was… wrong.

But the word was passed, and eventually the bellowing stopped.

The people and the animals moved on.

The beautiful gowns were quickly draggled with mud and water, for all the earth outside Great Saloe was wet and marshy now, salt-poisoned and dead. The ground was too wet for the wheeled carts to be able to roll over it, too wet for the people to simply drag them through the mud. At last they loaded as much of the food and their possessions as they could onto the horses and any animal that could carry a burden, and left the rest behind. The sucking mud quickly stole away one of Sais' glittering golden sandals, and in a fit of temper she unlaced the other one and threw it as far as she could.

The golden image of Sleeping Tar'atha they kept with them.

∗

They did not know where to go, or what they must do. They had lingered long, protected by the walls of Great Saloe, while others fled before them. The land had changed.

Tiny streams were now great rushing rivers of bitter undrinkable water. Fertile grasslands were dying swamps, the grass yellowed and sere.

By the time Ut-ash-atha sank toward the Halls of Sleep the

people were all sick and weary with walking, but a shepherd named Neshat had found a stream of water that was still sweet enough—just barely—to drink.

That night they finished all the cooked food they had brought with them out of Saloe. They lit their lamps, but the wind blew out the flames. It did not matter. Soon the oil would be gone as well.

That night Sais Dreamed.

She had not yet been admitted into the Sanctuary, where the Priestess-brides courted the wisdom of the Great Mother in sleep. Only last year had she begun to bleed as a woman. If the Salt had not come, this year she would have taken one of the Young Kings as a lover in the soft meadows of Spring, courting the favor and fertility of Sleeping Tar'atha.

She was still virgin, and so she should not Dream.

But she Dreamed.

She stood within the walls of Great Saloe. Water filled the streets, rose over the steps of Tar'atha's Temple. In the distance, the villages that had once looked to Saloe for wisdom could no longer be seen: only the waters of the Reed Lake, growing vaster with each death of Ut-sin-atha. The Younger Son shone down into the Sacred Courtyard, turning the sacred pillar to a dull bronze.

And she was not alone.

A figure stepped out from behind the orichalcum pillar. It was a man unlike any Sais had ever seen.

He wore the dancing-kilt of the Young Kings, but his beard was the long red beard of a man. In his hand he carried the Axe of Sacrifice, that only the Lady of Saloe might wield. And upon his brow…

It was as if one of the Young Kings had grown to manhood, and wore the horns of the Sacred Bulls upon his own brow.

She did not know what to do. This was a vision, Goddess-sent, but this was not the Goddess.

The Sleeping Goddess was the Mother of All, and in token of that they depicted her with her sons: Ut-sin-atha and Ut-ash-atha, the Tar'athanis, the Sacred Twins who watched by day and night. And since Sais' world was but a mirror of Her dominion, the Lady of Saloe had Twin Kings as well: five pairs, like the fingers of a hand.

But never did the Young Kings live into the fullness of bearded manhood. Should one be taken by the Mother from the bull-court, his brother must accompany him to Her sky-hall at once: it was the Law of the City. And the bulls were fast, and agile, and clever. Only the young could dance with them, and live.

"You do not know Me, Sais," the Horned One said. "I have danced for your pleasure and My Mother's many a time, yet still you do not know Me. But you will. You will need Me, and what only I can teach you. Call upon My name, when you are ready."

*

With a startled gasp, Sais awoke, staring into the darkness. The images burned strong in her mind and her heart.

But they made no sense. A man? A god-man? A man who was a god?

It could not be. There was only the Mother, alone and One. The Mother and her suckling babes.

Sleep did not come again that night.

*

Another day, their progress southward slower still. When they stopped at mid-morning to eat—slaughtering the young and the weak of the herds to feed themselves—it took a long time to find fuel to cook the meat, and the people lingered over the food. Worse, they made the water palatable by mixing it with the jars of beer and honey-wine they had brought, and so they slept after they had eaten, and did not move on again that day.

But Sais was too frightened to sleep.

When the sheep and the goats and the cattle are gone, what shall we eat? When the grain and the fruit is gone, what shall we eat? Why do not the Great Mother and the Lady of Saloe tell us what we must do?

She knew she should tell the Lady of Saloe of her vision, but she was afraid. She sat among the slumbering Court, and watched the herdsmen as they moved among the surviving beasts, trying to find them palatable grazing. Here and there a

57

tuft of hardy new growth arose in the blighted earth, but most of the grass was yellow and dead with the salt that had risen through the earth. Among them she saw the shepherd Neshat, standing among his beasts.

Sais could look back the way they had come and still see—faintly, in the distance—the gilded towers of Saloe. And along the way, the swath of broken grass that marked their path. It glittered with those things her people had carelessly dropped or discarded—a sandal, a painted fan, a shawl, a child's ball.

The day is warm, she thought. *But winter will come again. Our looms are behind us in Saloe. How shall we clothe ourselves when the cold winds blow?*

"You will need Me, and what only I can teach you. Call upon My name, when you are ready."

*

They were a handful of days upon the road when the first of the Young Kings died.

Sais had not Dreamed again since that first night, but she seemed to feel the presence of the Horned One with her always, waiting for the moment when she would do something she could as yet barely imagine. She was the youngest and most-untutored of Great Saloe's Priestess-brides. What could she do?

The way before them led through a marsh. They had looked for a way around it, and found none. They must cross it, or turn back. By driving the animals ahead, Neshat said, they could find the driest ground and the easiest way. And so it was: where cattle went, men could follow.

But one of the Young Kings turned aside, just for a moment, to pluck a clump of yellow flowers as a gift to the Lady of Saloe. There was so little beauty in the world now, but here in the marsh, flowers grew everywhere.

He put his hand upon a fallen tree to steady himself, and as he did, the trunk rolled aside, and an adder darted out from beneath it, sinking its fangs into his foot.

He died in seconds, gasping out his life, as his brother watched in horror.

The Lady of Saloe waited until they had all crossed safely to the far side of the marsh. Then she called for the Axe.

The Axe of Sacrifice and Tar'atha's golden image were all that they had managed to keep of the sacred things that had been Saloe's. The Axe was older than Great Saloe itself, it was said: its head was polished grey stone, smooth as a woman's skin, and its edge was sharper than any metal.

The dead king's twin came before her. He had known his fate from the moment his brother died. He knelt before her, consenting, and leaned back, offering his throat to the blade. In the shadow of Sleeping Tar'atha, the Lady of Saloe struck, sending him to the sky-halls to join his brother.

Their replacements should have been anointed at once and sent to dance with the sacred bulls in the bull-court. But the bull -court was gone.

Things are changing, thought Sais uneasily.

She did not mean their lives—those had changed on the day the Salt had come. She meant the way in which they were held upon the Mother's knees, and that was something Sais had not thought could change even if the Salt covered all the land below the Mother's sky-hall.

That day, when they stopped, she resolved to tell the Lady of Saloe of her vision, and beg for her comfort.

But that comfort did not come.

*

"These are virginal fancies," the Lady of Saloe told her implacably, when Sais had stumbled through her tale and brought it to its close. "What you speak of is not possible. An axe for men? It cannot be. Who have you told of this?"

"No one," Sais said, stunned and surprised. To whom should she speak of such horrors, save the Lady of Saloe?

"Speak to no one—or never speak again. And dream no more," the Lady said harshly.

Though she could promise not to speak, Sais could not promise not to dream.

*

That night He came to her again. Once more she stood in Drowning Saloe, in the Birth-Room of the Young Kings. Their bodies painted with the red ochre and the yellow, their faces painted as white as Ut-sin-atha's. Their bodies were bound with strips of fine cloth for their journey to the sky-halls, but she could still see the marks of the adder's bite upon the one and mark of the Blade of Sacrifice upon the other, for his head had been carefully set upon his shoulders again with a collar of white clay set with the teeth of bulls.

He was there.

He is no man, Sais thought rebelliously, for the Lady of Saloe's scorn still lay heavily upon her. *He is the Son of the Mother.*

"Do you know Me yet?" He asked.

"You are the Mother's Son," Sais said. She knelt before Him in reverence, though when she did, she knelt in icy water that came to her slender waist.

"My Mother is the Lady of all Beasts, and all that is wild and tame does Her reverence. Yet she has kept for Herself that which is tame, and given to Me that which is wild. You go now into My realms. Call upon My Name when you would accept My gifts."

Once more Sais awoke in the night, her heart fluttering in terror.

Her gown was sodden to the waist, as if she had been wading in a pool. She wrung it out and sniffed at her fingers.

Salt.

But I do not know Your name, Horned One! How shall I call upon You?

The darkness gave no answer.

*

They had been a full cycle of Ut-sin-atha upon the road. He had gone down into the halls of Death and been reborn victorious. In honor of his rebirth, the last of the bulls had been sacrificed in the name of Tar'atha, and the people had feasted, though there had been no incense, no oil, and only brackish water to drink, mixed with the blood of the slain bulls.

Since the death of the Young Kings, and the Lady's clear

displeasure, Sais was in disgrace, and so she heard things that others did not.

The Court—the surviving Young Kings, the Lady of Saloe, the Priestess-brides, the shadow-women, the great nobles and all their slaves and households—all grumbled constantly about the privations of the journey, but they trusted in their hearts to the wisdom of the Lady of Saloe, she who was the Hand of Tar'atha, and went on as if Great Saloe would rise again.

The others—the herdsmen, the farmers, the craftsmen—those who did not eat from the first cut of every sacrifice, but must make do with what the Court left… they doubted. They wondered if Tar'atha was displeased with them, if She had sent the Salt to scour them from the face of the world.

Neshat was first among them. He had even dared to speak out against the sacrifice, saying that if it was done there would be no bulls to put to the cows in the Spring, for they had been the last.

For that, the Lady of Saloe had had him beaten until the blood flowed, until he groveled for her favor and wept for her forgiveness

He had been foolish to speak, Sais thought. It did not matter. There would be no cows come Spring to stand to a bull. They would have eaten them all long since, just as they had eaten the goats and the sheep. The horses remained—for Tar'atha would not allow the killing of horses, or of dogs, even in sacrifice—but the horses were thin and sickly, and the dogs grew daily more anxious for meat.

And where Neshat had spoken and been rebuked, others would eventually follow. When there were no more cattle. When there was nothing left to eat.

Sais was in disgrace, so she had not been permitted to attend the feast of the bulls. She stood in the darkness and watched as the Court ate its fill, and then watched as the remains were dragged on flayed skins to the fires of the herdsmen and farmers.

She thought long upon the words of the Mother's Son. And as she waited in the darkness, she made her plan.

*

That which she bore, she carried wrapped in her shawl like a child, lest any see it. She walked boldly to the fires of the herds-folk, though her mouth tasted bitter with terror.

"I come seeking the herdsman Neshat," she said, stepping into the firelight. "I come to claim my bride-right, by the Law of Saloe."

A priestess-bride might claim any man she chose to be her lover. It was the Law.

"You have come to the wrong fires, little Goddess," one of the men said, not unkindly. "Turn, and choose again."

Almost, her courage deserted her, but fear and her visions drove Sais onward. "I come to claim my bride-right. I come for Neshat," she repeated, hugging her bundle tightly to her chest.

The men and women around the fire spoke among themselves, too low for Sais to hear. At last one of the women pointed. "He is there, little Goddess. He is yours."

Sais did not bow or thank her—that would have been wrong—but her heart leaped with gratitude. She turned and hurried off in that direction.

She found Neshat lying face-down upon a fleece beside a fire. One of the other herdsmen poured water from a jug over his wounded back. Sais knelt beside Neshat, cradling her bundle carefully.

The herdsman looked at her in surprise—and then in more than surprise when he saw who she was.

"I have come for Neshat," Sais said, summoning up the last of her courage. "I bring that which it is not proper for you to see. Leave us now."

The herdsman leaped to his feet and bolted into the darkness, his eyes wide with awe and fear. Now Sais was alone with Neshat.

He slept—or seemed to. Carefully, she unwrapped her bundle. The most important thing she set aside, out of harm's way. The immediately necessary items she took into her hand to use at once.

Even a virgin priestess-bride knew the secrets of the Temple, and so she knew that the base of Tar'atha's statue was hollow. She knew that it was filled with those things that the Lady of Saloe treasured—not gold and jewels, but things more valuable.

Medicines.

Sais had plundered that store ruthlessly.

A wooden box held an ointment of lamb-fat, honey, and distilled poppy-juice: she had compounded it herself many a time. It was sovereign for all hurts, dulling their pain. Now she laved it gently over the weals the shadow-womens' whips had left upon Neshat's back. He began to stir to wakefulness at her touch.

Into the sacred agate cup—which she had also stolen—she mixed poppy-milk, honey, and wine, adding a little water from the jug the other herdsman had left to thin it, and stirring it with her finger to mix it well. As she stirred it, she whispered the spells she had been taught, praying for the Mother's aid in healing—and for Her blessing upon what else Sais would do this night.

Neshat was awake now, watching her with glittering dark eyes.

"Drink this," Sais commanded. "It will ease your pain."

He sat up stiffly and reached for the cup, drinking its contents quickly. Then he reached for the water-jug and drained its contents as well. When it was empty, he wiped his mouth with the back of his hand and stared at her unspeaking for a long moment.

"Why do you come here, little Goddess?" he asked at last.

"I would claim you," Sais said. "It is my right," she added, when he said nothing.

"Are the Young Kings all dead, that you must come to me?" Neshat said. "Or have they cast you out of the Temple?"

"There… is… no… Temple," Sais said. Suddenly she felt sick with despair. He spoke the words of the Young Kings, of the nobles, of the Lady of Saloe. Somehow she had thought he would understand what she herself did not.

"No," Neshat agreed. "There is not. But woe to him who says there is not." For a moment he smiled, then he looked past her, to the other thing she had brought with her, and his face grew very still.

"It is death for you to touch that which you have brought here," he said, gazing at the Axe of Sacrifice.

"We are all dying," Sais said simply. "Come. Be the bull to my cow. It is my right—and it is you I would have, above all the kings and princes of Saloe."

*

I will raise you up—My Son, My Lover, My Consort—

The Voice echoed through Sais' mind. She felt as if she were borne upon the wings of the storm, and did not know if she spoke the words aloud.

I will give birth to You. I will take You to My golden bed. I will slay You in the harvest-year—

Neshat rocked between her thighs. Sais' nails dug into his shoulders, reopening fresh weals. His blood was on her hands.

The blood of sacrifice—

She felt the Horned One—near, so near. The Great Mother's Son, but sons grow to manhood. To father children and care for them, to teach them what they needed to know to survive in the world, no matter how harsh the world.

His hand reached out to her, to lift her up. And in that moment she knew His Name—hers to call upon, to seal a new covenant.

If she dared.

"Nis! Your name is Nis, Son of Tar'atha! Nis, help us!" Sais cried.

*

Afterward, when Neshat lay upon her, spent, Sais took his hand and clasped it about the haft of the Axe.

He did not die.

*

She Dreamed, and in her Dream, Nis came to her again. This time he did not come to her in Drowned Saloe, but in a great forest filled with beasts of every kind, and Neshat was beside her.

"Now I shall teach you what you need to know," Nis said to

them. "You know My Name and may call upon Me. The first meat of the kill is mine, as the blood is My Mother's, but the rest is yours, to nourish your bodies and your hounds. I shall lead you to a land of sweet grass and tall trees, and there you will flourish, but you must never forget Me."

"We will always honor You," Neshat said. "This I vow, upon Your Horns."

*

Before dawn, all among the herdsmen and farmers heard the story of Nis, Son of the Mother, from Neshat and Sais. They hid the Axe carefully, for it had passed from the Mother to the Son.

It was too late now to return it to the Sleeping Goddess. Too many would see. The Lady of Saloe's wrath would be as bitter as the Salt.

And it was no longer hers to own.

*

The loss of the Axe of Sacrifice did not go unnoticed. At the beginning of Ut-sin-atha's feast, it lay before the golden statue of Tar'atha. When Ut-ash-atha took his brother's place in the sky, it was gone.

No one could say how it had happened. It was impossible that anyone but the Lady should lay hands upon the Axe of Sacrifice and live. The shadow-women set up a great wailing, and the Priestess-brides added their lamentations, and the wives of the nobles and all their households howled like dogs.

In so much confusion, it was possible for Sais to replace the cup and the box and the medicines she had taken from the base of Sleeping Tar'atha's golden statue without being seen.

At last, the Lady of Saloe gave her pronouncement: she had Dreamed, and in her Dream, Tar'atha had come to her and taken the Axe of Sacrifice, saying She would leave it for them as a sign in the place they were to build Her new city.

She lies! Sais thought in shock. *She lies about a dream of Tar'atha! She puts words into the mouth of the Great Mother!*

65

She had not thought it could be so. But it was.

The Court was quieted, but the Lady's eyes rested keenly upon Sais' face.

"Do you say I do not Dream true?" the Lady of Saloe said for Sais' ears alone.

"You forbid me to speak of dreams," Sais answered, casting her gaze down upon the earth. *But Nis would have me speak, and what I speak of is no dream.*

*

To hunt was a small thing for herdsmen who had tracked lost sheep and goats through the high grass. To kill with the sling and the stick was a simple thing for farmers who had driven crows from the field and shepherds who had driven wolves from the fold.

At first their attempts went unrewarded, but they quickly learned. For a time—a very short time—their successes went unnoticed by the Court.

Each night Sais slipped away from the Court to go to her lover. Together they dreamed of Nis, and of the southern forests where they would raise His altar beside Tar'atha's own. From the horns and hide of the last bull of sacrifice, the artisans had fashioned for Neshat a Nis-crown, so that he might properly offer Nis His due portion of each kill. And Nis rewarded them, showing them new ways to reap His bounty.

But when Ut-sin-atha had gone down into the Halls of Death once more, and the nights were dark and filled with stars, Sais was summoned before the Lady of Saloe's face.

"The dogs no longer howl with hunger in the night," the Lady of Saloe said. Her voice was mild. In the red light of the fire, Sais could see her face, painted just as it had been in the halls of Saloe, though not even the shadow-women still painted their faces, nor did the Lady of Saloe paint her own face every day.

But tonight her face was as white as the face of Ut-sin-atha, and her lips and her cheeks were as red as the face of Ut-ash-atha. Her brows were as black as the hair of Tar'atha Herself, and the lids of her eyes had been carefully blackened as well.

"The dogs do not howl in the night," Sais agreed, though suddenly her heart beat fast with fear.

"And the smoke of the cook-fires of the herdsmen and farmers is black with fat and savory with roasting, though they have no meat to roast," the Lady said.

Sais did not answer. Two of the shadow-women stood close behind her, and in their hands were knives of the red orichalcum.

"They grow sleek and full of flesh while we starve and dwindle. Why should this be?" the Lady of Saloe asked.

"It is so because I wish it to be so," a new voice said.

Neshat stepped into the fire's light. Upon his head he wore the Crown of Nis. In his hands he bore the Axe of Sacrifice.

The shadow-women stepped back, gibbering in horror. The knives of red orichalcum fell to the earth.

Sais stepped to Neshat's side.

The Lady of Saloe stared at them both from behind her painted face, and her eyes were terrible to see. She stretched out her hand. "That is mine. Give it to me."

"It is not yours. It is not yours to give. It is not yours to take. It is the Mother's to give—and She has given it to Her Son: Nis." The fear Sais had felt was gone now. She knew that she spoke Truth—and Truth had once been honored in the Courts of Great Saloe.

"I know of no Nis," the Lady of Saloe said. But her voice quavered like that of an old woman, and she could not meet Sais' bright gaze.

"You know Him," Sais said, and now her voice was as hard as the Lady's once had been. "He has danced for your pleasure with the bulls. He has lain with Tar'atha in Her golden bed, and gotten Ut-sin-atha and Ut-ash-atha upon Her. As a goodly gift, She has given Him rulership over the wild things of the world. It is He Who gives the duck and the hare into our sling and our snare. Now it is time for Him to lead us."

A faint moan of fear escaped the Lady of Saloe's lips, and Sais knew that at last the Lady knew in her heart that Saloe was no more.

"But the Axe," the Lady whimpered. "It is Tar'atha's Axe."

"No," Sais said, more gently now. "Now it is the Axe of

AN AXE FOR MEN

Nis. Now it is an Axe for men.

♉   ♉   ♉

Rosemary Edghill is a New York Times bestselling, multiple-award-winning author. She has won the Cauldron Award given by Marion Zimmer Bradley's Fantasy Magazine numerous times. Rosemary Edghill's first professional sales were to the black & white comics of the late 1970s, so she can truthfully state on her resume that she once killed vampires for a living. She is also the author of over sixty novels and several dozen short stories in genres ranging from Regency Romance to Space Opera, making all local stops in between. She has collaborated with authors such as Marion Zimmer Bardley and SF Grand Master Andre Norton, worked as an SF editor for a major New York publisher, as a freelance book designer, and as a professional book reviewer. One of her short stories was nominated for the Rhysling Award, which is given for SFnal poetry, and she has been a Philip K. Dick Award judge and survived. Her hobbies include sleep, research for forthcoming projects, and her Cavalier King Charles Spaniels. In some circles, she is best known for her novels and short stories about Bast, a modern day, crime-solving, BTW Witch.

An Axe For Men was first published in Young Warriors: Stories of Strength by Tamora Pierce, Josepha Sherman, Random House Books for Young Readers 2005

By Ira Nayman

IN THE BEGINNING WAS THE WORD. The word was "flugbrartle." It made perfect sense to Anansi, probably because the word was only in his head, so his language needed only to make sense to himself. Loosely translated, flugbrartle meant, "I'm not going to tell you what this word means. It's my word. If you want meaning, make up your own word!"

Anansi looked at The People in the world, and he thought, *You know, I bet that they have words in their heads, too. Can't be sure, what with them walking into cave walls and setting their hair on fire. And,*

EPIK FLAYL CREATES THE WOR(L)D AGAIN

if they do have words in their heads, none of them will be as flugbrartle as flugbrartle. Still.

Anansi, a West African God who often took the form of a spider, loved The People, but he didn't always understand them.

Anansi noticed that The People made noises which could be interpreted as meaningful. For instance, when they walked into cave walls, they often said, "Oww!" or "Oof." When their hair was on fire, they frequently said, "Aaaaiiiieeee!" Loudly and at some length (usually determined by when they stopped making sounds forever). These sounds were made from a combination of the movement of their jaws and tongues and their exhalation of breath. This observation gave Anansi an idea. The next time he came across a man whose hair was on fire, Anansi shouted, "Flugbrartle!" at him. In this case, the word meant, "You're standing on the bank of a river. Why don't you dunk your head in the water and put out the fire in your hair?"

The man stopped yelling "Aaaaiiiieeee!" and looked at Anansi, who stood on the opposite bank, in incomprehension. Then, he collapsed and died because, of course, once fire—which has a voracious appetite—has burned through hair, it eagerly looks for other parts of a person's head to consume.

Anansi wasn't entirely satisfied with the encounter.

He realized that a single word could not adequately express all of the thoughts that needed to be expressed. So, he improvised. The next time he encountered one of The People with his hair on fire, Anansi said, "Crackison flugbrartle?"

This time, the man not only stopped screaming "Aaaaiiiieeee!" but put his hand up as if to scratch his head in thought. All this accomplished was that the man's hand caught fire before he died, but Anansi sensed that he was on to something.

Anansi spent some time giving objects individual names. The tall brown thing with the branches ending in small, soft, green things he called "stream." The round, hard, heavy, bumpy grey thing on the ground he called "pen." The clear, blue thing that constantly seemed to be moving and contained living things that The People caught and ate, he named "tree." *That should help the whole flugbrartle process,* Anansi thought.

The next time he encountered one of The People with her

hair on fire, Anansi shouted, "Tree! Tree! Tree! Tree! Tree!"

The woman looked at the tall brown thing with the branches ending in small, soft, green things in incomprehension. As she died, Anansi realized that naming things wasn't enough—you had to tell people what to do with them.

So, Anansi spent some more time giving actions individual names. To hurry from one place to another would be "to speculate." To put one's head into the clear, blue thing that constantly seemed to be moving and contained living things that The People caught and ate would be "to knock." To breathe words would be "to talkify." At the same time, he continued to give names to objects. The round bit on top of a person's body would be "hand." The things people used to grasp objects would be "graspers." The things people walked on would be called "bobs."

The next time Anansi encountered a man with his hair on fire (these were the early days of external combustion, and The People were having a rough time adjusting to the new technology), he shouted, "Speculate! Speculate! Knock hand on tree! Knock hand on tree!"

Anansi was mystified when the last action the man performed before dying was to hit the tall brown thing with the branches ending in small, soft, green things with his graspers. That wasn't at all what Anansi had told him to do! Perhaps… if The People didn't appreciate the meaning of the different breaths Anansi was directing at them, he should change the meaning of the breaths to what they did appreciate.

In this way, amid much confusion over a long period of time, oral communications was born.

SQUIGGLES

Brer Rabbit, a god who hippity-hopped here and hoppity-hipped there and was known all around Africa, watched as the spoken language of Anansi's The People travelled a great distance and was eventually adopted (with local modifications) by his The People. Fire had become pretty old school, so hardly anybody set their hair on fire any more, but, when they did, the people around them had lots of useful advice, such as:

"Dunk your head in the stream and the fire will go out;"

"Nod your head back and forth really quickly, and the fire might go out;"

and "Knock your hand on a tree. I'm not sure what good that will do, but it is a kind of tradition and, in any case, I will help your children mourn."

Of course, none of this advice was helpful when being confronted by a hungry mountain lion. Try it yourself if you don't believe me. But language would eventually grow to encompass advice for a wide variety of dangers.

Language was sneaky that way.

Brer Rabbit lived in a prickly old briar patch on a hill just outside the village of The People. This allowed him to watch what The People were doing when he wasn't pretending to be one of them in order to trick another one of them into giving him food or sexual favours. This was a satisfactory arrangement (except, perhaps, for the woman who was ambivalent about sharing her husband with a trickster god), save for one problem: when Brer Rabbit saw somebody about to do something foolish, he was not in a position to stop them. Such as using a handgun to break open walnuts.

To be fair, The People had not come upon this idea on their own. Brer Rabbit had used a handgun that one of The Pale People had left behind to create a large hole in the shell of a walnut, not to mention one on the side of his head. Well! Instead of seeing this as a cautionary tale of what not to do with a loaded pistol with the safety off, The People thought it was a behaviour that they should emulate! Not for the first time, Brer Rabbit marvelled at the ability of human beings to take from cautionary tales exactly the wrong lesson.

When Brer Rabbit saw a human, invariably of the masculine persuasion, laying nuts on a wooden picnic table and taking a handgun out of the locked wicker basket in which they were ordinarily kept, he shouted, "No! Don't do it! It was a cautionary tale!" Unfortunately, his briar patch was too far away from the village and his words were swallowed up by the distance, so he was never heard.

One day, Brer Rabbit gathered The People together and explained to them what a cautionary tale was, to much confusion, and advised them not to try to open walnuts with loaded handguns, which was much clearer.

Unfortunately, some of The People were away on a hunt or visiting their relatives in distant Fort York, so they missed the explanation and advice and, sure enough, continued to try to open walnuts with guns. Even more unfortunately, when the old people died and a new generation replaced them, the message got garbled, going from "You shouldn't try to open a gun with a walnut." to, "You should open walnuts with handguns." There was once a cautionary tale about a gun and a walnut that nobody understood that probably contained a good lesson but my eyes glazed over before Brer Rabbit got to that part; and so on.

Brer Rabbit—who preferred to teach in comic parables rather than town hall meetings—was disappointed to find that many in the new generation were back to opening walnuts with guns.

If only there was a more permanent way to get his message across!

The next day, Brer Rabbit was watching worms wriggle this way and that on the ground after a rainstorm. The squiggles of their shapes sparked something in him. 'Hmm,' Brer Rabbit thought. However, before he could make sense of the worms, children from the village stomped all over them, turning them into so much incoherent worm paste.

A couple of days after that, Brer Rabbit found himself staring intently at spider webs in the forest. The variety of shapes, which seemed random at first, soon settled in his mind as rather... squiggly.

'Hmm,' Brer Rabbit thought. 'I sense the emergence of a pattern, here.'

However, before he could make out what the pattern was, a stiff breeze blew the webs back to so much random dust.

Over the next few days, squiggles appeared to Brer Rabbit in the blood spatters of fallen warriors, the steaming entrails of slain deer and even a blanket sewn by an elderly woman with unsteady hands. Brer Rabbit's hmm organ got a real workout in those days, let me tell you! Still, just as he was about to make sense of it all, something disturbed the squiggles and stopped his hmm organ before it could achieve satisfaction.

Finally, one night, the Great Spirit appeared to Brer Rabbit in a dream. The Great Spirit seemed greatly annoyed—at least as annoyed as a nebulous cloud of dream stuff can be.

"Son," he said to Brer Rabbit, "I said, son. I been sendin' you signs and you cain't see the truth for the deer guts! You got the answer, I said the answer right there in your old cranium and you just cain't see it! Come on! Do I have to write you an instruction manual?"

The next day, Brer Rabbit woke up with the biggest erection he had ever had. Oh, and he also connected the breath of The People with squiggles, creating the first written language.

Brer Rabbit introduced his creation to The People. When they asked him what they could write on, he told them paper. Although paper had been created many generations earlier, The People used it primarily to wipe their bums and fold it into shapes that could fly if the right energy was applied to them, shapes that would later come to be known as "airplanes."

One of the village elders asked Brer Rabbit, "If we use paper to write on, what will we use to wipe our bums?"

Brer Rabbit responded that they should make two kinds of paper, one for each purpose.

"What if we run out of paper to wipe our bums with?" the elder continued.

Brer Rabbit allowed that, in such an unfortunate circumstance, it would be permissible for a person to wipe their bum with pages that had already been written on.

Thus, literary criticism was born.

Another elder wondered what they would write the squiggles on the paper with. Brer Rabbit took the beak of a passing chicken (which caused much squawking since the chicken was rather attached to it) and showed The People the motions with which they could use it to create squiggles.

Another elder—Brer Rabbit was beginning to wonder if, as you get older, you lose your ability to acknowledge genius—asked what would flow through the chicken beak to create the squiggles. Ah. Brer Rabbit gave the chicken back its beak (advising it not to go too far away), and went back to his home to consider this question.

Over the course of the next few days, Brer Rabbit tried many liquids with which to create the squiggles. Water did not make a sufficient mark on the page, and had the added disadvantage of making the paper useless for wiping one's bum. Deer's blood made a satisfactory mark, but had a tendency to coagulate quickly. One would have to kill an entire forest of the animals just to write a thank you note for that wonderful potlatch gift somebody gave you. Considering that the "wonderful" gift was usually an ill-fitting sweater, this seemed like an especially poor use of an important resource. Sap from the maple tree attracted flies, which, after a while, made reading thank you notes rather difficult.

In various places around the village, a thick black liquid oozed out of the ground. The People called it "ick." Brer Rabbit thought that if he diluted the ick just the right amount, it would be perfect for writing with. After much trial and error (some of which would take months to get out of his fluffy tail), Brer Rabbit created the perfect liquid. When he distributed his written instructions, The People misread "ick" for "ink," but this was a small glitch in the overall plan.

Brer Rabbit had just invented writing.

TYPE

Coyote, a God widely—worshipped may be too strong a way of putting it—warily watched out for by many indigenous tribes, including the Navajo, Chemehuevi, Paiute and Shoshone, stood in the desert. This was disconcerting. He had never seen so much sand in his life. He didn't think he would ever be able to get the small dune out from between his butt cheeks. (How Coyote had arrived in the middle of the desert was an amusing story involving a mechanical cat, twenty-seven mangoes and a baby born with a full head of hair, but that story has no metaphorical value, so it will have to wait for another time.) All he had to save himself with was a can opener and his wits.

Coyote was doomed.

In the shimmering distance, Coyote thought he could make out something standing upright in the sand. Could it be a man? Not caring if he was the butt of the third oldest joke in the cartoonist's repertoire, Coyote rushed towards the figure. As it happened, it was not a man: it was a pole stuck in the ground. At the top of the pole, somebody had used wire to attach a handwritten cardboard sign that read:

Gblasses – ES nilks.

Coyote shook his head. *That makes no sense*, he thought, and peered more closely at the sign. This time, he thought he could make out:

Kilbassas – ES rilke.

Now, Coyote was certain that his mind was playing tricks on him. For one thing, there were no delicatessens in sight, so how could he possibly get a kielbasa (tasty though the prospect may have been). And, while he was not an expert on German poetry, he was pretty sure Rilke had never written anything about east European sausages, although there was a passage in *Letters to a Young Poet* in which Rilke lyrically described a very painful bout of heartburn which academics conceded may have been caused by the too rapid ingestion of a blood sausage.

Dglassus – ES mikla.

EPIK FLAYL CREATES THE WOR(L)D AGAIN

Coyote took one last look at the sign, which now made even less sense. There was an arrow on the sign pointing to his left. Out of frustration and sheer orneriness, Coyote's first impulse was to go right. However, he reasoned that if he went far enough right, he would have ended up on his left in the end, so he may as well save himself all that extra effort and go left in the first place.

Coyote started walking.

Several days later (well, it felt like days—it may actually only have been four hours, twenty-three minutes and seventeen seconds), Coyote came upon the outskirts of a city of small wooden buildings.

Sitting on an overturned pail, an elderly woman wearing a long brown dress with an abstract red and white pattern sewn across the chest and something   angrily chirping in the rat's nest of her hair, watched him approach.

"Hello, old woman," Coyote greeted her.

"Hello, strange man with the head of a duck," the old woman replied.

"It's a Coyote's head, actually. I have the head of a Coyote."

"Reasonable people may disagree on this point. Still, you have the head of a bird where you should have the head of a man— even unreasonable people can see that you are an odd du—that you are strange."

Coyote resisted the urge to slap the old woman. "Where is this place?" he asked.

"This place is here," the old woman answered, a nod of her head suggesting the obviousness of the answer.

Coyote gritted his teeth. "What is the name of this particular place here?"

"Damascus. Although, strictly speaking, the city limits begin over there—" the old woman pointed to a gate set in a large wooden wall that towered over the small buildings a couple of miles away. "Here could be construed as more of an outer Damascus, if you will, perhaps part of some kind of Greater Damascus Area, or—"

"Thank you," Coyote wearily cut the old woman off. He was disappointed that he hadn't arrived in Jerusalem.

"Don't look so disappointed," the old woman continued. "Didn't you read the sign?"

Coyote slapped her. It was just a small slap, a love tap, really, something that would not have left a mark on a younger woman with more resilient skin. Yet, for all of its gentleness, the slap contained the great frustration Coyote felt at the difficulty of reading handwriting. The old woman, who did not know that the slap also contained Coyote's resolve to do something about this problem, furiously rubbed her cheek and shouted, "Hey! That's assault! Maybe it's okay in the land of the duck-headed people, but in the Greater Damascus Area, it's a crime! You should be ashamed of yourself, avian-man creature!"

Ignoring the old woman's ranting, Coyote decided the city wasn't worth the trouble and returned in the   direction from which he had come.

Coyote's return home involved adventures featuring mobile clay chipmunks, seven austere monks named Chip, a flute that played itself (but only songs that had yet to be written) and a Samurai assassin made up entirely of half-opened fans. Unfortunately, these tales were not merely of no metaphorical value, they had an absolutely anti-metaphorical quality: if you read one, a metaphor would be erased from your memory. So, to spare you the experience of an increasingly drab existence, I will pick up the story with Coyote back at his home in California, contemplating the deficiencies of handwriting.

Coyote gathered up some hen's teeth (the hen wasn't using them and, in any case, could no longer properly complain without any teeth) and carved letters into them. He dipped the carved letters into ink and pressed them onto paper. If the pressure he used was more or less the same, the letters would be imprinted more or less uniformly on the paper. Success! Now, he just needed to package the carved letters with a bottle of ink, hand them out to everybody in the world and revel in the uniformity of imprinting.

Coyote's plan fell apart after the distribution of just three sets. The first person lost the carved letter "m," making it impossible for her to spell "mother," "magic" and "muckity-muck." The second person had poor eyesight, and was constantly mistaking the letter "o" for the letter "a," "m" and "n" and, for reasons that would never be clear, "f" for "s." The third person couldn't spell, but had a lot of fun imprinting the letter "q" on everything: paper, floors, walls, and the side of the family dog. There was also the problem that to create a set of letters for every man and woman of writing age would take Coyote three hundred seventy-seven years. Clearly, this plan would not work.

A couple of weeks later, everything fell into place. Literally. Coyote gone on an adventure that culminated in the tweaking of the nose of Earth Mother, sending her into a spasm of angry volcanic activity that violently shook the ground. Such fun! When he returned home, he found the carved letters, which he had kept on a high shelf, had fallen into a box on the floor. They were in neat rows. At first, Coyote dismissed this because they were neat rows of meaningless gibberish. After a while, though, he realized that if he just rearranged the letters a little, they could form words. Sentences. Paragraphs. A complete, intelligible message!

Letters in a row in a box! Roll some ink over them and you could print out what they spelled as many times as you wanted! Better: you could change the letters and create a whole new message. Over and over again! You could create a message congratulating somebody on surviving a great battle. Then, you could create a message commiserating with the family of somebody who hadn't survived a great battle. Then, you could create a humourous message about the inevitable passage of time, especially as it pertained to the loss of sexual desire (or ability). The possibilities were endless!

Hens throughout the country involuntarily covered their beaks with their wings, although they didn't know why. It didn't matter. In this way, the greeting card industry was born! Umm, as was the printing press.

<u>IMAGE</u>

EXT. ICE FLOE – DAY
It is a vast, cold, desolate place. LOKI (in full ceremonial robes and helmet with horns) stares thoughtfully into the distance.

EPIK FLAYL CREATES THE WOR(L)D AGAIN

NARRATOR
(over)

Meanwhile, on a cold ice field in the far north in the depths of winter, Loki contemplates the accomplishments of his fellow tricksters and considers how he can build on their achievements to create his own brand of mischief.

Loki turns and faces the camera.

LOKI

Why must you assume that I am up to no good? For all you know, I could be considering how a certain Thunder God's actions contribute to violent shifts in the Earth's tectonic plates. That impish look on my face could be the result of some bad lutefisk I ate last night. The—

NARRATOR
(over)

You are a trickster.

Mischief is the largest
part of your job
description—the only one
that matters, really.

                LOKI
              (grins)

You know me too well.

Loki turns back to contemplating the
landscape.

              NARRATOR
               (over)

Although we might not be
able to tell exactly what
Loki is contemplating,
it's a safe bet that—
given that he is the god
of mischief—some kind of—

Loki turns back to the camera.

                LOKI

And another thing: why am
I so often portrayed as
existing in cold nothing-
ness?

              NARRATOR

EPIK FLAYL CREATES THE WOR(L)D AGAIN
(over)

You... you are a Norse god.

                    LOKI

Have you **been** to Asgard?
We have fire, you know.
And central heating. And
a temperate climate. It
really is quite lovely—
nothing like...

          (waves an arm)

...this.

               NARRATOR
               (over)

Fine. Where would you
like this scene to be
set?

               LOKI
               (smiles)

I thought you'd never
ask...

INT. JAZZ BAR - NIGHT
The scene is raucous: a trio is playing
on a small stage as a dozen people dance
in front of them. Drink flows freely as

people sitting at tables shout at each other to be heard. Loki, in a smart suit, fedora and spats, sits at the bar as the BARTENDER (fortyish, beefy) wipes dry a glass with a towel, eyeing him warily.

                         LOKI
                        (drunk)

Entropy, Joe.

                    BARTENDER

Naah. That was last week.

                         LOKI

I-what?

                    BARTENDER

Entropy   Joe   and   the
Jiving Shucksters. They
were in last week.
                         LOKI

Not what I was talking
about.

                    BARTENDER

Good. They drank half my
whisky and ran out on
their   tab.   Bastards.

Great bass player. Still.
Bastards.

Pause.

                    LOKI

     So,   yeah.   Entropy-the
     concept-Joe-you.   I   was
     saying-

                 BARTENDER

     Name's Seamus, pal.

Loki takes a moment to focus on the
Bartender.

                    LOKI

     I think we're straying
     from the point of what I
     wanted to say...

                 BARTENDER

     There was a point to what
     you wanted to say?

                    LOKI

     Uhh...

                    (pause)
I think I'm too sober for
this conversation. How
about another round?

                BARTENDER

It's your bottle, pal.

Loki looks at the bottle next to the shot
glass that he's holding as if it had just
materialized from a star ship in orbit
around the planet. He pours himself a
drink, but, after lifting his glass, he
plunks it back down on the bar, sloshing
the liquor all over.

                  LOKI

I'm an agent of entropy,
right?

                BARTENDER

You say so, pal.

                  LOKI

Indeed, I do say so. I
very   say   so.   Indeed.
Human   beings   build
t h i n g s—h o r s e l e s s
carriages, flush toilets,
societies. It's my job—

and, I will allow, my
pleasure—to remind them
that everything breaks
down. Nothing lasts
forever. So, why take it
so seriously?

                 BARTENDER

People didn't take their
shit so seriously, I'd be
outta a job.

                  LOKI

If people didn't take
their…lives so seriously,
I would be out of a job.

        (looks around)

Still, no danger of that,
is there?

Loki thoughtfully stirs his drink with
the little finger of his left hand, but
doesn't move to actually drink it.

                NARRATOR
                 (over)

Why was Loki drinking
that evening? He was
jealous of the work of
his… relatives. Sure. His

relatives. Coyote had recently bottled light. Light had just been sitting there, minding its own business, since the beginning of time. It took a trickster to capture it. Coyote called his creation a light-bulb—guy spent too much time in nature, you ask Loki.

                 LOKI
              (mumbling)

Still. Crazy mad genius bastard, Coyote.

              BARTENDER

Nobody by that name has ever come in here.

Loki makes to grab the Bartender's collar, misses by a wide margin. The Bartender shoots him a disbelieving look.

         BARTENDER (CONTINUING)

Hey! Watch the hands!

                 LOKI

It's not just that he captured light. He made it dance on a screen! What kind of demented genius would come up with something like that?

                    BARTENDER

Don't look at me. He's your pal, pal.

                      LOKI
                   (irritated)

Isn't that glass dry, already?

                    BARTENDER
                    (shrugs)

It gives me something to do with my hands.

Loki picks up the drink he had been contemplating and...contemplates it for several seconds.

                      LOKI
The problem with the cinema is that it only takes two hours out of your life a week. Where's the entropy in that?

Spider Woman was much more ambitious.

Loki looks up at the Bartender.

                    LOKI (CONTINUING)

You ever met Spider Woman?

                    BARTENDER

I knew a woman named Tessa once what fit the description.

                    LOKI

Naah. Woman I'm thinking about is from Arizona. She wove webs of electricity, first to transport text, then to transport sound. Hours of good, clean, entropic fun for the entire family. If only there was some way to improve on radio. If only we could...

As he trails off, a light-bulb appears over Loki's head and flares alight.

EPIK FLAYL CREATES THE WOR(L)D AGAIN

                    LOKI

          Brilliant!

                  BARTENDER

          Whuzzat?

                    LOKI

          We can use a light-bulb
          going off over somebody's
          head as a metaphor for
          having a brilliant idea!

                  BARTENDER
                 (skeptical)

          We got plenty of
          metaphors for brilliant
          ideas. Seems to me we
          could use more actual
          brilliant ideas.

The Bartender whips his towel at the
light-bulb, which dissolves in a puff of
smoke.

                    LOKI

          No, no! I have one of
          those, too.

BARTENDER

Un hunh.

LOKI

If we put Coyote's light-
bulb together with Spider
Woman's electric wire, we
can create the ultimate
timewaster! Cinema… in
the home! It will be
entropy off the scales!

BARTENDER

Riiiiight. Pardon me if I
don't help fund your IPO.

Loki jumps off his barstool and heads for
the door.

BARTENDER (CONTINUING)
(shouts)

Hey! What about your tab?

Loki waggles a thumb towards the camera.

LOKI

He'll get it.

EPIK FLAYL CREATES THE WOR(L)D AGAIN

As Loki runs out of the joint, the Bartender looks towards the camera.

                    BARTENDER

     That'll be twenty-seven
     bucks, pal.

                    NARRATOR
                    (over)

     I… I didn't bring my
     wallet

                    BARTENDER

     Then, we've got a
     problem, don't we?

The Bartender makes a fist with one hand and grinds it into the palm of his other hand meaningfully.

                    NARRATOR
                    (over)

        Now, now, no need to be
        like that. I'm sure we
        can work this out like
        reasonable—YIPE!

FADE TO BLACK. TITLE CARD: And that,

children, is how Loki got the idea to
create television.

<u>INTELLIGENCE</u>

P1. ePik Flayl was tired of playing pool by himself. It wasn't
that he was very bad at it, with each game lasting the better
part of a week (at which point he broke all of the cues in
frustration and vowed he would never play again). It was that
he was forced to banter with himself, and he hardly ever said
anything that he didn't already know (and, when he did, it
usually turned out to be wrong). The problem was that none
of the other gods wanted to enter ePik Flayl's hovel—even
though it had three pool rooms, a sauna, a barbershop (with a
trio—Phil the Tenor was off fulfilling his lifelong dream of
yodeling Tamino's aria from *The Magic Flute* at the top of
Mount Everest), a small petting zoo and a full service
McGreasy's restaurant. They worried, not without reason,
that he would use the opportunity to play a trick on them.
ePik Flayl's tricks usually involved gender switching, loss of
limbs, an unusual use of a highly personal orifice or some
combination of the three. You can understand their concern.

TO LEARN MORE ABOUT ePIK FLAYL: Go to
paragraph 2.

TO GET ON WITH THE STORY: Go to paragraph 3.

TO ABANDON THIS FAR TOO LENGTHY SERIES
OF PARABLES: Go to the next story in this volume,
starting on page 104.

P2. ePik Flayl was the black Angry Bird of the digital gods.
He was the great-great-great-great-great-great-great-great-
great-great-great-grandson of the aunt of the brother of the
great-great-… great-granddaughter of the third cousin three
quarters removed of the son of Coyote. Or, so his genial-ogist

had told him. He was so proud of this connection to the iconic trickster that there was a blank space in his portrait hall where he had been legally prohibited from displaying a painting of Coyote. Arrundel, the All Coder, looked upon ePik Flayl with indulgence; the rest of the digital gods thought him exceedingly strange and gave him a wide birth (his escapades often resulting in him being reborn). For his part, ePik Flayl wasn't keen on joining them in the Sparkling City of Digitaleusia because walking out of his hovel to wherever they might be **was work**, and who needs that?

TO GET BACK TO THE STORY: Go to paragraph 3.

TO REMIND YOURSELF OF THE SET-UP TO THE STORY: Go back to Paragraph 1.

TO CATCH A COLD: Go out of the house without your mittens and never wash your hands.

P3. Around the time ePik Flayl was trying to find a way to spend time with the other digital gods without, you know, actually **being** with them, he noticed that it took forty-three minutes and seventeen seconds for him to walk from the smoking lounge, where his telephone was, to the library that housed his typewriter; the trip took fifty-nine minutes and forty-nine seconds if he made a detour to the den that contained the nearest TV set (not counting the hours he spent watching it). *Wouldn't it be awesome*, he thought, *if all of these devices were one? Wouldn't it be sooooooo convenient?* And so, being a lazy sod, ePik Flayl set about creating one.

TO SEE HOW ePIK FLAYL CREATED HIS MARVELOUS COMMUNICATIONS DEVICE: Go to Paragraph 4.

TO SKIP A LOT OF SERIOUS UNPLEASANTNESS: Go to the point of the story, Paragraph 14.

TO GET TO CARNEGIE HALL: Practice! Practice! Practice!

P4. The machine would have to see what was in front of it, so ePik Flayl plucked out one of his eyes and placed it in front of a magnifying glass in front of a screen. It would have to be able to send and receive sounds, so he cut off one of his ears (no, he had never heard of Vincent van Gogh, although he was fond of sunflowers) and placed it in front of an amplifier. In order to input instructions into the machine, ePik Flayl followed Coyote's example and made a keyboard out of his sinews and teeth. To be able to process all of the information flowing through the machine, ePik Flayl took part of the part of his brain that dealt with logical reasoning (he was just silly enough to believe that he was just smart enough that he could make do without it) and created a CPU. In order to store information for future retrieval, ePik Flayl took part of the part of his brain that dealt with memory and created… memory. Several modifications later, ePik Flayl took many of the nerves out of his body (he was always accused of having too much nerve as it was) and connected some to an electrical outlet in the room (to power the machine) and some to the telephone jack (so that the machine could communicate with other machines). Finally, he encased the machine in his own skin because looking at all of those body parts loosely connected in ways they hadn't been created for was, even he had to admit, pretty gross.

P5. Then, ePik Flayl invited some friends over to see what he had created.

WAIT A MINUTE! WAIT JUST A MINUTE! DIDN'T YOU SAY NOBODY EVER WANTED TO VISIT ePIK FLAYL'S HOVEL?

TO FIND OUT WHY SOME GODS WERE WILLING TO VISIT ePIK FLAYL: Go to Paragraph 6.

EPIK FLAYL CREATES THE WOR(L)D AGAIN

TO FIND OUT WHAT ePIK FLAYL'S FRIENDS DISCOVER WHEN THEY ARRIVE AT HIS HOVEL: Go to Paragraph 9.

TO REMIND YOURSELF OF WHAT HAS LED TO THIS DISGUSTING POINT: Go to the beginning of the story on page 69. Then, when you read ePik Flayl's part of the story, skip over Paragraph 4 and go straight to Paragraph 6.

TO EARN A MILLION DOLLARS IN THE STOCK MARKET: Start with two million dollars to invest…

P6. While it's true that none of the Digital Gods were keen on visiting ePik Flayl in his hovel, other trickster gods were happy to. Brer Rabbit, for example, was always delighted to avail himself of the all-you-can-eat salad bar. Loki enjoyed a good game of no-holds-barred-snooker. Coyote (who wasn't able to make it because of a toothache that had wracked his entire body) was always happy to avail himself of the all-you-can-eat rabbit bar. Because they were different aspects of the same universal human impulse, what one trickster did to another he did, in a sense, to all, including himself. This didn't stop them from tricking each other, of course, so over the millennia the tricksters developed a code of honourable conduct.

P7. According to the Tricksters Code of Honourable Conduct, RULE THREE THOUSAND SIX HUNDRED TWELVE AARDVARK: Never pull a trick on a fellow trickster, especially one you have invited into your home. Unless it's really funny. RULE THREE THOUSAND SIX HUNDRED TWELVE BATS read: Never play a trick on a fellow trickster who has invited you into their home. Unless it's really funny. Not every rule in the TCH ended with "Unless it's really funny." Some ended with "Unless it's really, really funny," "Unless it's uproariously funny," or even "Unless it's so side-splittingly funny that you may not make it to the hospital to get your side sewn back up before you die." As you might expect, this didn't stop them from tricking each other, either. But, just the fact that a code of conduct existed made them feel more at ease in each other's company.

P8. Silly tricksters.

TO FIND OUT WHAT ePIK FLAYL'S FRIENDS DISCOVER WHEN THEY ARRIVE AT HIS HOVEL: Go to Paragraph 9.

TO GET TO THE POINT OF THIS PARABLE: Go to paragraph 14.

TO NEUTER YOUR PET RHINOCEROS: Make sure that your insurance is fully paid up. Your beneficiaries will thank you.

P9. To make things easier, let's assume that Anansi, Brer Rabbit, Coyote and Loki arrived at ePik Flayl's hovel together. Each availed himself of the food or beverage of his choice. ePik Flayl was nowhere to be found, but they assumed that the trick he was about to play on them was funny and, in any case, the rabbit tart in a white wine sauce was delicious—I think I'm going to have to go back for seconds! The tricksters eventually assembled in ePik Flayl's laboratory, where they found their host barely recognizable, his cannibalized body having great difficulty standing erect, feebly waving a hand at a small box of skin with some truly disgusting peripherals. ePik Flayl mumbled something that nobody could understand; later, he would explain that it was an invitation for each of them to do the same thing to their bodies so all of the tricksters could "network."

TO FIND OUT ANANSI'S REACTION TO SEEING ePIK FLAYL'S MACHINE: Go to Paragraph 10.

TO FIND OUT BRER RABBIT'S REACTION TO

EPIK FLAYL CREATES THE WOR(L)D AGAIN

SEEING ePIK FLAYL'S MACHINE: Go to Paragraph 11.

TO FIND OUT COYOTE'S REACTION TO SEEING ePIK FLAYL'S MACHINE: Go to Paragraph 12.

TO FIND OUT LOKI'S REACTION TO SEEING ePIK FLAYL'S MACHINE: Go to Scene 1.

TO FIND OUT ePIK FLAYL'S REACTION TO HIS FRIENDS' REACTION TO HIS MACHINE: Go to paragraph 13.

P10. Anansi looked upon ePik Flayl's creation and said, "Flugbrartle," which, in this case, probably meant something like, "Okay, that's an image I'm not going to get out of my head any time soon. Thanks. Thank you so much for that!" (It's all in where you place the emphasis of your breath.)

TO FIND OUT BRER RABBIT'S REACTION TO SEEING ePIK FLAYL'S MACHINE: Go to Paragraph 11.

TO FIND OUT COYOTE'S REACTION TO SEEING ePIK FLAYL'S MACHINE: Go to Paragraph 12.
TO FIND OUT LOKI'S REACTION TO SEEING ePIK FLAYL'S MACHINE: Go to Scene 1.

TO FIND OUT ePIK FLAYL'S REACTION TO HIS FRIENDS' REACTION TO HIS MACHINE: Go to paragraph 13.

P11. Brer Rabbit excused himself from the room and hopped madly to the nearest bathroom. Unfortunately, it was a five minute, thirty-seven second hop from ePik Flayl's laboratory, and Brer Rabbit didn't quite make it. As he wiped himself off and started to make his way back to his fellow tricksters, Brer Rabbit hoped the hallway in *which he had made the mess wasn't much used...*

TO FIND OUT ANANSI'S REACTION TO SEEING ePIK FLAYL'S MACHINE: Go to Paragraph 10.

TO FIND OUT COYOTE'S REACTION TO SEEING ePIK FLAYL'S MACHINE: Go to Paragraph 12.

TO FIND OUT LOKI'S REACTION TO SEEING ePIK FLAYL'S MACHINE: Go to Scene 1.

TO FIND OUT ePIK FLAYL'S REACTION TO HIS FRIENDS' REACTION TO HIS MACHINE: Go to paragraph 13.

P12. Coyote resisted an urge to pluck his own eyes out with his beak—sorry, I meant snout. That old woman can be quite persuasive! He didn't think that it was physically possible; perhaps he could detach his beak from his face to accomplish the task. He had done stranger things to his body. In the end, realizing that ePik Flayl had done something more bizarre to his body than Coyote could have possibly imagined, he settled for shaking his head sadly. *Don't you have access to hens?* he thought.

TO FIND OUT ANANSI'S REACTION TO SEEING ePIK FLAYL'S MACHINE: Go to Paragraph 10.

TO FIND OUT BRER RABBIT'S REACTION TO SEEING ePIK FLAYL'S MACHINE: Go to Paragraph 11.

TO FIND OUT LOKI'S REACTION TO SEEING ePIK FLAYL'S MACHINE: Go to Scene 1.

EPIK FLAYL CREATES THE WOR(L)D AGAIN

TO FIND OUT ePIK FLAYL'S REACTION TO HIS FRIENDS' REACTION TO HIS MACHINE: Go to paragraph 13.

S1 **INT. ePIK FLAYL`S LABORATORY—DAY**

The room appears to be full of a Rube Goldberg contraption of pipes, wires, Bunsen burners, cogs, cams, weights, counter-weights and even a mousetrap. In a clearing in the centre, ePik Flayl stands, well, staggers, more like, his mutilated body looking like something George Romero would have rejected as too horrific. Next to him is a small, humming box made out of… no. Really? Just—no.

Brer Rabbit hops out of the room. Anansi looks disgusted. Coyote shakes his head in sadness. Loki sternly puts his hands on his hips, looking like he is about to deliver a long, long lecture. After a couple of tense seconds, Loki bursts out laughing.

                    LOKI

        You know, we can do all
        of this with space age
        materials now.

    Anansi chuckles. Coyote smiles to himself. ePik Flayl wheezes in what he hopes comes across as an amused way.

TO FIND OUT ANANSI'S REACTION TO SEEING ePIK FLAYL'S MACHINE: Go to Paragraph 10.

TO FIND OUT BRER RABBIT'S REACTION TO SEEING ePIK FLAYL'S MACHINE: Go to Paragraph 11.

TO FIND OUT COYOTE'S REACTION TO SEEING ePIK FLAYL'S MACHINE: Go to Paragraph 12.

TO FIND OUT ePIK FLAYL'S REACTION TO HIS FRIENDS' REACTION TO HIS MACHINE: Go to paragraph 13.

P13. After his guests had left, ePik Flayl made his body whole again. No permanent harm was done to it, although for the next few years every time he sneezed, a vein in his leg would come loose. Still, he felt it was worth it. Having gotten the basic design down, ePik Flayl was able to recreate his machine in silicon and plastic.

P14. And that, children, was how the computer age was born.

TO READ THE STORY OVER AGAIN FROM THE BEGINNING: Go to Paragraph 1.

TO QUIT THIS STORY AND START A NEW ONE: Turn the page.

TO EAT A SANDWICH: Make yourself a sandwich and eat it.

MMMMMMMMMM, SANDWICH: Are you going to finish that? Because I gotta tell ya, parableizing is hungry work, and if you're not gonna finish that…

Ira Nayman is a humour writer who stumbled into speculative fiction over a decade ago and decided to hang around. His latest novel, *Bad Actors*, was recently released by Elsewhen Press; it is the seventh in his Transdimensional Authority series, the second in the Multiverse Refugees Trilogy. He was the editor of *Amazing Stories* magazine for two and a half years. In the first week of September, 2022, he will celebrate the 20th anniversary of *Les Pages aux Folles*, the website that features weekly updates of political and social satire.

Between Fire and Infinity

By James Dick

OUTSIDE THE AIRPLANE WINDOW, the clouds parted to reveal a dying nation. Though it gave few outward signs of its decomposition—the trains ran on time, cars packed the roads, and the ants on the sidewalks went about their business—Dawn knew for a fact the sun was setting on the Soviet Union. She was the proof: an American citizen, a rocket scientist, invited into Russia to pick over the bones of the military research bureaus.

The United States told the world it won the Space Race, but Dawn and her colleagues viewed it as a tie. Growing up, she'd watched the USSR claim one title after another: first nation to put a satellite in orbit, first to put a man in space, first to put a woman in space, first to conduct EVA, first to operate multiple spacecraft simultaneously, first to photograph the dark side of the moon. America had won the moon landing, but even that turned out to be a near thing. With the fall of the Berlin Wall, a flood of footage had spilled out of the Soviet Union, most shocking of all being the grainy, washed-out film reels of a rocket that defied imagination, a monster that dwarfed even the mighty Saturn V, a god which bore the enigmatic name "N1". If not for the death of the chief Soviet rocket designer, Sergei Korolev and the ouroboros of Soviet bureaucracy, the USSR may have taken the moon as well.

The burgeoning western rocket industry quietly acknowledged this and was hungry for the secrets of the engines the Soviets had used to so roundly embarrass America for nearly ten years. Getting those secrets was Dawn's official assignment, given to her by her superiors at Aerojet. She was part of the first wave of scientists being let into Russia. But she had another reason for coming.

Opening her carry-on briefcase in her lap, Dawn took out a folded copy of a letterhe'd received three weeks ago, the original being held by the US State Department. She'd read and re-read it so many times the creases were starting to wear through. Soon, she'd have to tape them to keep the pages from falling apart. With a light touch and a heavy heart, she read it once more.

Dear Dawny,

Dawn inhaled sharply. Those two words never failed to sting. Steeling herself, she continued.

Forgive me for addressing you so familiarly, your father assured me it was the only way you would know to trust me. He told me that was your nickname, one that only he and your mother used. He also told me to remind you never to wind grandpa's golden watch, to keep your fire truck close in case your bookcase catches fire at night, and to check your math over and over until you feel like socking Newton in the eye.

Dawn, it grieves me to have to tell you this, and perhaps you've suspected the truth for a very longsome time, but your father is dead.

Dawn always had to pause at this part and fight back tears.

My name is Perun. You do not know me, but I had the honour and privilege of working with your father while he was undercover at OKB-456. Later, we were transferred to OKB-333 to begin work on something I must show you <u>in person</u>. Your father recruited me very early into his infiltration of Valentin Glushko's program, and I helped him acquire classified information for many years. Frank was a truly brilliant engineer.

That he was, Dawn thought.

The KGB discovered your father's identity two weeks after he transferred to 333. They came to the complex early one morning looking for him, but found only me. After they left, I departed the lab and sought him out to tell him he was in danger, but I was too late. Perhaps the CIA told you this, but your father was given cyanide capsules in case he was ever discovered. He swallowed one before they could get their hands on him. He was never tortured or interrogated. I swear this on the name of my own father.

For many years, I have felt responsible and lived with the guilt that I survived and your father did not. I am not a good man. He was. He deserved to live far more than I. I cannot bring him back, but at least at the very least, I can show you what he died for.

At OKB-333, we built an engine. This engine may be is the key to the future unlocking the cosmos. I wish to give you this engine, Dawn, before it is lost in the churn of civilization death throes of the Soviet Union. <u>Come quickly</u>, I beg you. The USSR may be dying, but it is not yet dead. The cords of power are loosening, but they are not yet undone. In this land, there are still forces that would see us turn back towards the past, to never change, who would steal the future from you us. I don't know how much time I have.

I will enclose a map with this letter.
<u>Come quickly.</u>
Perun

Dawn reached into her briefcase and took out the map, which depicted a forested region about four hours' drive north of Moscow, and east of Tver. Perun had drawn several lines branching off from the highway with an engineer's exactitude, complete with notes on turnoffs, gas stations, and road conditions.

Upon receiving the original letter, Dawn had taken it straight to her boss at Aerojet, who in turn reached out to the

State Department, who then connected her with her dad's old handlers at the Central Intelligence Agency. The CIA did indeed have records of someone named Perun being recruited by Frank Spencer whilst he was in the Soviet Union, but there was no mention of OKB-333 in any of Frank's intelligence reports, nor was it on any list of Experienced Design Bureaus disclosed by the new Russian government. That meant one of two things: either OKB-333 didn't exist, or it had been targeted for liquidation.

There was also the little matter that Perun was most definitely a codename. By happenstance, Dawn had discovered it was the name of a Slavic god of thunder and war. *Appropriate for a rocket scientist.*

Whatever the case, Dawn wanted answers. Her father had left his life in America to try to steal the secrets of Soviet rocketry. Dawn had made peace with her father's departure and subsequent disappearance, and now some stranger had just dredged the loss up all over again.

If Perun doesn't have a good reason, there'll be hell to pay. Dawn intended to meet Perun, but she wasn't going alone. The CIA had detached two of their best operators to watch Dawn's back. They were on the plane with her right now, across the aisle, a man and a woman, playing the role of lovebirds off to see Europe.

Dawn glanced to her right to check on them, only to find her view obstructed by a big-bellied man who was the spitting image of Jolly Saint Nick, complete with a full snowy beard and a twinkle in his eye. He'd been looking at the letter and the map in Dawn's lap, but when Dawn's eyes met his, he blushed and held up his hands. "Oh, forgive me," he said, his voice coloured by a Russian accent. "I did not mean to pry." He looked like he'd been caught with his hand in the cookie jar.

Dawn smiled, hastily folding the letter and map and stowing them in her briefcase, which she then shut and latched. "No worries," she said. *When did he get there?*

"I hope you don't mind," Saint Nick said. "I came from the back." He jabbed a thumb over his shoulder. "My neighbour is a kind old woman, but unfortunately—unbearably—flatulent." He rolled his eyes.

Dawn chuckled. "It's okay." She leaned forward and scratched her ankle while stealing a discreet look at the Lovebirds. The man—Dawn didn't know his name, the CIA just told her to call him Grey—turned toward the woman (Rosy) and nuzzled her, but his eyes were trained on Dawn and her visitor.

"A lover?" asked Saint Nick.

That brought Dawn up short. "'Scuse me?"

Saint Nick nodded to her briefcase. "The letter. I could tell from the creases you've read it many times. In my experience, the letters re-read the most are composed by lovers."

Many responses came to mind. "An… opportunity," Dawn said at last. "One I've been awaiting for a long time."

"Mmm." Saint Nick nodded sagely. "This is a time of opportunity. *Perestroika*, *glasnost*, and now the Wall itself has come down. As I have said for years: there is much to be gained from our comrades across the Atlantic."

Since Father Christmas had been so good as to pry into Dawn's affairs, she felt it was only right to return the favour. She studied his slate-grey three-piece suit. "Let me guess… you're a businessman."

Saint Nick pointed a meaty, well-manicured finger at Dawn. "Correct." He opened the rest of his fingers, offering his hand. "Mikhail Volosov, Ikon Korp." He lowered his voice conspiratorially. "I specialize in hostile takeovers."

"Dawn Spencer." She shook his hand. "Aerojet."

"Ah!" Volosov's face lit up. "You're here for our rockets."

"Right on the money."

Volosov chuckled. "Aerojet. If many more of you make the crossing, there will be more American rocket scientists in Russia than Russian ones."

"That wouldn't surprise me in the least. Some of the machines we've seen since the Wall came down are beyond belief. Are you connected with rocketry, in any way?"

"Oh, only tangentially. My concerns are minerals, precious metals, earthworks, much of which is probably used in rocket-building. But as for the engineering aspects, I truly could not get my head around it."

The PA system chimed. The pilot thanked the passengers for their patronage, informing them that the plane would be touching down at Sheremetyevo Airport in ten minutes, *"and could everyone please take their seats."*

"I suppose I should go back," said Volosov, sighing. He shook hands with her one more time. "It was a pleasure, Ms. Spencer."

"Likewise. See you around."

"I should hope so," Volosov chortled as he headed back down the aisle. "In fact, I am sure of it."

Dawn frowned. *What do you mean by that, Saint Nick?*

*

Upon landing at Sheremetyevo, Dawn procured a slate-grey jalopy, some snacks for the road, and began the drive to OKB-333. A yellow Lada kept pace behind her, the Lovebirds at the wheel. They never drew close enough for it to be obvious they were following her.

The brutalist concrete hives of Moscow gave way to lush green pines and golden fields. Fat fluffy clouds rolled across the skies, casting shadows on the forests and farms below. Russia was a vast country. Dawn imagined the land in winter, covered in ice and snow, and began to understand why it was the grave-yard of so many conquering armies throughout history.

Dawn caught herself speeding and eased her foot off the gas. She wanted the revelations to be over, for better or worse. All her life she'd been a woman of action, working herself to the bone to get a degree in engineering, battling tooth and nail for a job at Aerojet, and manoeuvring herself to be one of the first to get a look at Soviet engines. She'd made peace with her dad's departure from her life. The sudden appearance of this Perun felt like an insult from the universe, the work of a malicious trickster trying to take her down a peg. Dawn was eager to put this affair in the rear-view mirror, right next to the deadly Lovebirds where it belonged.

Before making the final approach to the OKB complex, Dawn stopped at a gas station to drain her bursting bladder. As she got back in the car, a navy-blue Lexus pulled up to the pumps, and none other than Mikhail Volosov stepped out.

A chill shot down Dawn's spine at the sight of the jolly big man. *Now, what are the odds that he just happens to be driving the same route as me and stops at the same gas station at the same time I do?* She glanced across the lot. The Lovebirds had parked just beside the station. She couldn't see them very well, but they surely must've noticed Volosovtoo.

The big man opened the station door for an elderly gentleman, then followed him inside, letting the door swing shut behind.

Dawn wasted no time. She double-checked the route on her map, started her engine, and got back on the road. In her rear-view mirror, the Lovebirds mounted the highway behind her. She kept one eye on the mirror for the next few kilometres, but Volosov's Lexus didn't reappear.

*

Following the route on Perun's map, Dawn turned off the highway into what looked like a small copse of trees, but which turned out to be the tip of a large forest. It was mid-afternoon, and the angle of the sun combined with the heavy cloud cover endowed the forest with an ancient, dusky atmosphere. Dawn glanced in the rear-view. She could no longer see the Lovebirds.

The road was gravel, and was clearly intended to be used only by large-tired military and industrial vehicles, not a civilian sub-compact like the clunker Dawn was driving. She took it slow, wary of sharp rocks and deep potholes.

Perun's full of shit, she decided. *This road isn't paved. There's no way it could service a rocket lab.*

By her estimation, she only had another kilometre to drive, though, so she decided to see where this wild goose ran.

The trees abruptly ended and a clearing opened before her, dominated by a monolithic administrative building, all angles and sharp corners. Just past it, a couple kilometres further on, was an even larger concrete structure, a raised platform suspended over a cliff, covered in snaking pipes and fuel tanks. Dawn identified it instantly as a test stand, a fixed stage upon which to fire rocket engines to see how they behaved.

Okay, not so full of shit after all.

A man stood at the top of the steps leading to the front

door, wearing a white lab coat over drab army fatigues, holding a mug in one hand. He waved at her.

Dawn checked her rear-view mirror. The Lovebirds trundled up the road behind her, keeping out of sight of the main building. Confident of their protection, Dawn let the downward slope of the road carry her into a parking spot beside the front entrance. She put the car in park and stepped out into a warm breeze.

The man came over to meet her. As he drew closer, Dawn saw that he was broad-shouldered, narrow-hipped, brown-eyed, and curly-haired. Handsome, all things considered. His lips were curled into a cocky smirk. "Ms. Spencer?" he asked.

Dawn nodded. "Are you Perun?"

"I am." He offered his hand."It's a pleasure—"

"Let me clarify two things," she interjected, putting her hands on her hips."First, I don't much care for the way you've used my relationship with my father to bring me here."

Perun's smirk vanished. His hand fell to his side.

"I made my peace with his loss a long time ago. Second, my superiors at Aerojet and our contacts at the State Department know where I am and what I'm doing. If you try anything funny, there isn't a corner of this planet where they won't find you."

As Dawn spoke, a cloud stole over Perun's face, darkening it. "I'm sorry if I've caused you pain," he said softly. "It was of the first importance to get you here, to show you…"

Dawn crossed her arms. "What's your name? I mean your real name."

"Perun is my name. I have no other."

Dawn's nostrils flared. She shouldn't have been surprised the man wouldn't tell her his name. Russian politics were a maelstrom, and someone who was a hero of the Soviet Union might be a criminal in the Russian Federation. Perun was playing it safe. She couldn't fault him for that.

"I have something," Perun said, reaching into his lab coat with his free hand. "A gesture of good faith." He produced a thick sheaf of papers, double-folded, held together by a steel ring at the corner, and held it out to her. "And to show I'm genuine."

Dawn reached for the pages. When they passed from Perun's hand to hers, an expression of—was it relief? satisfaction?—crossed the man's face. Unfolding the pages, Dawn saw that they were numbered, with the first being a title page and table of contents. Printed large in bold letters across it was "**RD -271**". That was a Soviet rocket engine designation.

But not just any engine.

Heart hammering, Dawn scanned the table of contents. Her Russian wasn't great, but she knew enough to identify the words "cycle diagram", on page ten. She went straight there. On this page was a simple cross-section of an engine, with all its fuel and oxidizer tubes laid out in a readable manner. Dawn traced the pipes with her finger, and when she got to the engine nozzle, she looked up.

Perun was nodding. "Now you understand."

"We thought only one was ever built."

"No, there was a second." Perun stepped aside and gestured to the front door. "Come and see."

*

The halls of OKB-333 were dusty and deserted. The place looked as if it had been empty for a couple years. Perun led Dawn down a long hallway toward the heart of the facility, guiding her around broken glass and exposed wiring. "This place is a victim of Valentin Glushko," Perun explained. "When the N1 moon rocket failed, he ordered many design bureaus to close their doors and scrap their engines. Some scientists, like Kuznetsov, disobeyed, preserving their creations. That is what I have done here."

Dawn shook her head. "So typically Soviet. Create the best machines in the world and then scrap them just to save face."

"This country is full of paradoxes. You get used to them." Perun glanced over his shoulder at Dawn. "You're familiar with the RD-270?"

Dawn's eyebrows rose. "Are you kidding? I've read every word I could find on it. In America, we always thought full-flow staged combustion cycle engines were impossible to build. I remember how shocked we all were to find you not only had a working prototype of one, but that it could also be fuelled by either RG-1 or Pentaborane."

Perun's cocky-ass smirk was back. "In this place," he said, gesturing at the walls around him, "we were charged with building the RD-271, only it wouldn't be fuelled by RG-1 or Pentaborane."

"What, then?"

The hallway terminated in a pair of imposing steel doors. "Liquid methane." Perun pushed the left door open as if it weighed nothing and held it open for Dawn.

She stepped through and found herself on a catwalk overlooking a cathedral-like assembly room. On the factory floor, fifty feet below the catwalk, rank upon rank of rocket engines reposed. Each engine was fifteen, sixteen feet tall, easily, and unlike most Soviet rocket engines that split into two or four nozzles, these were single nozzle giants that could swallow the car Dawn drove here in with room to spare.

Perun ushered Dawn towards a staircase that led to the factory floor. Dawn approached the nearest engine and ran a hand over its smooth grey-green nozzle. The analytical side of her brain revved up as she studied the tangled snakes' nests of pipes crowning the engine. "Why methane?" she asked. "It's not an easy fuel to work with. It's a pain to store and you can't load as much of it into a rocket as standard kerosene-based propellant."

Perun joined her beside the nozzle. "Frank and I said much the same when we arrived here. Neither of us could imagine that the Soviet Union was looking at a picture beyond the Earth and the moon. Think for a moment, it'll come to you."

Beyond the Earth and the moon... oh my God. "Mars," said Dawn. "They chose methane because it's the only fuel that can be synthesized on Mars."

Perun's smirk widened into a glowing smile, and he nodded. "Shocking, isn't it? Someone was actually thinking that far ahead." He placed his hand beside Dawn's. "Imagine a rocket, equipped with the most efficient engine possible, that could refuel and re-launch from Mars, which only has a third of Earth's gravity. Any nation with access to space on that basis would have the keys to the universe." Perun looked at Dawn.

"This is the secret your father was killed to protect. This is the future, and it doesn't deserve to die in a landfill."

Dawn held out her hand and approached the engine. Even earthbound and unfueled, the machine exuded power. "Has it ever been tested?"

Perun chuckled. "I was so hoping you would ask that." He opened his mouth to speak further, but a series of faint, far-away *pops* cut him off.

Dawn listened, trying to identify both the source and the nature of the noises, and from the intent expression on Perun's face, she guessed he was trying to do the same. "Sounds almost like… firecrackers," Dawn said.

Perun's eyes suddenly widened. "No," he said, his tone low and deadly. "It's gunfire." He started moving towards the stairs.

Dawn trailed after him. "How can you—"

"It's gunfire," Perun repeated, running up the stairs. The certainty in his voice unnerved Dawn.

*

Dawn and Perun dashed out the front doors of the research complex. The Lovebirds had driven their car into the parking lot and parked it perpendicular to the road, forming a makeshift barricade. They crouched behind it with semi-automatic pistols drawn, firing into the treeline.

Grey looked back at Dawn and Perun, eyes wild. "Get down! We're surrounded!"

"Right flank!" Rosy cried, sending two rounds into a tree trunk a hundred metres away.

Dawn kept low and scanned the treeline. She didn't see or hear anyone returning fire. A hand touched her shoulder, and she looked up. Perun was standing upright, unconcerned. He shook his head. Then he strode down the steps to where the Lovebirds crouched and touched the backs of their heads. They both collapsed into a heap on the asphalt.

"What'd you do?" Dawn snapped.

"They're not hurt," said Perun, "just asleep."

"Is that some KGB trick?"

"Far from it."

Before Perun could elaborate further, the Lovebirds' car took flight, lifting bodily off the ground and flipping end-over-end to land at the edge of the parking lot. Standing in its place was Mikhail Volosov. He smiled, cheeks dimpling. *"Naytitebya,"* he sang.

Dawn translated Volosov's words: *Found you.*

Perun squared his shoulders with Volosov, hands curling into fists. Dawn could only see Perun's back, but when he spoke, he did so with a deadly current in his voice. *"Ostavlyat,"* he said. *"Pryamoseychas." Leave. Right now.*

The clouds above the lot began to darken, gathering and congealing into ferocious thunderheads. A chill wind tugged Dawn's skirt.

Volosov's eyes twinkled with mischievous glee. His belly bounced with barely suppressed laughter. *"Da poshel ty, nesnosny-yublyudok!"* He made a fist and swung at Perun.

Perun ducked and retaliated with a jab which struck Volosov's eye. The instant it connected, a white light blinded Dawn and a sound like a crack of thunder deafened her.

After that, it was pandemonium. Flash after flash and blast after blast battered Dawn and sent her to her knees. She closed her eyes and covered her ears, but the light and sound seemed to assault her on a more fundamental level, as if each shock-wave from the confrontation pushed her atoms further and further apart. Soon, she would be dust. Soon, she would be nothing. She opened her mouth to scream, but vomited instead.

Dawn curled up on the ground in a foetal position, unable to move, barely able to breathe. She opened her eyes, but saw only grey. She heard nothing. *I'm blind and deaf,* she thought. Her head rang like a bell.

Then she felt something new: an arm slipping under her knees and her back. She was borne aloft, and felt the motion of air against her skin, but gentle, and not at all harsh. She was moving, but to where?

Time soon lost all meaning, and Dawn drifted on the periphery of sleep. She might've crossed over but for a voice that, rather than hear, she felt with her heart and her bones.

"…just a little longer, please, Dawn. You'll be all right.

"You'll be all right.

"You'll be all right."

*

Dawn had no idea what she was drinking, but it was hot and fragrant and each sip seemed to bind her frayed body a little tighter together, and restored her sense of hearing and sight. She lay on a sofa in a staff lounge inside the OKB. The schematics of the RD-271 lay on her lap. The Lovebirds, unconscious but breathing softly, lay on a larger sofa against the wall opposite Dawn. And sitting in a foldable chair beside her, holding her head up to drink, was Perun.

"Your bodyguards will be all right," he said softly, kindly, "but it'll take a while longer for them to heal because they were much closer to the combat. They likely won't remember the 'firefight'."

When she felt strong enough, Dawn pushed herself into an upright seated position and took the ceramic cup from Perun. She sipped some of the drink—tea, she decided—and scrutinized Perun. He looked like nothing more than an ordinary, if ruggedly handsome, man. "What did I see out there?" she asked.

"A pointless brawl between two old men." Perun clasped his hands and leaned over in his chair, looking unspeakably weary. "The Slavs called us gods, but in this age of spaceships and weapons that can obliterate entire cities in a second, the line between a god and a man is fairly blurry, don't you think?"

Now Dawn had yet another question to answer: whether the man in front of her was out of his mind. "I think I don't believe in gods," she said after a moment's consideration.

Perun nodded. "All right. Questions of godhood aside, all I can tell you is that I'm old, very old. I don't remember my birth, though I'm sure neither do most people, but I can remember a time when the people of this country hunted with stone arrowheads. I'm not omnipotent, but I do have power over lightning, metal, and I've helped a great many couples conceive a child."

Dawn brought her legs up to her chest and tugged her skirt over her feet.

Perun's face broke out in a bashful smile. "Not what you

think. Besides, I'm certain you're more interested in your career than conception."

"Exactly, so no funny business." Dawn was acutely aware that, if Perun *did* intend funny business, then based on his display in the parking lot, there was probably very little she could do to resist. But she *would* resist.

Perun raised his hands. "No funny business, I promise."

Dawn tapped her finger on the side of her mug. "And Volosov? You have beef with him?"

Perun snorted. "'Volosov'? Is that what he calls himself now?" He shook his head. "He's becoming more unimaginative all the time." He steepled his fingers in an upside-down triangle. "His name is Veles, and we've 'had beef,' as you say, ever since he stole my cattle and kidnapped my wife and son."

Dawn swallowed hard. *What the hell have I gotten into?* "I'm sorry."

Perun sighed. "Me too."

"Where are they now? Your wife and son?"

Perun met Dawn's gaze, and in his eyes, she saw an unspeakable sadness. "I don't know," he said. "I spent ages trying to find them. Searched the world many times over. Never found any sign of them."

He sounds like he at least believes *what he's saying… and there's still the matter of the strange blasts I felt…* Regardless of Perun's nature, Dawn knew when it was time to move on from a painful topic. "Why were you building rocket engines for the Soviet Union?"

Perun leaned back in his chair. "The answer to that begins on the day I gave up hope of finding my family." He looked out the window. "I settled down on the banks of the Dnipro, in a small community. There were many chieftains, many predatory tribes all around, in those days, and the Dnipro was a highway to foreign lands, which meant foreign invaders. I grew quite attached to my people, and eventually taught them metallurgy to give them a better chance of survival. Later I taught them warfare, so that they might defeat those who tried to take what was theirs. Ultimately, they became conquerors themselves. All that time, Veles never stopped tormenting me. He stole the secrets I gave to my tribe and distributed them across the lands, leading to many unnecessary wars. I fought him, killed him many times, but—"

"Killed?" Dawn interrupted.

"Death is not so lasting for us."

Dawn lowered her eyes and sipped her tea. "Lucky you."

"You wouldn't say that if you had a few millennia's worth of mistakes to look back on. Besides, we're not the only creatures in this world for whom death is not a serious impediment. Anyway, Veles would always come back. He doesn't make anything for himself, only takes what I make for me and mine. His soul is defined by envy. Eventually I gave up trying to help my people, believing that all my works would simply be perverted by him in the end. I stopped believing my actions made a difference, so I stopped acting.

"Then a renegade scientist from a far-away country gave the secret of nuclear weaponry to the Slavs, and I witnessed a power I could never have imagined my adopted children possessing, a power which could turn this world and everything in it into a ball of lifeless ash. I realized I made a grave mistake in disconnecting from the world. I'd missed so much. I could no longer be a recluse.

"I was always adept at mastering new weapons, and the rocket was, initially, just another weapon. But any warrior or hunter will tell you that employed correctly, a weapon can become a tool for preserving life rather than taking it. Knowing this, I set to work helping the OKBs build engines that could loft more than just bombs into space."

Dawn found the notion of a thunder god suddenly showing up for work one day, clean-shaven and dressed in a lab coat, extremely comical, which made it even harder to buy the story Perun was selling. "So, this," Dawn picked up the schematics, which Perun had placed on the sofa beside her. "This is a penance for you?"

"In part, but it's far more than just that." Perun leaned toward Dawn, and his eyes took on earnestness and intensity in equal measure. "This planet is a miracle. It gave me life, and you, but one day, it will have no more life to give. One way or another, whether by the eventual swelling of the dying sun or the sudden flash of nuclear war, this world will end. You have to have a new home by then, a place among the stars where life can continue. All I have to my name is a thousand generations of bloodshed. I am responsible for suffering that exceeds the bounds of nightmare. I can't take back the gift of war, but I can at least give you the chance to live beyond me, and others like me."

For a long while, Dawn could say nothing. The depths of pain she saw in Perun's eyes was greater than any she'd seen on a living face. "And Veles? Why is he still after you?"

The pain was replaced briefly by anger, then simply exhaustion. "I made yet another mistake. I sought out the others of my kind, the few that I could find, including Veles, and tried to explain to them the finite nature of this world. Most of them turned away. Maybe immortality has closed their minds to the idea that something as vast as the Earth can die. But Veles..." Perun's voice hardened. "He laughed at me, and began hounding me again, destroying my works. He feels threatened by the instruments of science. His domain was always magic and trickery—that's how he made your body-guards behave the way they did—and he suffocates in a world of reason. He wants to destroy my last gift to you because, not only is it something I care deeply about, but because it represents ultimate freedom from the old ways.

"To put it another way, there are two fathers: one who wants to control his children, and one who wants to give his children independence."

Dawn looked towards the window. Beyond it lay the test stand, and beyond that, the forests of Russia. "He'll come back, won't he?"

Perun nodded.

Dawn looked back at Perun. "What will you do when he does?"

"Kill him again." It was a simple, direct statement of fact.

Unwilling to discuss death any further, Dawn looked over the schematics. "It's so elegant," she breathed, reading the cross -sections and turbo-pump diagrams. She understood them, if not all the accompanying Cyrillic notes. *No matter what Perun believes, this engine is real.* "So clean... I've seen blueprints for the original 270; it was nowhere near this economic. *This* almost looks easy to build."

And cue the cocky grin. "You'd be surprised what a god can do when he's motivated." The grin faded somewhat. "I don't think we have time to arrange transport for the engine that's currently on the test stand, but before you go…" He flashed his teeth in a proud smile. "Would you like to hear it roar?"

Dawn looked up and leaned forward eagerly. *He's serious.* "It's ready to fire?"

Perun winked "Oh yes."

"How'd you get it onto the test stand by yourse—?" Dawn checked herself the moment the question was out of her mouth.

Perun's shoulders hitched with laughter. He stood up and offered Dawn his hand. Rather than belittle her question, he simply replied, "Very carefully."

*

Ensconced inside the test stand control room, Dawn watched as Perun flitted from one console to another, fingers moving so quickly they were nearly a blur. He was doing the work of ten or twelve people and making it look effortless. "Methalox flow is good," he said. "Engine chill down commencing." He looked over his shoulder at Dawn, who stood at the back of the control room, out of the way. "We're moments away," he said, almost apologetically, as if he felt the rate at which he was performing miracles of engineering wasn't satisfactory.

If time and a malicious god of magic weren't against them, Dawn would've told Perun to slow down so she could enjoy watching him. *Great, I'm already thinking of these guys as gods.*

Dawn thought she ought to be freaking out at how her world had been upended in the last hour, but truth be told, it was thrilling. For her, the joy of being a rocket scientist was building great big things that served to expand humanity's horizon. She felt no fear in the face of discovery, and Perun and Veles represented one hell of a discovery. Add to that the fact that Perun was a fellow builder, a kindred spirit, it actually made a lot of sense why she was unperturbed.

"Water deluge, is…" Perun threw a switch. "Active."

Outside the huge, panoramic window, below the test stand,

two ranks of four nozzles like firemen's hoses opened and sprayed jets of water into the trench below the RD-271's bell. The purpose of the water was to soften the vibrations given off by the engine, which had the power to shatter concrete and shred metal.

Finally, Perun turned to Dawn. "Would you like to do the honours?" He pointed to a green button at the centre of the console.

Heart hammering, Dawn stepped forward. She kept her eyes glued to the engine as she hovered her finger over the button and pushed.

There was a green flash inside the engine, and all the dust and soil lying atop the shoulders of the test stand leaped a foot in the air as a ragged tongue of yellow fire shot down into the flame trench. The water vaporized, and steam billowed away from the fire towards the northern edge of the forest, faster than a car on the freeway, in an infinitely unfolding mushroom cloud. A half second later, a dull roar filled the control room and reverberated inside Dawn's chest.

Perun reached out and turned a dial found next to the green button, bringing the engine to a hundred percent power. The ragged flame surged, transforming into three translucent pink beads, each one curving into and through the other, with the third half-buried in the roiling steam. A three-looped infinity sign. It looked nothing like fire, but rather like a watercolour painting suspended in midair by some cosmic artist, applied to the canvas of the atmosphere itself.

Giddiness bubbled in Dawn's chest and she laughed at the sheer beauty of a machine created to carry life to the stars.

Five minutes later, though it seemed like no time at all, the control room automatically terminated the test. On the closed-circuit cameras, the structure of the engine was intact. It looked as unruffled as if it had never even been switched on.

Breathless, Dawn threw her arms around Perun and squeezed him. He hugged her back. "Now you know it works," he said.

"It was…" Dawn laughed again. "I have no words." She broke the embrace and looked again at the engine. "I wish all my friends could see this."

"They will. The schematics I gave you are for the very engine we just fired. They're correct in every detail." Perun's joyful expression darkened. "We shouldn't waste time. I'll get your bodyguards into your car. They'll sleep a while yet."

"Wait a min—"

"There's a service road that leads north out of the complex." Perun was in motion, resetting switches, loading more methalox into the test tanks. "Take a left when you come to the highway at the forest's edge. You can get to either Tver or Moscow from there—"

"Stop." Dawn put her hands atop his, arresting them. She made him meet her eyes. "Come with me," she said.

Perun smiled sadly and shook his head. "I can't."

"This engine—"

"Dawn." Perun turned his hands over and held hers. His fingers were rough and calloused. "There is no government on Earth that can conceal me from Veles, and there is no barrier that he cannot breach. You felt the consequences of our fight. That was only a drop in the cup of our power. If we were to fight in a more populated place, a town or a city, it would be as bad as if an atom bomb had detonated at its centre."

Dawn swallowed. "There's so much you could teach us."

"Maybe there will be a day when I can, *maybe*, but it's not today." He looked out the window at his creation. "Human beings have had many symbols for *us* over the millennia, but if I had to choose one for *you*, it would be the rocket." He looked at Dawn. "Fire on one side, infinity on the other; the very knife's edge between death and possibility. At any moment, it could tip to one or the other. And yet…" Perun beamed. "Capable of far more than even gods can imagine."

The tears Dawn had resisted since she'd first opened Perun's letter now spilled forth. She hugged him one last time. "You *are* a good man."

*

Her words still rang in his ears. *"You are a good man."* Secretly, he didn't believe her, but he did feel closer to a good man today than he did yesterday.

Perun sat on the upper level of the test stand, his back to the now-quiescent engine, his legs dangling over the hundred-foot drop to the ground. He liked it up here. From this platform, he could see for miles and miles, the forest turning to farmland and thence into horizon and sky. Even for one as old as he, nature never ceased to be beautiful.

Thick clouds were gathering over Tver Oblast. It would rain, soon.

Soon.

Perun watched as Dawn pulled away from the research complex, driving her car over the gravelly wastes that lay between the test stand and the treeline. In a minute, she was out of sight.

The catwalk behind him clanged with footsteps. He heard the *ting-ting* of knuckles rapping on metal. "It's good for fireworks," said that familiar, insufferable voice. "I'll admit that."

Perun glanced over his shoulder.

Veles stood next to the rocket engine, thumbs tucked under his belt, studying the machine. He looked at Perun and smiled.

Perun shook his head and went back to enjoying the landscape. Thunder rumbled above.

Veles sat down at his side, swinging his feet over the precipice.

Neither of them said anything. After so many thousands of years, what could they possibly have to say?

Well, perhaps one thing… "Good for fireworks?" Perun asked.

"Yes," said Veles. "Of that much, you can be proud."

Perun's lips parted in a cheeky grin. He looked at his ancient rival. "You should've paid more attention when I told you how it works."

Veles frowned. "Why should I? It's all so much hot air, much like yourself."

Laughing, Perun jabbed his left index finger skyward, directly at the fuel tank above his head. A bolt of lightning arced out of the sky, passing straight through the fuel tank and touching Perun's finger.

And the air grew very hot indeed.

A fireball leaped up over the forest, followed a full three seconds later by a low *boom*. Dawn saw it through her rear-view mirror. She didn't know if the explosion had caused the two immortals any permanent injury, but no matter what kind of being you were, a conflagration like that probably didn't tickle.

In the back seat, the Lovebirds continued to sleep. Dawn wasn't sure yet what she would say to them when they awoke, nor was she certain what she'd tell Aerojet and the State Department, for that matter, but whatever story she presented to them, it would be pretty close to the truth, and the truth was this: a rocket scientist at an abandoned OKB numbered 333 had indeed made contact with her, and presented her with schematics to a revolutionary new rocket engine. Feeling his life was threatened, he made her leave the bureau post-haste, but stayed behind to hinder his antagonist.

The Lovebirds would want to know why they were unconscious for the entire visit, and why so many rounds in their weapons were missing. Dawn would have to get creative there, but again, she didn't foresee any difficulties. Collapsing nations were dangerous places, after all.

She cleared the trees and turned left onto the road that led to Tver. She'd stop for gas and catch her breath there before pressing on to Moscow. The sun was setting over the Soviet Union, lighting the western sky ablaze. Above Dawn were rainclouds, with the occasional flash of lightning. Dawn thought of her father. *Did Dad know who Perun really was?* She wished she'd thought to ask Perun when she had the chance. There'd just been so little time.

Dawn told herself that knowing for certain her father was dead, and what he had died for, made no difference, but she knew it to be a lie. *And he didn't die for nothing,* she thought, as her hand drifted to the folded schematics in the pocket of her denim jacket. *It might be many years before we successfully recreate Perun's engine, but one way or another, we will do it.*

A new world awaited, and the first gentle drops of rain tapped against the car's windshield, washing it clean.

James Dick

James Dick is an actor, author, screenwriter, and director living in Toronto, Ontario. He is a student at Ryerson University's Creative School, working toward a degree in Media Production. James's media and acting studies inform every aspect of his writing process, from ideation to finished story. His work has appeared in Improbable Press, Ghost Orchid Press, and Blank Spaces Magazine. You can follow him on Instagram @james.patrick.dick, and find more of his written work and collaborations at www.storystation.net

Inheritance

By Seth Augenstein

IN THE NIGHT, I SAT listening to the summer insects off in the trees singing, mating, and dying. My rocking chair creaked on the century-old boards of my wraparound porch. My wife and older kid were across the state line, at a motel in the countryside with no cell service. My younger boy was asleep safely upstairs. I listened to the crickets and to my heart, their rhythms combining to lull me into a sort of stasis, a waking dream. The mescals wished softly in my tumbler, the citronella candle on the round side table flared some tangy smoke. I had almost drifted to sleep.

Footsteps coming up the walk roused, startled me. Someone approached, but the motion sensor had not been triggered. My eyes adjusted to catch a pale figure advancing toward my front steps. In the cloudy moonless dark, I could not see who—or what—it was.

I sat rooted, not rocking, clutching my tumbler and ready to throw it at this unnamable shadow, this unseen threat.

"Who's there?" I called out.

The figure reached the steps and slowly lurched up onto the porch. I noted the familiar, ancient limp. And before he even stepped into the tiny glow cast by the candle, I knew it to be my Dad.

I breathed a sigh of relief, but then confusion hit me as he neared the rocking chair next to me.

"Dad," I said, my voice raspy, uncertain.

"Yes, Son," he said, his voice a whisper.

"What are you doing here? Mom told me you were sick in the hospital."

"I'm better now," he said, slowly lowering himself into the other rocking chair beside me. I could only see his outline, his vague shape.

"How is it you're walking around? You're Stage IV. You were in hospice," I murmured.

"I decided to visit, since we haven't been on the best of terms," he said, ignoring my question. "I've come to clear some things up. To tell you some things."

I turned away, but kept talking. "I meant to visit," I said, voice quavering. "But I figured you wouldn't want me there."

"How are the kids?" he said, again ignoring me. "Are they here?"

"Why do you ask?" I asked, my defenses raised once more, still refusing to look at him. "What do you care?"

"They are my grandchildren," he averred .

"You've only met the younger one once," I muttered. "Bet you don't even know his name."

I shook my tumbler, and then lifted the glass to my lips, where the last drops of smoky mezcal hit my parched tongue.

"That's what I'm here to ask you about," he said. "What's the younger one's name?"

"Why should I tell you?" I sneered. "Shouldn't you have figured it out in the two years since he was born?"

"Andy," Dad said, snapping his fingers, ignoring my tone. "I remember now. Andy."

I clapped soundlessly, slow, still not turning to face him. "Congratulations. You're a model grandfather."

"Great. It's settled. Andy is the one," he said. "If he's here, we can do it right now. Is he here?"

Confused, I finally turned to him. When I saw his ghastly face in the onyx dark, I knew nothing would ever be the same. But I had to hold my ground.

"What the fuck are you talking about?" I snapped.

"You remember the Anasazi?" Dad said, again ignoring my question.

I was so taken aback, I stared in stunned silence into the darkness between us. Anasazi. The word seemed like an unworldly incantation from another planet, from another lifetime entirely.

"You really don't remember? The pueblos out west, the camping trips, the thousands of miles of terrain we crossed every July when you were a child?" he asked, surprised. "The Anasazi, the natives who built those magnificent cliff dwellings, those huge houses of mud, stone, and sand that lasted longer than entire European empires. The natives who just vanished, like this." He snapped his fingers again.

"I do remember seeing the monuments: Chaco Canyon, Mesa Verde. Montezuma's Castle," I murmured uncertainly.

"Wupatki."

The very word made my head swoon. I had not thought of that place for decades. I raised the empty glass to my mouth with trembling hands. Something had happened at Wupatki, but I could never remember exactly what.

"I see you remember the day of panic," he said. "The blown radiator, the empty waterskins. Heat. The thirst."

"I remember nothing."

"Yes, you do," he said, tapping his temple. "But what else can you recall, I wonder? I wonder…"

"I was ten fucking years old, Dad," I barked. A familiar scratching nestled in my throat that was not the mezcal, and my heart started to hammer. "I remember nothing."

"No, you wouldn't remember everything, would you?" he said. "You were somebody completely different, really."

I tilted my head at him, baffled. "No, that was me, Dad. I remember the pueblos, the no-water thing, the broken-down car, some kind of panic… I just don't remember what happened at the end."

"The Anasazi did not call themselves by that name, you know," he said, ignoring me. "That was what the Navajo called them. Do you know what it means?"

"No. Can't remember that," I said, setting the tumbler on the table. My hands cradled my head, my throat suddenly dry as a desert.

"'Ancient enemy,' that's what 'Anasazi' means," he said. "It was because of what they became.

"The Anasazi were a peaceful farming people, in prehistory. They lived off the land, and they were nomadic. They moved with the rains, and sleepy centuries passed.

"But warrior-priests from the south, from what is modern-day Mexico, arrived one searing, parched summer," he said."Everything changed.

"The warrior-priests brought the rains with them. But they also brought the gospels of extinction," he said. "The need for sacrifice, to enflame the sun with human grease so as to make it turn over the horizon. The blood for the rains, an even trade. The suicide ball games, the thrill of the cull."

I remembered the ball court at Wupatki. I tried to remain expressionless. I knew I failed. Fear spread across my face as his words opened before me.

"I see you are remembering," he said. He leaned in closer, and his pale flesh seemed to incandesce. "Do you remember the blowhole? The darkness that starts so small, but increases to everything entire?"

The hole in the earth. The wind. The blackness swelled in front of my face even at the thought. I felt the cool wind once again, I smelled the entrance to the deep recesses of the earth, nameless and numberless. I pictured that yawning hole in the ground, just large enough to stuff a body if it had been disarticulated at just the right angles. The perfect joints, the choicest tendons. I laughed out loud at the insanity of all this.

My lungs froze up at that moment, like an enormous vice had enveloped my chest, my arms, everything. I gasped, as I saw the blackness and I felt the way down.

He stood to loom over me. His enraged smile made his eyes sparkle with some stellar light, but not from the sky. I could not breathe.

"You see, they centered the community around that fissure in the earth. They only knew it as the breath of XipeTotec, the Flayed Lord, the Bearer of the Skin, favoring them with cooling air blowing from below, a cooling salve for those who had survived the bloodsport games of sacrifice held at the ballcourt just a few yards away. The cool wind from within the well-tended hells of the satiated god.

"But it is not always so. You see, it works both ways. The atmosphere had a surfeit of pressure that day we made our pilgrimage to Wupatki. Things were in reverse. The blowhole was not blowing. It was sucking air in. XipeTotec was not a giving mood that day."

He chuckled, shaking his head. He waved his fingers in a strange motion, and I could suddenly take little sips of air. Just enough to keep me alive. But I was still otherwise paralyzed in my seat.

"It was just when we were arriving at Wupatki, engine nearly on fire, that I realized we were not alone," he said. "My father, your grandfather, was in the backseat. His phantom shape hovered in the rearview mirror. You could not see him. You may remember that he was dying right at that moment, on that very day, back here in New Jersey, thousands of miles away. We had taken the trip despite him being on his deathbed."

I panted, unable to answer. I did remember. It was all returning, with each new utterance of madness.

"So your grandfather sat in the backseat. I told you nothing. But when you went to look for water, he leaned forward and whispered to me.

"He had just died, he told me. But he was not totally gone just yet. He could stick around. He could have another turn. And it was all up to me.

"We needed to continue our lineage of centuries. I needed to clear a young vessel from our same bloodline. A sheath for his continuance."

Dad leapt up so he was crouched atop the porch railing, light as a feather. I was powerless. He loomed over me like a gargoyle in shadow, and as he leered down I saw he was emaciated—drained, desiccated utterly.

"And I saw you—my son—in the rearview mirror returning

down the desert trail from the locked bathrooms," said Dad. "My Dad kept speaking in my ear. All I needed to do, he said, was stop my son's heart for a second, and it was enough for him to merge with the existing corporeal form, to make our bloodline whole.

"It was not killing my son, he said. It was making our lineage complete by continuing his own merging. It would merely be two souls of the same line commingling. The brain, the memories, the everything would be the same otherwise. My son would still be my son—but it would also be him."

I wanted to scream, but my mouth wouldn't move.

"The voice of my Dad went silent when you opened the door. Silence, except for the hissing of the overheated radiator. I suggested we get out of the car and explore.

"The day was searing hot, easily a hundred degrees, and there were no visitors. While we waited for someone to arrive and rescue us, we took in the sights. You grabbed one of the brochures and we made the grand loop, the tour of the ancient village, so long abandoned.

"You narrated our walk through the kivas and great houses and ruins standing up only to our knees, though they once boasted splendor not seen in our hemisphere since the Maya. You read aloud about grains and farming techniques and climate and intertribal disputes and all sorts of other things which I tuned out.

"Because I was listening to that other voice.

"The entire time, my spectral father spoke into my ear. He walked on my right, narrating things as they actually were as we made the tour. We passed the pueblos, the magnificent temple which was left as nothing more than a pile of stones, the ball court for the sacrificial games, and, of course, the blowhole. He spoke of the truth with a strange cancerous warble to his voice:

"*'The Anasazi were a slow, peaceable people by nature. That's why they so easily knuckled under when the warrior-priest death cult came to them from the south, from the ruins of Tula, the Toltec capital,'* he said. *This was the faith of Xipe Totec, He of the Flayed Skin, who made the renewal of life from death possible, from Teotihuacan until the arrival of the Spaniards at Tenochtitlan.*

"*His followers are an elite race of fearsome leaders with feet in both worlds: the seen, and the unseen. Their Lord controlled rains, kept the skids of the sun greased on its way along the sky.*

"'These warrior-priests changed everything about these sleepy farmers. XipeTotec was convincing, the results undeniable. The harvests were bountiful, the births soared and the deaths plummeted. But the debts mounted; the whims of the Flayed Lord needed to be cultivated as carefully as any crop.

"'Blood and meat and skin were in arrears. The warrior-priests finally unveiled the unthinkable price to the stunned farmers: human sacrifice, cannibalism and routine atrocity, the extraction of the hearts and the wearing of the skins. The warrior-priests directed them to strike out in every direction to vanquish their enemies. It was the only way to ensure success. And for more than a century, they were correct.

"'The farmers made enemies, but they vanquished all. Their numbers and territories grew. The Navajo and others simply came to call them The Enemy.

"'But the sacrifices were not just outsiders. This ball court here at Wupatki, now so unassuming, was the site of ritualized slaughter of their own kith and kin. The losers of the contests were skinned alive and then eaten, in banquets to the honor of XipeTotec. The bones were tossed aside as so much chaff. And it was the blowhole which was the earth's mouth that swallowed it all. The blowhole, though just a geological anomaly to us, was the pathway to whole other dimensions in their mythological firmament. It was the portal to the eternal, the power current driving the sun.

"'So when the climate turned sour, and the enemies turned on The Enemy in a victorious alliance, the final stand was a pathetic show indeed.

"'Two members of the once-elite death cult stood at either side of that portal, obsidian knives in hand, with two of the last Anasazi children, trussed up like sacrificial animals. Because that's what they were— sacrifices. But in a whole new way.

"'After some quick consecrations, the first priest pushed the little boy facedown into the hole. The pressure that day was high, and the blowhole took, not provided. And the child drowned in air, gasping for that which was sucked out of him by the very earth.

"'The child stopped breathing. The priest turned him over and lay him gently on the ground. And then he raised his obsidian knife and—slit his very own throat from ear to ear, and was dead within moments.

"Moments later, the boy again began to breathe, and opened his eyes, and smiled. The transference was complete. The boy then helped the other

priest with the same ritual on the terrified little girl.

"'Thus it was when the enemies of the Anasazi came over the ridge some days later, they found the putrefying, flayed bodies of the last two warrior-priests of XipeTotec—and two innocent children who whimpered and begged for mercy—but who laughed behind their merciful conquerors' backs because they had ultimately found their new skins.'

"My father spoke to me like that for an hour, spinning out the sordid last days of the Anasazi, XipeTotec, the last strands of the faith.

"We were still marooned. No one had come, for hours. The heat seared. You asked for water. But we had none. You looked sick. You kept asking. Finally, you swooned and collapsed from dehydration, your face and shoulders burned from the sun. We had reached the final location on the map: the blowhole. Your voice flighty, you asked me what was within the blowhole to make it pull in air like it did.

"My father whispered in my ear that it was time.

"So I told you, this boy, there was water down in the hole.

"You should lean far down in and take a look, I said.

"When this boy did, I pushed him down, with my hands around the throat. The struggle was brief.

"Needless to say, when you again opened your eyes, it was a different boy. It was you, but not you. It was my father who now inhabited your body.

"You, my father. Once again my son, for these last twenty years."

The grip on my lungs and body abruptly lifted. I could breathe again.

"You're a maniac," I exclaimed. "You must be delirious from the hospital."

I rose to grab him. But as I lunged forward, my hand passed right through his arm like it was so much air. I gasped. He scoffed at my importunity.

"Come now, Son," he said, words dripping with irony. He bared phantasmal teeth. "Or should I say, Dad?"

He started toward me. He moved in herky-jerky motion, like an animation missing frames. I staggered away, knocking into the table, the empty mezcal tumbler shattering on the porch. I backpedaled until I hit the front door. He stepped forward without sound, the shadow approaching soundless. I quickly opened and ducked in the front door, and then slammed it shut, quickly shooting the lock. I was only halfway down the hallway to the kitchen when he emerged through the same door I'd just locked, his form not even breaking stride. My heart nearly stopped. I ran back into the kitchen as he pursued.

"I drowned my son—I drowned my son in the air to those ancestor spirits of Wupatki, in that small oasis," he said. "I drowned my son so the father could once again be the son, as it has been so many times since we swapped bodies in that final sacrifice of the Anasazi, the final murders and suicides setting our cycle in motion.

"We two last inheritors of the Flayed Lord priesthood, holding true to the rituals after all these centuries."

I rounded the kitchen and ran into the dining room. I ran to the other side of the big old table, as if it would stop his advance. But when I stopped, he did, too.

"If your brain wasn't paralyzed with terror, you'd probably be able to figure out on your own why I'm telling you this," he said, smiling grimly. "But let me just make it plain: I want Andy's life."

He raised his spectral hands front of him, like he meant no harm.

"That little grandson of mine. He's upstairs, isn't he?" he said, pointing up at the ceiling. "He's sleeping upstairs in his little jammies, dreaming of baseball and cartoons and whatever else."

"You stay the fuck away from my kid!" I shouted.

"Come on, Dad," he said. "Were you not listening to me? Can't you feel it?"

I did feel a stirring within me. My breath shortened, all oxygen robbed by the blackness of the fissure in the earth so long ago. A rage rose within me that was not my own. I felt intimations of immortality, the flitting memories of a hundred prior lifetimes cascading through me. Violence and lust and boredom all at once. I gritted my teeth, I closed my eyes. I wanted none of this. It was overtaking me, all of it. It was irresistible. It was inevitable.

"Can't you understand that you are the inheritor of a truly

incredible lineage we have shared through the centuries?" Dad continued. "Even as the Europeans arrived and we melded in with their society, their DNA, we have kept true to the tenets of XipeTotec and his changing of the skins, the cycles of renewal."

I circled around the table to the right, but he followed me. I circled around to the left, and he blocked my way there, too.

"It's simple, and it must be done," he said. "Just put that nice Spider Man pillow over Andy's face, just for a minute or so, snuff him, and then I can inhabit his body. He—I—will remember nothing. And we shall continue the dance for another generation."

He was drifting right through the heavy oak of the table. I instantly dashed to the left, back into the kitchen.

Instead of continuing down the hallway to the stairs heading up toward my helpless son, I flung open the door to the basement. There was only one way to stop it all. I jumped down the stairs, turned to the right, and grabbed the bag with my Mossberg. I yanked the shotgun out and rushed over to the workbench. From the drawer I snatched out a double-aught buckshot shell and dropped it in the action, and racked the gun. Only one way to stop it all. Flipping the safety off, I turned the barrel to my mouth.

"I wouldn't do that if I were you," he said softly, a hint of menace there, as he stood on the wooden stairs. "If you strand us both in the spirit world, we will be punished to wander the earth forever. We will never again be able to cross into the mortal realm, to wear the other skins. If we do not continue the cycle, XipeTotec will not be pleased."

"Good," I said.

I pulled the trigger.

Seth Augenstein is a writer of fiction and non-fiction. His debut novel, Project 137 (2019) was called "an involving, tense and visceral near-future thriller" by Kirkus. His short stories have appeared in numerous magazines and fiction podcasts. He spent a decade writing for New Jersey newspapers, witnessing many tragedies and triumphs. He was also the editor of Forensic Magazine, a tour guide at the James Joyce Centre, and a student in Saul Bellow's final class. His second novel is Lama with a Gun, published in 2023 by Pandamoon.

By L.A. Selby

DISGRACED FORMER GENERAL MILTON Howard patted his pocket before he unlocked the lab door to Quality Management. He squinted into the pre-dawn mist one more time, but the stray dog he'd been feeding wasn't there today and the fat rolled in oats might melt before he could find the dog again.

Milton? Ares' voice vibrated like a rusty wire in Milton's head, weaker than it had sounded two years ago, but not weak enough.

Leave me alone, Milton thought back. He squeezed the bridge of his nose. He wanted his head to himself again.

*

Inside, the air of his weapons lab tasted metallic. Its stillness was broken by the same quiet hiss of air as the mile-long commuter tunnel he walked each morning. Wall monitors covered every wall, filled with diagrams of the SAT Twenty—the only peace-keeping satellite still able to do what Ares demanded. Its circuitry and schematics gleamed in familiar dull certainty from multiple screens.

The disjointed static of florescent lights added a layer of agitation to Milton's unsettled thoughts.

If he did what Ares wanted him to do, today might be the last time he used that tunnel, limping past adrenaline biosensors—anger detectors—called Red Eyes that scanned each worker like vultures watching from fence posts. He'd ask his sister to feed the dog once he was gone, or his wife if he could get word to her before it was too late.

Milton's regulation blue jumpsuit did nothing to keep out the laboratory chill, and its course weave scratched uncomfortably over the twisted hunch of his shoulders. His back had been straight once, taller than most men, until Ares, God of War, had cracked his foot, twisted his spine, and forced him to do as he was told.

He felt the pressure of his unexpressed anger like a paralyzed dreamer who struggles to fight in his sleep.

He unhooked his electropad from the wall and opened the screen by signing his fingers above it. He imagined hurling the electropad against the far wall and hearing it shatter the way he meant to shatter the god's hold on his mind. No matter who he had once been, and no matter what he'd promised to do for Ares, Milton would never help Ares start another war.

Ares said, *I've waited long enough. If you don't reprogram the SAT Twenty today, I will fill your ears with my voice until you die. You will never hear another soft word, another song, another voice but mine. You will cry for silence from your bed, but you will never find it.*

Milton signed his second level clearance code over the electropad with shaking fingers. That got him to the security warning page. His chest tightened. *Get someone else to approve your weapon*, Milton said, but he only said it to delay his choice a few more minutes.

Ares barked a laugh that sent a pain like needles behind Milton's eyes. *No one believes in waging war the way you do, Milton.*

Milton gripped the electropad hard enough that its corner dug into his palm. *I'm only stalling because your plan isn't going to work. Everyone's on Valdol.* Valdol—the universal pacification drug—was mandatory for anyone who spiked enough adrenaline to alert the Red Eyes. Mandatory for all except for Peacekeepers and government workers who had to keep a clear head. Like Milton.

Ares said, *The underground resistance is not on Valdol. If they were angry enough to keep me alive, I'd leave you alone. Sadly, they fight too cold for me.*

I'm doing what you want, Ares. Go away. Milton imagined stomping his electropad into jagged crystals all over the white tiles.

Ares still lived because Milton was special. Because he'd discovered he could lock rage over his father's death behind a thick wooden door in his heart where the Red Eyes couldn't find it, the same rage that kept Ares alive.

For now.

I picked today as a gift for you, Ares said.

Milton's hands trembled and he entered the third level security code wrong. *You don't do anything for anyone but yourself.*

The seven-year anniversary of your father's arrest. I can't imagine a day more filled with anger. You make me feel so alive.

If Milton hadn't been *special*, he could not have left his apartment today without being pumped full of Valdol and shoved in a cell.

He didn't know the name or face of the clerk who'd reported his father to the State for anger-speak seven years before, but he imagined a pasty-faced coward with tiny raisin eyes set too close together. He imagined a furtive smile and a hand reaching out for the reward.

Milton rubbed his forehead with the back of his hand. He didn't want this rage. He hadn't asked for it. *"Wherever you are,"* he said to the clerk in his mind, *"run. Run. I am coming."*

Ares brought him back to the present. *I have a feeling you're going to stall again.*

Milton asked, *How can you genuinely expect anyone who remembers the Great War to follow you like before?*

I know they will.

L.A. Selby

As long as it's not me. Milton spat on the tiles. A familiar needle-like pain jabbed the center of his spine. He stiffened; eyes wide. He grabbed the thin metal table beside him to steady himself. Sweat formed on his forehead. He let his eyes unfocus so he could pay attention to his back, to see what the pain would do.

I can make it worse, Ares said evenly.

Yes, Ares could make it worse.

Milton had had no warning the first time one of his vertebrae disintegrated. He and his wife Chari had been riding bicycles at Last Coast, swerving around abandoned tanks at the edge of New Angeles. They'd raced under the skeletons of shattered trees. Radiation hadn't come yet. People hadn't learned to cover their skin. Birds had cried louder than any place he could remember. The air had been heavy with an incomparable, sharp sweetness of dying jasmine. Her laughter had been sweeter than the air.

He could still feel echoes of stabbing pain when Ares had broken his spine, the way he tumbled beneath his bicycle, how his mouth stretched to take in air with lungs too painful to move. He remembered the red sun searing the sky like a waiting forge while the medics loaded him in an ambulance and took him away.

No jasmine grew anywhere in New Angeles now, except in the domed Peace Garden where he sometimes walked with his sister, Thalia. As a Peacekeeper, she had three days leave every two weeks. She was getting out of the Peacekeepers tomorrow. After that, they could go to the gardens every day. He allowed himself a smile.

I will miss sharing your head, brother, Ares said.

Milton's smile disappeared. He concentrated on staying upright on his weakened legs. *I'm not your brother.*

Your heart keeps me warm.

Milton ground his teeth and pain flared in his jaw. He imagined shredding Ares with the same weapon that had turned humans into confetti-sized strips.

Ares said, *I enjoy the way your head fights against your heart. If you agree to keep working for me, I could make your life easier.* Ares did that at times, suggested new bargains. *I can straighten your spine, heal your voice, and return your peace of mind. Your wife would come back, and I could guarantee you she'd never leave. You can alter the bargain that much, if you choose. I will grant the modification.*

No, said Milton.

Their current bargain was simple. After Milton made three changes to the SAT Twenty and certified it as safe, Ares would give the clerk to Milton.

Ares promised that the war he started with the SAT Twenty would be limited, but Milton knew the truth about the word "limited." He remembered the limited strikes of the last Great War. He remembered the piles of bodies and the constant smoke. He remembered what it felt like to have medals pinned to his chest under an orange sky where the sun coughed its way through the clouds.

Ares said, *If you let me stay with you after today, I'll protect you.*

I don't care what happens to me.

You would care what happens to you if your neighbors found out you had a shrine to me in your apartment. You would care if you were arrested for worshipping the God of War. You would care if they threw you in prison. Or Silenced you. Silenced, the way Milton's father had been the day he died alone in prison. His father's death had been announced with a text.

Milton said, *I don't worship you. I tolerate you.*

The shrine gives you away, retorted Ares.

I keep it to remind me of who I'm not anymore and who I'll never be again.

The lab door slid open behind Milton.

He jerked. A bolt of pain shot up his leg. He bit his tongue to keep silent and turned. He hadn't expected Sipra so soon.

Now was his chance. If Sipra found the clerk for him, he wouldn't have to fulfill his bargain with Ares to get his revenge. Milton intended to listen to Ares scream in his head forever. Milton meant to suffer anything to have his vengeance without giving Ares the war that would destroy more innocent people. Hadn't two-thirds of the world's population dying in the Great War been enough? *Never again.*

"Meeting here on a Rest Day." Sipra watched him from the doorway with crossed arms and a false smile. "I hope it's for what I think it's for." The lights reflected off her shaved head.

The folds of her gray jumpsuit hid her whipcord body except for the barest outline of her hips.

He pressed his lips together to keep himself from snapping at her. If Sipra reported that Milton had come to QM on a Rest Day with no reason to be there, the State would torture him for a confession and he wouldn't survive it. His plan would be ruined.

"What, are you Silenced now?" She stepped inside, the door sliding closed behind her.

Sweat beaded under his arms despite the chill. I need your help," he said steadily. Could she see his sweat? Smell it?

Sipra rolled her eyes and slouched against the wall, partially obscuring a monitor covered with electronic scribble, his own hated equations and formulas for the SAT Twenty. "Why should I help *you*?"

"I'll have you promoted to QM. More money than being a targeting tech." In his mind he screamed at her and shook her and begged her to agree.

Sipra moved closer. Her nearness made his skin crawl. "How, Milton?"

"There's going to be a job opening here in QM. I have connections." He tried to sound like this favor didn't mean much.

"You don't have connections. Otherwise, you wouldn't be here, you'd be sipping grappa with the Oligarchs."

Milton listened for Ares. Nothing. "I swear I can get you promoted. But even if I'm lying, maybe you'd do it for fun."

Sipra grinned. "Tell me more."

"Help me find someone. A man." Milton cleared his throat. He'd waited so long. "He was a Food Distro Three clerk seven years ago. Disappeared on the first Mandatory Peace Day and never came back. He rang up orders on ground level, that's all I know about his job. His records should be easy for you to find. I can't do it. My clearance doesn't leave QM anymore." Sipra knew data the way Milton knew weapons.

"Gods, Milton. You mean the clerk who ratted out your father for pro-war speech?"

Blood rushed to his face. "Yes." The story was too well-known for him to lie.

His father's punishment had been an *example*, and Milton's demotion had been the State's form of mercy. They'd taken Milton's stars, taken his status, and hidden him in QM where Ares wanted him to be.

Ares.

Sipra said sardonically, her eyebrows rising, "If I find the clerk, you'll get me promoted? That's it?" Yet there was an eagerness beneath.

"Name and location."He fake-yawned to hide the way his lips curled in disgust. If she saw how important she was to him, she'd never help, not until he gave her everything she could think of.

She rolled her eyes again. "Maybe I will, then. If I feel like it."

"Sure," he said, forcing his twisted body to stay relaxed, to mimic a man who didn't care.

Sipra took another step closer. "Listen—" She reached to touch his arm. He flinched. She smirked and let her hand fall. "Your home-wife's been gone awhile." Home-wife. Because everyone else had lovers on the side."I thought you'd want to know she's just fine."

"What?" His stomach tightened.

"I only thought you'd want to know."

Milton, said Ares.

Milton blinked. Hard to track mentally with both of them there.

Ares said, *I promised you I'd give you the clerk. Key in the codes to the satellite and you're done. Sipra is nothing but a targeting tech.*

Milton pressed his elbows into his sides as if that would keep his thoughts and feelings from spilling out.

Sipra tilted her head. "I don't think you got what I just said. I've been watching your home-wife for you."

"I don't—"

"Right *here.*" She moved to Monitor Seven and signed her fingers over the vid control panel next to it. "I found out if I knew your home-wife's basic Corps mission—easy to find—I could key on her." She rotated the monitor so he could see.

Milton's thoughts buzzed like flies trapped under a bowl. He limped closer.

On the screen, a two-story concrete building crouched between towering palm trees. The palm leaves were green; probably signal towers. Windows on the building were free of metal shades, so the location must be somewhere the radiation was not so bad. An orange sky reflected off the metallic sign of the Peace Corps Coalition stenciled around the top. There were no other buildings nearby. Just sand.

Sipra signed her fingers over the control panel. The screen brought him close to one of the windows. Through it he saw a thin, unmade bed and standing at the foot, Chari.

He bit down on his tongue to stop himself from calling her name. She tugged a soiled and faded shirt from her shoulders. He couldn't look away. His need to be with her threatened to weaken the anger he needed to keep. Every part of her called to his heart. He reflexively touched his thumb to his calloused ring-finger.

Sipra signed over the controls again. Chari's face filled the screen, a dark smear of fatigue shadowing her green eyes. Lines deepened the corners of her mouth. The dullness of her skin told Milton she was back on Valdol.

He swallowed against his feeling of hollow loss. *This is my fault.* Driving Chari away had seemed like the only way to keep her safe from Ares. His wife had loved him even as his body had started to fail; it had been too much for Milton to imagine putting her in worse danger.

Yet she'd known him too well for his deception to work. At dinner, she'd asked why his back was stiff. At breakfast, she'd asked why he ground his teeth and pushed the palms of his hands hard against his thighs. Then, when he'd kissed her with open, distracted eyes, she'd stepped away, her hands on his shoulders, searching his face for reasons.

The last week she'd been with him, her eyes had been red, her lips thinned, and her body stiff at his touch. She'd stayed as long as she could, months longer than she might have. The day she said she couldn't take his silence anymore, her voice had been as frayed as an old sheet. She'd held her back straight when she walked out the door, but Milton's back was bent, his heart caved into itself.

Milton shoved aside his longing. *That was then. This is now.*

He waved the electropad at Sipra. She stepped back.

"Get out." He moved in front of her and shut down the screen.

"What?" Her raised brows affected false surprise at his rejection. "Home-wife is fine without you."

He let his anger at Sipra burn away the pain of seeing the emptiness in Chari's face. Sipra wouldn't help him get his revenge. It had been stupid of him to hope. He was still at the mercy of his bargain with Ares. But Sipra hadn't left. He said coldly, "What exactly is it you want?"

"You're here. I'm here." She rubbed her fingers across the rough khaki belt at her waist. Everyone in the government labs had home-wife and work-wife—or work-husband—except Milton. He couldn't do it. He would never do it, even if Chari stayed away the rest of his life. And he was not fooled. The gleam in Sipra's eyes was not lust. It was contempt. Sipra did not want him: she needed arguments to relieve her emptiness. She also needed a promotion, or his job.

"Stop watching my wife," he said.

"I thought you'd be grateful."

"If you watch her again…" He paused. "Every code you entered is there. It's your code you used for private reasons."

"No one cares, Milton. No one."

"Get out."

"You sound angry."

Milton leaned back. He saw she meant to trap him into admitting forbidden emotion. He would be Silenced, and she would be entertained when it happened.

That's right, said Ares. *It is only a matter of time before someone like her figures out I'm in your head. You've stalled me for the last time. If you do not act now, the next target is your wife.*

Milton gestured at the door, unable to speak.

"Peace always." Sipra laughed on her way out.

Do you understand? Ares resumed. *I know you meant to cheat me out of my war. Threats against your body meant nothing, I see. Change the SAT Twenty for me now, or I'll keep you alive long enough to watch your wife and sister die voiceless in prison.*

Milton turned back to the monitor. His fingers shook when he signed to open the screen. The images were still there.

Chari faced away from her window, her ribs a testament to hunger and to the pacification drugs in her food. She was addicted again. It might take months for her to recover.

For a moment he thought he could feel her warm hand holding his like before, her lips touching his own. A lump burned in his throat. *When I'm dead, she'll get the food rations I saved. She can restart the kitchen garden. That'll cut the Valdol in half at least. She'll have a voice and a home and a chance for life.*

He wiped at his eyes with the back of his hand. The electropad waited for his choice. He expected Ares to say something else. The chill air made his legs ache. He shifted his feet. Milton's conscience protested, as though a frightened chorus chanted in time with his heart: *Stop this stop this stop this stop this.* Buthe was a man capable of making hard choices.

Milton code-keyed the three computer sequences that Ares demanded. Instead of its advertised pinpoint strike, the pulse from the SAT Twenty satellite would take out a building. Instead of the target on screen, it would fire a fraction to one side. And the third change protected Milton from immediate discovery. After the changes he'd made, SAT Twenty would always fire the way it was supposed to in lab tests, but always misfire in the field. Ares had promised no one would track the changes to him, but he wouldn't say how.

Milton believed Ares had enough power left to make good on his threats against Milton's family. His ravaged body was proof.

He spoke into his electropad, his voice hoarse with this proof of what he was willing to do to save his wife and sister. "SAT Twenty. Safe. Record. M3387."

He attached the electropad to its charge holder and rubbed his hands on his jumpsuit as if he wiped off stains no one else could see. He'd expected to feel different once it was over. To feel something more than this great, numbing loss.

If Ares had targeted a building full of innocent people, Milton couldn't have obeyed. No matter his rage, he would never harm an innocent. But Ares had promised the SAT Twenty would only blow up an empty building. Just Gov Center One on a Rest Day. It would be a *slap*, something to let the Oligarchs know the resistance could reach their protected weapons when they wanted.

He shook his head and took a deep breath. Ares was wrong. Ares might think the Oligarchs would blame the underground resistance for the explosion, that Milton's part could be hidden forever. Ares might think the tension would escalate to battles, return his power, and save his life. Milton disagreed. Everyone knew now how to suppress feelings. They'd avoid the level of anger that powered a god.

But Milton had done his part now. Ares would leave his mind. Chari and Thalia would have their lives. That was the promise Milton chose to believe.

He listened for the chorus of his conscience. It was missing, as though he'd Silenced himself.

Milton kept tight hold of his deeper thoughts. Though Ares lived inside him, Milton still hid his secret.

He had forged an iron door deeper in his heart than the door that hid anger from Red Eyes. He'd painted the door the blue of his childhood skies and covered the thick iron handle behind a mat of vines and a spray of bright white jasmine. In front of the door, he'd raised acres of arched stone fountains filled with clear water. He'd imbued them all with an air of grief. He'd raised more acres of thick green grass leading away, as tall as his hips and as straight as spears to show no trace of him there. Then, with a sharp coldness to mask the burn behind his eyes, he'd locked his plan to destroy Ares inside.

*

He didn't see Sipra or anyone else on his way out.

The stray dog who'd adopted Milton stood behind the giant waste bin outside. Milton stopped. His eyes stung. He wiped his eyes with the back of his hand.

The dog slunk out to meet him, its patchy hide stretched too tight over its ribs. Food coupons were too precious to use for the few animals that survived since the Great War. This one had one black paw and one white one, like the puppy he had as a child. Milton felt in his pants pocket for the lump of fat rolled in oats. He'd go hungry a day to make sure his friend was fed. The dog's eyes widened and long tail wagged. Milton tore the lump into three pieces so the dog wouldn't choke.

"Just this today, boy." He dropped the first piece and it was gone faster than he could see. "I don't know when I'll be back." He dropped the next two. Jaws snapped twice. "I'll tell Thalia about you before they come for me. Please stay out of sight till she comes." He cleared his throat. "And peace to you." He thought about what he'd like to do with the Oligarch who decided food coupons were only for humans.

He walked twenty steps under the hazy orange sky to the concrete wall and metal door of the commuter tunnel. The Red Eyes watched him from above the door. Inside the tunnel he breathed recycled air tinged with old sweat, safe from the radiation above.

His twisted foot sent pangs to his hip with every step so he stayed close enough to the concrete wall to catch himself, in case he stumbled. Red Eyes stared at him. He felt like they knew what he'd done. He imagined bashing them with a forge hammer and listening to them fracture and splinter to dust.

Around a corner, he almost bumped into a woman, her hair in a regulation braid and wearing a shapeless dun jumpsuit. She barely glanced at him despite his twisted frame. The flickering blue light from inset ceiling panels gave her face a pallid cast of illness, and she smelled like rancid cooking oil.

Milton's empty stomach lurched. Her dose of Valdol was too high. Or perhaps she was one of the Silenced, like his parents, her voice box removed for wrong-speech. Or a second offender, with even the prosthetic voice taken away. Or a third offender, with her fingers paralyzed. He clenched his fists. Then he unclenched them in case anyone noticed.

It was fifty steps from the end of the commuter tunnel to his one-room government apartment. His windowless apartment was colder than the lab. He'd run out of heater coupons months ago. He'd traded them for food rations and then saved most of those on his empty bookshelf like a monument to futility.

He was always hungry.

Milton's front door opened directly to the kitchen. Above his cracked formica countertop the faucet dripped gray water and smelled of sulphur. He turned the faucet so the drip hit the side of the basin where he couldn't hear it. He placed his one dry plate in the barren cupboard. The light bulb over his head gave enough light to know where he was but not enough to be useful or warm.

Milton moved around his small plastic kitchen table and pre-formed chair. He scowled at his modest shrine to Ares in the vid area next to the kitchen.

A miniature brass helmet, glittering and delicate, rested on a red plastic sheet draped over a broken card table. Propped against the helmet was a chewed toothpick representing a spear. Behind them burned a four-inch orange candle he'd forgotten to put out when he left that morning, its color symbolic only to Milton of his long-hidden rage. Milton snuffed it with his fingers.

As shrines go, it was purposefully and deceptively shabby. A simple act of defiance against the State, an acknowledgment of his truth, and a slap at the god who ruined him. He could be killed for having it. But Chari was gone. Thalia was on her own. Who would ever see it?

Milton fell into the hard kitchen chair and put his head in his hands. He'd done what Ares wanted. He felt numb. The soft tick of an ancient mechanical clock in the viewing area punctuated his thoughts. That clock had been his mother's, and her mother's before that. She'd taught him how to polish it when he was only five years old. It was dusty now.

Milton couldn't afford the time to think about his parents. He'd had to stall Ares by sabotaging the SAT Twenty. Now he had to stop Ares from starting a war.

What would happen if Ares fired the SAT Twenty now? Would he feel the explosion from his apartment? And when would it happen? Days from now? Weeks?

If blowing up the empty Gov Center One didn't start a war, then what would Ares do? Would the god die? Would he come back to force Milton to do something worse, holding Chari and Thalia hostage until Milton obeyed?

Still, there was a chance, a small chance to his mind, that the explosion of Gov Center One would go as Ares wanted.

He groaned into his hands. *I should have tried harder to fight him. Has he made me so weak? I won't give him this. I can't.* A single tear cooled into a patch on his cheek.

He jerked up straight. *I won't. Tomorrow. I'll go to Gov Center One tomorrow.* The Oligarchs would be there. *I'll carry a knife.*

Someone, if he was lucky lots of someones, would record him on vids trying to enter the building armed without clearance. He had to do it there, where the most vids were. Where security was tight. Where he'd get the most vid coverage.

He went to the kitchen drawer and yanked it open. The only knife he had was a dull table knife.

He picked it up and turned it in his hands. *So small.* When the State had taken his stars and his medals, they took his weapons too. He'd never said a single word for war after the declared peace, but when his father died, they erased his stories from the histories and packed away the swords decorating his walls.

Milton sliced the tiny knife through the air and laughed the way one does when it is too late to succeed. All he needed was to be seen by as many people as possible. *Victory has more than one definition.*

All it had taken for his father to be arrested was a pro-war joke. In a food line. And he was gone.

Milton would have been demoted to Food Distro services himself, if he was not one of a handful left alive who still understood the satellite systems. Or if Ares hadn't needed him to be there.

Tomorrow he'd yell the warning, tell anyone and everyone that an explosion was coming. He would explain at the top of his lungs that the explosion was not a real attack by the underground; no one should fire in response. He felt like he was trying to convince himself of something he didn't believe.

If only he knew when Ares meant to fire the SAT Twenty.

He'd call Thalia before he went on his mission. The State might come after her but she could hide with the underground—but would she? *To stop a war, she would. Today is her last day with the Peacekeepers. The tracker chip will be out of her arm.* He exhaled loudly. *At least one of us will be free.*

He put the knife on the counter and tried a vid call to Thalia.

No answer.

He tried again. He didn't dare leave her a message. If she didn't call him tonight, he'd have to go back to the lab tomorrow morning and look normal.

He scraped the kitchen trash bin across the floor to his shrine. The spoiled scent of three breakfast tins and three dinner tins assaulted him when he opened the bin cover. The small helmet made no sound when it landed on old coffee grounds. He pushed in the toothpick and the candle before wadding the tablecloth and shoving it on top, as if clumsily hiding evidence of a crime. The purpose of his shrine, whatever it might have been to Ares, would soon be of no matter.

That night, Milton lay sleepless. His wrinkled linen nightclothes, still rough from yesterday's hang-dry, bunched awkwardly under him. He had only a tattered blanket for cover. On the bedroom wall, the dim outlines of family holograms hung in a neat row across an otherwise empty space. The three of them under the climbing roses of the Garden Dome when Thalia was younger, before Valdol dulled her skin. His arm around Thalia when she joined the Peacekeepers, her bright eyes free of Valdol now that she worked for the State. Chari looking up bemused from a deflated bicycle tire with the dark green ocean behind her, flat as a lake, and her dark hair curled like a raven's wing next to her strong cheekbones and generous lips.

Pain jabbed his lower back no matter which way he turned.

Milton started at a faint rustling. He sat up and listened past the ticking clock. The rustling resolved itself into a low, delighted chuckle, not in the room but in his mind. He tensed. Ares had never laughed like that before. *He's supposed to be gone. Why is he laughing?* His empty stomach clenched.

Milton's vid screen flickered to life across the bedroom and Ares' laughter faded to nothing. He wanted to feel relieved but he didn't. The charcoal gray static onscreen arranged itself into the features of his sister. Thalia's picture sharpened, her regulation braids in tight rows showing below her broadbrimmed hat and her voice gruff and clear through the speakers.

"Milt, are you awake?"

"Thalia. Peace." He pushed up on his elbows, tried to straighten. The sight of her reminded him of what he'd done. He wanted to be happy to see her but he couldn't. A part of him was missing.

"Shouldn't you be eating breakfast?" She'd lived with him before and knew his habits.

"It's okay," he said. He'd never been as completely devoted to anyone else in his life as he'd been to her, until he met Chari. Then he'd learned it was possible to love beyond any limits. Why couldn't he feel anything now?

Thalia smiled, as she always did when they were together. She'd never looked at him any other way, even after his spine began to twist. "Guess where I am? Guess." She sounded much younger than her twenty-five years. It was part of what he loved about her.

"I'm no good at—"

"Department of Prosperity. Food line."

The picture from her handheld vid swung around. White marble columns, gleaming orange and red under the meager daylight, stretched above to the slanting tiled roof. A row of dusty marble steps stretched up from where she stood. The line of people in front of her wore their hats pulled low and covered every part of their bodies with gray jumpsuits. They waited in a listless queue that disappeared into a shadowed alcove. Children stood in docile rows next to their caretakers like tiny statues, their faces indistinct as though blurred by the screen, all joy lost to Valdol.

Milton imagined what he'd like to do to the functionaries who approved Valdol for the calming of *children*. He swallowed the bile in his throat.

The vid swung back round. "It shouldn't take me more than a couple of hours to get us something to eat. Better than last time."

"You're standing outside," Milton said. Then he realized his mistake: of course, she would have to stand outside for food now, like everyone else. *She's not in the Peacekeepers anymore.* The Peacekeepers always had access to the safety tunnels. Their bodies were government property until discharge.

"Tunnel closed for graffiti removal." She grinned under her hat.

He frowned. "I don't understand."

"I get extra rations for re-enlisting. I'm just up the street from you. I'm stocking up on oranges and I'll bring you some bread. Two loaves, if I'm lucky."

Cold sweat formed under his arms. His throat tightened. *Re-enlisting? Ares knew she wasn't leaving the Peacekeepers. He's laughing at me. She's only two blocks away from Gov Center One—*

Milton cleared his throat. "You're buying at Food Distro Three? What about Valdol?" Small amounts of Valdol had been added to all Distro food except bread.

"Peacekeepers get grapefruit pills. Stops the Valdol action. We still eat food with Valdol, but it doesn't slow us down."

Milton grimaced as though he could mask the twitching that started next to his eye. "I thought yesterday you got out of military—I mean, Peacekeepers?" His voice rose. *Someone might be listening to us. We'll be reported.*

Thalia's head tilted as though she noticed the brittleness under his words. "Medical benefits. And I don't like Valdol."

She jokes. "You said you were getting out." His vision narrowed to the circle around her face. He couldn't go yelling at Gov Center One with Thalia still in the Peacekeepers: the State would hunt her down the moment they discovered who he was.

Thalia shrugged.

Milton said, "You could stay here with me. Why don't you spend a few days here at home? Come today?" Fear made his thoughts swarm. His hands twitched as if he could swat away the static in his mind. *I'll have to tell her what I'm going to do so she can hide.* Milton's secret plan would only work if he lived. It would only work if Ares didn't find someone else to use.

Thalia looked at something he couldn't see. "Next number. One step forward," an automated voice demanded from loudspeakers in her background. She moved one step and turned back to the vid. "There are three Peace parades this afternoon. I'm meeting some friends at the last one. I'll show up later. If you're not there, I'll leave bread on the table."

Milton put a hand on his empty stomach. His skin was clammy and cold. He told her he liked to save bits for a dog outside of QM. He said it in passing. He hoped she'd remember, after.

"Later, Milt."

"Careful speech," was all he could say.

"Peace at all costs," she answered.

The vid went dark. Milton rose. He pulled a robe over his bedclothes on his way to the kitchen. A new chill in his body from more than lack of sleep. He set his kettle on the stove with shaking hands and returned to his bed to wait until it boiled. *I can't confess until I tell her the truth.*

He sat on the edge of his mattress. Waiting for water to boil. Staring blankly at his bedroom wall.

When the vid screen chirped again. This time, it was Sipra. The muscles in his neck tensed and jaw thrust forward. There could be no good reason for her to call him here. None. He rose, tightening the thin tie of his robe. The idea she had seen him on his bed, in his private space, starting anger much stronger than he felt it should be.

"Shouldn't you be at work already?" she asked. His lab equipment stood out behind her like a miniature city of tubes and gauges.

He clamped his anger down, hoping he'd hidden it well, yet could not help speaking through clenched teeth. "Don't call me."

"I found something."

Milton stared flatly to mask his spinning thoughts. "Get out of my lab. You don't have authorization to be there."

"I'm only helping you." She vibrated with excitement on the vid. He didn't expect that. She was a sociopath.

"What have you done?" he asked.

"It's what I found out. The clerk. Found him."

"Who is he?" *So fast. So fast.* He steadied himself on the back of the padded vid chair.

"What's it worth to you?"

"Just tell me."

"Turns out he got promoted for loyalty. He works in Gov Center One. Look."

Sipra shared her screen. Gov Center One squatted like a bloated Oligarch one block away from Food Distro Three. A shadow moved at a central window and the vid followed, zoomed in on a man bent over a desk, at work before offices should be open.

"That's him. Right there," she said.

Before Milton could see more than hazy detail, the vid image flickered away. Sipra's teeth seemed to fill the screen.

Milton clamped down on the howl in his throat. *I'll kill him. Today.*

"Now give me my promotion, Milton."

He kept his voice free of emotion. "You'll have it." He'd kill the clerk. Pretend to attack Gov Center One. Go to prison. Sipra would get his job. He'd listen to Ares shrieking until he died. He imagined how it would feel to put his hands around the clerk's throat and shake—

Sipra interrupted his thought. "How about we take care of this together?"

Milton blanched. "Stop." Vengeance was *his.*

"The SAT Twenty upgrade is fantastic. Elegant. If I just program this in here—" She signed her fingers over the SAT Twenty controls. The hum of activation rose behind her. "And if I use this pinpoint focus here—"

"Don't." Sweat beaded on his upper lip. *Thalia is two blocks away. Two. Sipra won't listen to me. I'll hang up and call—*

"The job promotion will be great, and since I'm doing this extra favor maybe you'll share a little of those food rations. Bet you'll have more time for me too, once we're working together. I'll test out the new SAT Twenty system—since tests are my job—but it's beyond simple," she winked, "to accidentally activate the pinpoint while I'm testing—and he's dust. No more clerk."

Milton stretched his arm toward the screen as though he could grab her hand. "They'll know it was you."

"You're not the only one with secrets." Her teeth glinted. "I can do what I want."

His right eyelid twitched. He couldn't help it. *Has Ares whispered to her? Promised her something? I have to make her listen.* "Sipra, don—"

"And... done."

Sipra shared her screen again, her gloat still visible in the square picture inset.

Gov Center One.

The explosion stabbed the air like a thousand guns firing outside his door. He put his hands over his ears and hunched to the shaking floor. The bulb of his ceiling light arced wildly. His holograms winked out. His heart struck his chest like a desperate prisoner.

Dust billowed over Gov Center One on the vid where concrete and steel fell from the sky. When the dust blew away, Gov Center One was standing.

Sipra's mouth hung open. "What? I—" She panned the vid slowly, tracking the rubble to the pillars of fire and smoke that had been Food Distro Three.

"Thalia!" shouted Milton.

No nononono

Then he thought he was begging Sipra to send help but he could not hear his own words.

He couldn't feel his tongue. He couldn't feel his teeth. Surging emotion demanded he bring his hand to his mouth but his hands would not rise. The life or death of one clerk ceased to matter. In the remains of his heart a wooden door crumbled to dust.

"You did this," Sipra said. Her teeth started to chatter making her harder to understand. "You approved SAT Twenty. You. They'll Silence you and worse. I had nothing to do with this." Her eyes widened with understanding. "He said they wouldn't know. But they'll see I was here—no, it was an accident. Something went wrong—"

The vid went dark. The walls next to the screen receded as though a cameraman moved away with the lens, stepping too far for focus. Milton did not mean to fall but his spine would not hold him. He did not feel himself hit the floor, and he did not reach out to break his fall.

Thalia's death had been meant only for him. Ares's answer to his hubris. His delay. All Ares had had to do was whisper to Sipra. Nudge her. Promise her.

*

Six months later, Milton still lay on the hospital bed like a crumpled shirt discarded at the end of the day. He tried to remember Thalia's face. He only remembered a chaos of concrete and dust. He searched his memories for her laughter, but it was drowned out by the drumbeat of guilt. *My fault. My fault. My fault.* And beneath the guilt, behind an iron door, he still stored the fuel that kept his enemy alive.

Ares had been silent, but Milton knew Ares was only weak, not dead.

I'll open the second door, Milton vowed numbly to himself. *This time I'll make sure the biosensors will detect the adrenaline. The nurses will dose me with Valdol. Ares will die.*

But he couldn't find his iron door. He wandered the desiccated fields and rotted forests of his heart, but grief and guilt hid the secret door that would open to the last of his rage.

Nurses placed a shrine to Asclepius next to his bed and near enough to touch, had he been able to move. Across from his bed, a vid screen played morning and night programs from long ago. No one talked about the explosion where he could hear. His constant hunger to find out if bombings had started, retaliation of the State against whoever they'd chosen to blame for the destruction of Food Distro Three, made his brain hum like a band-saw.

Milton couldn't speak. He couldn't control his hands. He knew what needed to be said but was unable to share the truth—that War himself was coming. But he could see and hear, and the nurses made sure he always faced the vid.

Someone finally told Chari where he was. She visited on screen. His eyes teared. He could only see the blurred outline of her jaw next to the curl of her coal-black hair.

"I hope you can hear me. I'll come. I promise. As soon as the contract lets me out."

He didn't want her to come. He didn't deserve it, unless she came to put blame where it should lie.

She called again a month later. "Vids are restricted to minimum at the village, but I'll come. I will."

He didn't deserve to see her. What if she guessed the truth? What if she knew it was him? He couldn't bare it if she forgave him.

*

Milton's day nurse stood in the door, his face creased with

surprise. "There's someone here to see you."

Chari appeared in the doorway. She'd chopped her hair regulation-close to her head. Her pale face gleamed gray under the hospital lights, punctuated by dark circles under her eyes. In Milton's mind he surged from his bed to throw his arms around her, to bury his face against her shoulder.

She pulled the chair next to his bed and stared. She still wore the charcoal drab uniform of the Coalition. Its monotone utility clashed with the anguish in her eyes. She smelled like jasmine. He longed to hear her breathing, but the sounds of a hospital never stopped. Had she come a few months earlier, he felt he might have died of the need to speak to her. Since then, he'd changed his mind. Forced silence was just punishment for what he'd done.

Chari wiped her eyes with the back of her sleeve. He wondered if she would touch him.

Milton. The voice was thin and far, like a plucked wire in a distant room.

Ares.

Milton's chest spasmed. A line of pain throbbed between his eyes. *You can't still be here. Get out. Get out. Get out.*

I have another job for you, Ares said.

You killed her. You put me here. You killed her. I killed her. Milton thought the force beneath his words might throw him from his bed, but he wasn't moving.

Chari glanced at the biosensors. He couldn't read her thoughts, and he couldn't stop Ares from talking.

Firing on the Food Distro didn't work, Ares said. *Sipra's action made the explosion look like an accident. No one wants war for that. I'd thought at least a few would blame the underground or the Oligarchs, but no. Everyone is pickled in Valdol. Even when they found out the SAT Twenty upgrade caused the mess... And Sipra has no anger. She feels nothing. They won't bother to Silence her.*

"This was the soonest I could come." Chari said.

Ares whispered, *So, we're not done. I'm giving your legs back. QM will put you where I need you. There are more peace weapons coming. Get up now or I'm taking Chari.*

Milton could barely hear his wife through the tumult in his brain.

Chari bowed her head for a moment. "I thought you stayed at work to be away from me. Thalia told me back when I left that I was wrong, but you wouldn't talk to me." She closed her eyes. Squeezed her lids tight. A muscle twitched by her jaw. Her shoulders rose with a deep breath and dropped. She opened her eyes. "I left because I believed it was what you wanted."

Wanted? He had wanted it but not in the way she said it. The pain etched on her forehead made him want to weep.

"You were never good at emotions, Milton." Her frown made her look years older. What she said was the truth. They used to laugh about it together. "I couldn't think of any other reason why you wouldn't come home. Why you wouldn't tell me what you were thinking."

He'd stayed at work to silence Ares. To have peace in his mind for a few more minutes. To make Chari move away so Ares would leave her alone.

Get up, Ares said.

Milton would remember her this way. The way she'd become because of him.

He had to find the iron door and open it, but Ares was still inside, ready to come back. Ares was supposed to be too weak to know what Milton was about to do. He clamped down on his fear before the nurse could see it on his chart. If he failed now, Thalia's death meant less than nothing. Blood pulsed at the sides of his neck.

A tear formed in the corner of Chari's eyes. She tightly gripped his hand.

Nerve impulses he shouldn't have felt pricked his skin. He made the first small voluntary movement of his lips since the night they placed him in bed. The thumb of his right hand twitched. He felt an answering pinprick in the muscle of his right forearm.

Chari rocked gently on her metal chair but didn't seem to notice a change.

Ares repeated as though from a great distance, *I said you're going to have to get up.*

Chari's hand gripped tighter. If she thought Milton was getting better, she wouldn't do what he needed her to do.

The nurse leaned in from the door. "You're his wife?"

"I am," Chari answered.

The nurse came in the room frowning at his hand-vid. "Your husband's not in any pain, but the biosensors read adrenaline spiking."

Chari blinked rapidly, the gray of her thin cheeks paling further, dark circles under her eyes deepening. "He hasn't been taking Valdol?" Milton would have done anything to bring back the color to her face and the fire to her eyes.

"He works—worked—for the State. Peace Department. We haven't had to dose him. If we had, I would know."

What are you doing, Milton? asked Ares.

Milton focused on finding the place inside, the walled-off cavern behind the iron door, the place where rage fueled by deep grief hunched like a vagabond. Milton thought to himself, *It must come now. The nurse must see.*

Ares raced through his thoughts like a demon, slashing through his memories. *What is this inside? What have you hidden?*

Milton forced himself to remember the moment he sabotaged SAT Twenty. The moment Sipra fired. The children at Food Distro Three. Thalia's last smile for him. Chari on the day she'd left him. His father's melted voice and paralyzed fingers and brain full of Valdol.

The nurse checked his electropad. "No Valdol before today because no reactions, but he's having a reaction now."

Chari gripped Milton's hand. He knew he could flex his fingers and let her know he was still there. But he had to be still. The nurse was going to ask. He felt it coming. Heat bubbled in his chest. He had to keep still. Chari wouldn't allow Valdol if she found out he could move, that there was still a chance. He had to be *still*.

The nurse said, "If adrenaline keeps spiking, and if he starts to improve—"

Chari nodded. "Silenced." Her voice was hoarse, as though she spoke around a rock in her throat.

Stop this, said Ares. *You know you'll never let yourself be dulled. You'll never let them take away your anger. You need it. You need me.*

Milton ignored Ares. Milton watched himself move toward the deepest door in his heart. He was not afraid.

Where are you, Milton? Where have you gone?

THE LAST GRASP OF WAR

Milton imagined crushing tall grass under his massive boots. Flicking away clear crystal water fountains with his thick, strong fingers, the illusory fountains he had built in his head to distract Ares from his secrets. Yanking down jasmine, clawing away with hardened fingernails the matted vines and filling his nose with their sweetness. Grabbing the iron handle of the deepest door. Drawing it open with a shuddering groan.

Rage roiled forth unchecked from the secret places of his mind.

Adrenaline pounded his heart like the giant fist of a blacksmith god.

The nurse studied his tablet again. "It's worse, these readings." He frowned as he glanced between Milton's body and the spiking on the screen. "I've never seen adrenaline this high. He has to have Valdol." The nurse's hand shook as though he feared Chari would try to stop him. "He'll be much happier."

Chari's eyes dulled.

Blood surged in Milton's legs. His feet. Ares woke Milton's body limb by limb. Anger made him ache to move as if he'd been chained and would now be free. He had to be *still*.

His thoughts scattered in bursts of confusion like explosions on a vid. Without Milton's rage, Ares would wither and die. The world had to have a chance to heal if it could.

Ares tore at the roots of Milton's will. Milton saw the blinding light of his love for Chari and Thalia. He grasped it to his heart while anger rolled across the top of it. He had to do this. He'd held on to his darkness to use it now. It was time to make his anger *mean* something.

Chari's warm hand trembled in his. Her Valdol must be wearing off. "I know you can't hear me, but I miss you, my husband. I miss you." A tear glittered under the fluorescent lights; the last one he would ever see.

The nurse leaned forward. A knot of coldness the size of a cat's eye grew in Milton's forearm. It pushed its tendrils through his veins. He felt it reaching his fingers and branching near his shoulder. He was going to win. His heart swelled with the knowledge.

Ares, his voice louder as Milton's anger fed him anew, shrieked in Milton's mind with the sound of a thousand sword-points scraping steel plate, *Rise!*

Milton's tingling hands needed to jerk like the last moments before sleep. He forced them limp at his sides.

Ares covered his face with thin lines of pain like scalpel cuts across his cheeks. Under his eyes. *Get up! Move! I'll kill her!*

Milton howled inside, silent and motionless on his bed. When Ares was dead, Chari would have nothing to fear.

With the parts of his mind he could still use, he concentrated on his wife. He wanted to remember her while was still himself. He saw her as she had been in the beginning; eyes like shadowed pools framed by dark hair wild in the winds, her body angled toward him, and her voice full of whispered passions. Her skin smelled like toasted almonds.

Numbness spread under his breast-bone. Weight like a leaded blanked pressed him down. The florescent lights burned unaccountably bright.

Ares' screams came from somewhere through the ceiling. The pain in Milton's face subsided.

He tried to move his tongue to see if he could, but it was frozen like before.

Chari pressed her lips hard against Milton's as if she chased the fire dying in his eyes. He imagined he could feel their warmth.

The only sign he had that Ares meant to break his bones was pressure, and even that began to disappear. Ares called from far away like gulls crying over the sea; too distant to understand.

Colors leached away. Milton hadn't been prepared for that. Brown faded from Chari's hair and redness from her lips. Green turned to gray in her eyes. He pushed away the sorrow that might have dulled his anger: he meant to hold it until the end. Until he felt it ripped away. The only way to be sure Ares was dead.

Color faded from his memories. Gray crept up the tangled flowering vines in his hidden places until the last white petal faded, leaving only the memory of a fragrance.

His muscles slackened. Chari pulled away, yet her love stayed with him. Reminded him of the reason he'd held anger so tight and so deep. This was the way to spend it.

THE LAST GRASP OF WAR

Rage shrunk to anger. Anger to irritation. Irritation to nothing.

Ares tightened a fist around his lungs and squeezed. Milton gasped but it was not his own. Ares struggled for air until, as the last of Milton's secret crumbled to ash, Ares had nothing to breathe.

Milton's lips relaxed into a smile. Ares was dead. Chari was safe. And, for a moment, Milton was still himself; alone inside his own head.

The sweet scent of dying jasmine hung on the air and was gone.

L. A. Selby finds passion for writing in the darker tales of the human heart. Drawing from more than twenty years as a trauma therapist, her stories often carve unsuspected channels through loyalty, love, and loss. She divides her real life between coasts and enjoys foreign travel to abandoned or haunted places. The first city she ever loved was Venice. Ten years ago, she fell in love with Rome. Her newest passion is Transylvania—all of it. If you ask her about gods, goddesses, and archetypes, she will talk a very long time.

Dark Fantasy. Speculative Suspense. Supernatural Horror. www.LASelby.com

By Jeff Provine

TU WATCHED THE LITTLE MAN fail in his oration at the hotel conference center. Through his many years, Tu had stood in grand coliseums of granite and limestone, palaces leafed with gold, and decks of battleships wooden and steel. Now, here he was in an air conditioned cold room that stank of cleaning fluid with carpet worn thin. It was almost as pathetic as the speaker.

This whimpering man-child had been given every tool: a proud title, a moment of attention, even bright colors cast behind him from the projector. Yet he failed so thoroughly in his long, stumbling, quiet words. He barely looked his audience in the eye, not that many even paid him attention now. The little man had already defeated himself, yielding to his own weakness.

Conquering him would be too easy.

"Not a challenge in itself," Tu muttered, "but if it helps me against my brother, so be it."

A low thunder of applause broke out, though no one meant any of it. The little man's miserable song and dance at the conference room podium had ended. He stood silent, nodding his head and waving at the room, his shoulders slinked. The applause died after only a few beats, and the audience members grabbed up their bags and papers from their tables and chairs.

Tu sighed at the little man and added a rumble of disgust from his throat. The real challenge was going to be stirring up action out of such frailty.

He studied the little man fidgeting with his computer, practically hiding behind it. There must be strength in him somewhere. His skin was pale with splotches of red to match the fiery hair that ringed his over-sized head. He was of Celtic stock. The Celts were strong. They had even driven back those iron-shelled Romans, at least from the corners of their realm. Tu smiled.

In those days, this little man would have been among those in camp, counting stores and sharpening weapons. If it had come down to him raising a weapon against foes he could barely see with his weak eyes, the battle had already long been lost.

Now the human had glass mounted over his eyes so he could see as well as any. He might even fight as well as some with modern weapons throwing their metal bullets across the battlefield. *Did he have the heart to raise a weapon? No, this little man's part is still better played at camp where his head could fight with theories and numbers.*

The conference center was clearing. It was time to act. If Tu could make that short, thin brainbox from Corsica into the mighty Napoleon, conqueror of an entire continent, he could harden even this runt into action. And if this little man's weapon worked…

Tu scooped up one of the pamphlets left behind on a coffee -stained tablecloth covering the information by the humans who didn't care about the little man's scheme. Colored drawings and symbols danced over the printed paper. Paper, the desecrated sheaf of his brother Tane's precious trees smeared with ink and tossed aside like it was never alive. That made Tu's smile widen.

Perhaps now, after all these years, his last brother would fall.

Dr. Joel Healey pulled the USB drive from the port on the conference laptop even before his PowerPoint was closed. He held it tight in his sweaty palm.

The IT guy working the conference computer made a face. He stood behind Healey, hands full of cords that he had already rolled up while walking up the stage.

Healey grimaced back at him, not wanting to hear it, but IT went on anyway.

"You know, you should really wait to pull that about until after you've ejected the drive digitally."

Healey shrugged. "Does it really matter?"

The IT guy rolled his eyes and shifted his stance to show how done waiting he was. "Yeah, it does. Otherwise, the drive thinks it's still plugged in, which can lead to data corruption."

Healey's throat went dry. He didn't have anything to come back with, so he just made a mumbling apology and retreated to tucking things into his old, brown leather satchel. There was a hole in the bottom, so he had to carefully tuck his pen and USB into one of the inner pockets. Then he hurried off the stage and out among the tables to escape.

There were so many handouts left on the tabletops, standing out like pink, yellow, and blue flowers amid the dull beige of the conference hall. Healey had made a big order at the print shop since the coordinator had sounded so excited telling him he would be the climate conference's last speaker. He thought it meant he'd keynote. Instead, Healey had been the speaker people could skip to get to the airport an hour earlier. The conference hall had been packed this morning when Dr. Karris called out her rhetoric about the need to act for climate change while not specifying how. After the break, only a few tables still had people, and most of them were on their phones.

Healey sniffed and readjusted his thick glasses. What did he expect? He's just some wack-job spouting sci-fi that no one took seriously.

Something deep within Healey, something hard, shouted back at him. *It's fiction now, but it is science! And it can save the world.*

"If only people would listen to me," Healey mumbled back

at it.

A wide shadow fell over the table beside him. Healey looked up. A tall man stood above him, wearing a suit that suggested limitless resources. He was enormous, broad-shouldered with muscles that pressed against the fabric. His skin was tanned, and his black hair was long, pulled back in a way that was professional yet refused conforming.

He didn't even have to say anything. His presence alone commanded attention.

"C-can I help you?" Healey asked.

The tall man had one of Healey's handouts in his enormous fist. He held it up to show the rough schematics of the Parasol on the second page. It was a rough doodle Healey had done with the computer graphics department showing the orbit of Earth, mobile water-vapor blocks, and squiggly solar rays being partially reflected.

"This is yours?" the man demanded, his tone deep and serious.

Healey shivered and nodded. He cleared his throat. "Yes, I'm Dr. Joel Healey."

"And it can do what you say? Influence the weather?"

Healey blinked. Had the man not listened to his presentation at all? He grunted. "Of course it can."

The tall man looked at him with deep, dark eyes.

Healey shivered again. His voice became softer. "It's basic meteorology, really: block the incoming solar energy, and you can decrease solar heating of a region. The only major innovation is the microwave heat-sink. Otherwise, solar energy would excite the enclosed water molecules and they'd drift off into space. Well, most would fall back to Earth—"

"You ramble," the tall man said. "Be firm and precise in your words."

Healey stood silent for a moment and rearranged his glasses. When he looked up again, he asked, "Who are you?"

The tall man directed a hand at his chest. "I am Tu."

"And what do you want from me?"

"You should be asking what I can do for you to meet your goals," Tu said, his tone again deep and serious.

"My goals?" Healey looked at the man's firm face. He wasn't

kidding. "I just want to make the world a better place."

Tu rolled his head back and growled a scoffing noise. "That is not a goal! That is a wish, a feeling. What is your goal?"

"I, well, I was hoping…"

"Stop your stammering!" Tu commanded. "What do you seek to achieve?"

"I want to build the Parasol," Healey said. He looked away, surprised at himself. It had been so long since he had been so concrete. Had he ever actually been so frank? That hardness in his chest seemed wider now, like a foundation.

"You *want* to?" Tu ask, dragging out the word "want" like a verbal sneer.

"Uh, of course I want to," Healey stammered. "I've dedicated the last seven years of my life—"

"Who cares about your past?" Tu said.

Healey felt his face grow hot. "How dare you! I have a Ph.D. in Physics and a professorship at Hudson University."

Tu started smiling again. "Now that is your present. Who you are. *That* is much more important to me. Give me the present and the future. Tell me you will build this." He held up the image of the Parasol again.

Healey stammered. A lump grew in his throat and stopped up even that noise.

"*Can* you build this?" Tu asked. For the first time, his voice sounded unsure.

Healey nodded in fast, short movements that shook his glasses. He grabbed hold of them. "As you can see on page four of the pamphlet, I've already thought out the necessary components with the ground-base for launch, the control station, everything."

"All you are saying is that it *can* be built." Tu leaned over Healey. "Can *you* build this?"

Healey blushed again, now out of embarrassment. He said softly, "Of course I can build this, if I had the right team."

Tu peered at him. Healey could feel the stare going through him like an x-ray, searching for something solid. Part of him wanted to back way, even run for safety. Yet there was such an air of power about this man. He wanted that feeling. Healey stood up as straight as he could and took in a breath to swell his body.

Tu slid the handout into a pocket inside his suit coat and crossed his arms over it.

"You make excuses," Tu stated. "Nevertheless, I will find you that team. There is much to be done with you, but I will have you lead my campaign."

"Campaign?" Healey echoed.

A loud whine made Healey jump. He turned toward the sound to find a janitor starting up an industrial vacuum in the corner. When he turned back, the tall man disappeared.

Healey looked around for him, but the conference hall was empty except for the janitor vacuuming. The IT guy had vanished, too. The tables were folded up, standing like ranks of soldiers.

"Mr. Tu?" Healey called. How could a man that big just have disappeared?

The janitor looked up at him and shook his head.

Healey clutched his satchel like a protective stuffed animal and hurried out of the room. The long hallway that had been filled with vendors in colorful booths was now empty, stripped down to the carpet and wood paneling. How long had he been talking to Mr. Tu?

His phone pinged. It was an email from the Department of Energy, "Re: Project PARASOL."

*

The next weeks came as a blur. Healey's inbox flooded with emails from federal offices and NGOs that had never gotten back to him before. Meeting after meeting populated his calendar until he had to begin turning people down and made media appearances only for the highest rated news channels. The Physics Department secretary at Hudson forwarded so many calls to Healey's office that the dean finally awarded him his own secretary along with the chair of a new endowment from some benefactor that had popped out of nowhere. Graduate teaching assistants seemed to materialize out of the air to take over his classes. Everything became about the Parasol.

Through it all, Mr. Tu had been at his side, prodding him,

coaching him. He had been literally by his side at the news-magazine interview, standing just out of frame until the red recording light on the camera went out. They were in Healey's new office, the big one with the wide oak desk and the shelves built into the walls. It smelled like an ancient library, not at all like the tar-and-concrete smell of his old office. The cameraman from Marketing and Communications broke down the camera, took the lapel mic, and wound up the wires. He left without saying more than a few words to Healey. He never spoke to Mr. Tu at all.

"A whirlwind," Healey said cheerfully. "It's been simply a whirlwind!"

Tu stood beside him, looking into the sky out the broad-paned window, lost in thought.

"I always believed people would do the right thing if they had the option," Healey said, straightening his collar where the lapel mic had pinched it. The interview had ended with actual applause from the pundit. "They're finally listening."

Tu laughed loudly. "Humans won't do anything they don't have to."

"What?" Healey chirped.

Tu still laughed, a beat of war drums between his words. "Humans act only to improve their survival."

"That's a pretty cynical thought!" Healey said. His throat felt tight, but he tried to speak up over wheezing. "People obviously help each other. Altruism isn't a myth."

Tu nodded. "They work to help because they want a world where they themselves would be helped when in need. Show that need, and people will act. Don't show it…"

"…and I guess they wouldn't know to act," Healey finished. He thought of the millions starving across the world while grocery stores threw out old produce. "They couldn't."

"So you must show that need," Tu told him, "and explain to them what they must do. *Make* them act!"

Healey's mind spun. He kept thinking of counterexamples. Grandparents doted on their favorite grandchildren. Nonprofits promoted literacy. People built homes and gave them away to the needy. Yet there was an echoing response from a hardness deep in his chest for each of them: grandparents want vibrant family lines, literacy strengthens the wealth of the community, volunteers are swayed by promoters with sweet words.

The office landline phone on Healey's desk rang and interrupted his thoughts. It would be another meeting, another step up the ladder of resources. They came seemingly from nowhere, but his background in Physics reminded him "nowhere" was a myth. There was some causality.

"You've been getting people to act on the Parasol project," Healey said to Tu.

The tall man nodded.

The phone rang again. Healey just stared at it and then went on, "I tried everything I could to get people interested in the Parasol. The need to act is obvious, but people never cared." He looked up at Tu, his tone almost begging. "How are you getting their attention?"

"I do what I must to make them act," Tu told him. "I have my own goal."

Healey wanted to ask, but the incessant ringing made him answer the phone. The phone displayed, "Senate."

"Hello?" Healey asked into the phone.

Tu cocked an eyebrow at him.

Healey cleared his throat and answered more firmly, "This is Dr. Joel Healey."

*

The committee chairwoman, a senator for Alaska, banged her gavel on the long desk where five senators sat. Healey was at a small table in front of them, surrounded by charts and piles of documents. Mr. Tu stood beside him.

Healey looked around the chamber, the "Kennedy Caucus Room" one of the aides had called it. Huge marble pillars lined the walls to the high ceiling trimmed with relief and gold leaf He thought he had seen it in a movie. The carpeting smelled of shampoo. Flags were everywhere and in every size.

He sat at in a blocky wooden chair behind a wooden table across from the senators at their green-clothed table. All the wood was polished. Aides slipped like phantoms between tables and around chairs, filling water glasses and handing folders to other aides. Cameras hummed. It was like the inside of a beehive.

No, Healey thought. *That'd be too organized toward some goal. This a corpse of maggots all trying to get their own bites.*

He winced. The thought was too dark. Was Tu influencing him?

"With all those pleasantries completed, let's get on with the hearing," the chairwoman said. "Dr. Healey, we've all read your statements, so no need to go into those details. Certainly your project has gained national attention lately. I want to hear your thoughts from your own mouth."

Healey straightened up in his chair. All eyes were on him. Why didn't they look at Mr. Tu? He towered over Healey, but he was silent. Tu raised his eyebrows over his dark eyes at Healey as if offering the floor.

"Well, senator," Healey began. He looked her in the eye and spoke loudly so he didn't have to bow into the mic. "The world is in a dire situation. Global temperatures are rising consistently with new record temperatures almost every year. Glaciers are breaking up faster than scientists ever predicted. Storm systems are becoming more powerful and striking more often. We have to do something."

One of the senators, an older gentleman from Oklahoma, huffed and crossed his arms. "I don't even get why we're here. We don't have enough meteorological data to know this isn't a natural cycle. And where I come from, we know a thing or two about wild weather!"

Healey glanced up at Tu. "How can I argue with someone who won't even admit there's a problem?"

The senator from Oklahoma cleared his throat. Healey swallowed. Looking away from the senator must have been odd and disrespectful. He took hold of his water glass and drank to cover his gaffe.

"What does he see as a problem?" Tu replied.

Healey turned back to the senator. "Maybe all of that is all too abstract. Senator, what if you could stop a tornado?"

The senator sat up in surprise and cleared his throat. Stammering, he asked, "I'm sorry?"

"What if you had the power to ensure a tornado never

struck your state again?"

Oklahoma wrinkled his nose. "I'd say you'd be playing God."

"Not at all!" Healey held up one hand like a boy scout making a pledge. "All we'd be doing is managing nature. It's no different than irrigating the plains to grow crops or building a dam to control a flooding river."

The senator from Oklahoma squinted. "We do enjoy our lakes. You're saying something like that could stop a tornado?"

"Once the Parasol system is in orbit, the solar-energy buffers could be moved to block sunlight in trouble spots, cooling down warm fronts, decreasing the chances a tornado could form at all. When the danger's gone, those blocks can be moved, and together we can give everybody a beautiful day at the lake."

Oklahoma hummed and nodded. "Together. I like that."

Tu grinned.

The senator from California spoke up. "But we're not just talking about slowing down storms. You could effectively control the weather, correct? When it rains?"

"Not complete control," Healey admitted.

Tu hummed in his throat, a warlike guttural sound like the beating of drums.

Healey flushed. Was that too much weakness? It was honest. He swallowed and began again. "While we can't prescribe the weather totally, we can certainly influence it where needed. Droughts would be a thing of the past, along with all the suffering from farmers and destruction from widespread forest fires."

California looked dreamily into space.

"And who decides all this?" the senator from Massachusetts asked.

"We already have the National Oceanographic and Atmospheric Administration," California said. "Their work could be expanded not only to predict weather but to manage it."

The senator from Oklahoma clapped his hands. Massachusetts made notes in her binder.

"We are looking at an investment of tens of billions of

dollars, not including annual expenses in maintenance," Alaska said. "Isn't there any way to scale this down?"

Healey started to sneer, but Tu put a hand on his shoulder.

"See the fret of money upon her?" Tu whispered.

"So I comfort her?" Healey replied. He addressed the senators, "While the initial cost may seem high for the launching system, maintenance is cheap, and we gain an inexpensive way to move cargo into orbit as well as…"

Tu squeezed the little man's shoulder to stop him. "No, use her fear."

"As well as," Healey picked up, "saving untold trillions of dollars in destruction, as I mentioned to the senator from California. No more hurricanes. No more state-wide floods. No more nation-wide fires. Not making this investment will cost our country, our people, dearly."

The senator from Alaska nodded.

Tu grinned at Healey. He made a quick smile back.

Healey studied the senators' faces while he spoke, just as Tu had taught him. Oklahoma and California were smiling. Alaska kept flipping through her schedule, likely already agreeing and ready to move to the next meeting. Massachusetts's eyes were down at her notes. Tennessee leaned back in his chair. Those final two were his opponents.

Healey aimed for Tennessee first. He watched him during the other senators' questions and his own responses. His face was blank, dismissive. What inspired him to act?

"Is it the business of the United States government to fund fantasy projects?" Tennessee asked at last. "There have been people building weather machines for ages and cloud-seeding and all that. Isn't this just more snake-oil?"

Angry bile bubbled up inside Healey. *I've been showing the benefits for over an hour, you useless—*

Tu glared down at him.

Healey took a drink of water to calm himself. He had to work toward the man's survival. Lowering his voice to make it as dark as he could, Healey said, "If the United States doesn't take the lead on this, other countries will. Imagine the Russians becoming the world's breadbasket by warming up Siberia."

Tennessee's eyebrows shot up.

"Imagine the Chinese dictating weather patterns across the Pacific, controlling how much rain the West Coast gets."

California winced.

Healey went on. "Imagine Iran destabilizing–"

Tennessee cleared his throat. All he said was, "I see."

Healey nodded. Of course he did now. He'd won.

Tu grinned.

The chairwoman from Alaska called for final comments. The senators made speeches echoing Healey's points, until it came to Massachusetts.

"I appreciate the efforts toward making a dent in global climate change," she said. "But I'm concerned about the potential mismanagement in the long term."

"Mismanagement?!" Healey sank in his seat as if she had slapped him in the face. "Don't you trust your own government, the very thing you've dedicated your life to?"

"I trust many things about it," she said with a nod. "But I am also skeptical on things that seem to have no downside. It makes me wonder who will benefit most from it, and who will lose out. If we're bringing more rain to the American Southwest, where is that going to come from? Will the northwestern states of Mexico suffer?"

Healey sputtered.

Tu kicked him.

"I, uh, senator, thank you for your thought," Healey said. He was sweating. He had to take back control. "However, we can generate that moisture from the Pacific with energy reflection."

"Wouldn't warming the waters there be a danger to local sea life, especially sensitive coral?"

Healey's mouth was too dry to speak.

"New technology doesn't have the best record for minimizing economic impact," she said, "although what truly concerns me is that there might be interests who actively misuse the system. We could see the destruction of whole habitats by drying out rainforests or greening up deserts."

Healey blinked. There really could be environmental disasters, if the wrong people…

Tu kicked him again.

Healey looked up, his eyes watering behind the thick glasses. "She's right."

"Admitting defeat?" Tu asked. "All you've worked for, gone because of a few comments?"

Healey rubbed his head. "How can I win her over?"

Tu turned his dark eyes to the senator. After a moment, he shook his head. "She cannot be moved by the likes of you. She is much stronger."

Healey let out a soft sound like a balloon losing air.

Tu's strong hand slapped him between the shoulders to make him sit up higher. "One defeat is not the loss of the war! Win this. I demand it!"

Healey looked at Tu and back at the senators. None of them acknowledged the slap at all. They kept staring at him.

That hardness in Healey's chest felt firmer. He brought himself back to his microphone. "With respect, senator, I hear your fears, but I must say they are as unfounded as they are un-American. What evidence is there that it would be mismanaged? Don't we already have laws in place to protect our sensitive biomes? And don't the lives of American citizens lost in hurricanes and fires, or farmers suffering from drought mean something to you?"

He prattled on, glorifying land management. She remained still, her lips tight and eyes calm. Around her, the others seemed to back away from her. Oklahoma and Tennessee nodded with Healey.

When he was done, Healey felt sick. Did he even believe half the things he said?

Alaska's gavel banged. "Let's call this to a vote."

Four hands raised yea, and one nay. Healey's heart pounded against the hardness, stilling it some.

"Very well, we have our recommendation to the Budget Committee," Alaska said. Her voice was nonchalant. "We'll take a recess and…"

Healey didn't hear the rest. He just breathed in his chair. After all these years, the Parasol would become a reality.

Beside him, Tu held his fists tight, pressing them to flex his arms. After all these millennia, he had a weapon for victory.

*

Healey's dean had begged him to take a long sabbatical instead of resigning. There would an extensive study into potential conflicts of interest as Healey took on his directorship of the Parasol program, the dean had said, but he assured Healey that they wouldn't find anything. Even if they did, they could find a way to work around it, the dean added.

"I'm never there, but they put my name on every new program that comes up," Healey said on the flight to Honolulu. He sat in first class, lounging in the spacious chair and sipping a cocktail he couldn't remember the name of. The sabbatical stipend had paid for the upgrade.

"What you do for them is little compared to who you are and what is believed you can do," Tu replied. The giant man stood in the wide walkway between seats, leaning over Healey.

Healey wasn't sure where Tu's seat was. Tu had simply walked past the curtain from the rest of the plane. *They weren't supposed to do that, were they?* Healey was afraid to ask.

"They want to be by your side, in your glow," Tu told him. "That is conquest. Power."

"I don't need power," Healey muttered.

Tu sneered at him. "Don't be a fool. Without power, you never would have come this far. Power is everything."

Healey blinked. He didn't know what to say.

Tu nodded. The silence proved his point.

*

From Pearl Harbor, a small flotilla of Navy support ships sailed fourteen hundred miles to Jarvis Island, a hunk of coral near the equator. Guano and sand had accumulated to make something of a soil where some scraggly plants grew. There were a few wrecked buildings left from the guano-mining days and the weather station in the 1930s, but it was nearly a blank slate. Its highest point was only seven meters. If nothing were done about rising sea levels, it would disappear in a few decades. The thought of rescuing it made Healey smile.

The island changed over the coming months. The fleet

established a makeshift port on the island's west coast, out of the incessant eastern wind. Once the airstrip was laid down, crews from the Army Corps of Engineers flew in from American Samoa. Construction turned the quiet reef into an anthill. The saltwater-fed nuclear plant was the first major addition, then spartan housing and offices, and finally the track for the two-mile coilgun along its widest path that would launch the water-vapor pods into orbit. Everything was packed close together, nearly piled on top of each other, and hung out over the water into the ocean on piers and rafts.

Once in space, the pods would come together by magnets and move on ion-drives fueled by captured solar energy. Even though it would be years until the Parasol was fully unfurled with its mutable clouds of pods orbiting the earth, breaking up and rejoining as NOAA commanded, Jarvis Island was forged into reality.

Healey was the director, but there was little for him to do outside of signing papers. The construction crews scurried outside of his office, which had evolved from a canvas tent to a sprawling room with glass walls. Everyone seemed to know exactly what they were doing, working off blueprints based on his designs from years ago. Sometimes he would send out emails of encouraging words to motivate them. The crews worked just as hard on the days he didn't send the emails out. Tu went among the workers; his bulky frame seemed to be everywhere at once, urging them on, stoking their warrior spirits.

The little man started drinking expensive scotch just to fill the time. Tu did not need him, so he left Healey to sit with the others who played soldier without courage for a fight.

*

Tu's ear pricked. He looked up from where he stood among men welding, patching together the bones of the earth, encouraging them with whispers of glory.

Healey was angry. Tu looked up at the office window.

The colonel, his hair thick but stone gray, sipped his tumbler of scotch. "'Parasol' is going to mean something very different very soon. It'll make people sit up straight when they hear it, like we did back in school when somebody said 'ICBM.'"

Healey tried to laugh, but he couldn't make more than a huffing sound. He sat in the huge executive chair behind his equally huge desk. They were so large they made him want to curl up. "What?"

"Mutually-assured destruction, nuclear proliferation, shock and awe, all those words the PR guys cook up," Col. Bradbury said from the wall of glass that served as a window for Healey's office. He waved his tumbler at the construction.

Healey narrowed his eyes. He couldn't have been that drunk, even if it was two in the afternoon. "What do you mean?"

"It's a weapon, doc. You know that, right?"

Healey's glass shook in his hand. He set it down as fast as he could but not before some of the scotch spilled onto the cork tabletop. The puddle turned a dark red.

"Shit, Healey, you look like you saw a ghost," Bradbury said. He grabbed Healey by the shoulder with his free hand. "Maybe you've had enough."

Healey shook his head. "No, that's impossible."

"I've been to enough bars in my day—"

"No!" Healey shouted. "Not that!"

The colonel backed away a step.

"You can't weaponize Parasol! It's a tool for peace!"

Tu laughed as he listened. The humans around him heard nothing.

"Doc, call it what you want, but we're going to weaponize this thing. 'Tool for peace,' I like that. So was iron and nuclear fission, I'll bet." Bradbury took a sip and gestured with his glass again toward all the construction beyond the massive window. "What we have here is a better deterrent that the Bomb. Somebody crosses us, and we can just park a glob in orbit cutting off sunlight to their whole country. Morale devastation and economic sanctions all in one packet without wrecking any infrastructure. Genius."

Healey squeezed his hands into fists in his lap.

Bradbury went on. "And what are they going to do, shoot it

down with anti-satellite missiles? Go ahead. We'd have whatever was taken out replaced in a matter…"

"A matter of days," Healey finished for him.

"Right." Bradbury took a sip.

"Get out," Healey told him.

"Hm?"

Healey pointed toward the door and roared, "Get out!"

Bradbury rocked back on his heels. He nodded, gulping down his drink while he did, and set it down on the soaked desktop before he slipped out the big door to the hallway.

Healey stomped his feet under his desk and slumped over his desktop with the scotch-stained red.

"Tu," he said aloud. "You can probably hear me. Come here! I demand it!" He grabbed a handful of pens and notebooks from his desk and hurled them across the room.

Tu opened the door and came inside with a casual strut. He patted the pockets of his suit and closed the door behind him. His dark eyes flashed while he grinned. He strolled like a used car salesman to stand in front of Healey's desk.

Healey glared at him. Then his lip quivered.

"Should I even bother with you now?" Tu asked.

"Are—" Healey began. He had to say the words slowly through gritted teeth to ensure he didn't stammer. "Are you the devil?"

Tu's smile widened. "What makes you think that?"

"The speed everything's progressed, just a matter of months when government projects take years or decades or… It's supernatural. And just now, you could hear me. I didn't even know where you were, but then you were here. You're always here, even though it's like other people can't see you."

"I am everywhere," Tu said with a nod. He then winced and sighed. "Almost everywhere. There are those who resist me."

"So you are the devil!" Healey shrieked. He shrank back into his chair.

Tu grunted."No, I'm hardly anything like that, working to corrupt human souls for whatever sentence in the afterlife. That's all a waste as far as I'm concerned. I only care about the living world. I am a warrior, and I seek to defeat it."

"Defeat… what?" Healey asked in a whispering voice.

Tu crossed one huge arm over the other. "Everything."

Healey shivered. He realized he was sitting with his shoulders curled, like he could hide behind them. "Why?"

Tu took in a long breath. He began to pace. "It is fitting that we are here on this Pacific island to build the weapon that will defeat my final brother. The people here tell the story more clearly than others.

"When the world was new, Father Rangi, the sky, rested on top of the Earth Mother, Papa. All was darkness, like a cavern. My brothers and I could only crawl between them. Eventually we discussed what to do, and I made the obvious answer: kill them both and fashion a better world from their corpses."

Healey gasped.

Tu sneered at him. "I expected such a response from you. So weak. My brothers, too, refused. Tane, father of trees and birds and insects, said we could move our parents apart to give us room to grow. We did it, he pushing and me cutting their tendons, and light poured forth onto the earth. It was a time of celebration, except that slippery impish Tawhiri fled to Rangi's side."

"Tawhiri?" Healey asked.

"My brother, father of wind and storms." Tu growled. "He's attacked us ever since, leveling Tane's forests. He drove Tangaroa and his children into the sea. Papa hid Rongo and his crops and Haumia and his ferns under the ground so they would survive. I was left alone to face Tawhiri, and I did face him. I sank my feet into the earth and stood against Tawhiri's mightiest blows. I fought back, even though my brothers would not heed my calls for aid. I fought until Tawhiri slithered away once more. Every day since I have worked to get my vengeance.

"First; I defeated my weak brothers. I trained up my humans to use tools to capture and slay every one of their children. You fell trees, dug up roots, trapped birds in snares and fish in nets, and then you…" Tu grinned unlike anything Healey had ever seen before.

Healey's chest ached.

"You eat them," Tu said, never interrupting his grin. "How beautiful, how thorough, is that for defeating your enemy? To take their strength and make it your own?"

Healey only shook his head. "N-none of that really happened."

"It did," Tu said with a firm tone, "though your mind cannot understand it. These words are metaphors, the best you can fathom."

Tu spread his arms, showcasing himself. "Like me. This is not my true form. I am myriad, every aspect of conquest. Many do not know me by name, but they see me. Sometimes it's a banner or an obsidian ax or a supersonic jet, but, to you, I'm a man in a business suit. What an odd way to envision a god!"

Healey shook his head so fast he had to close his eyes. "No, no, no. I'm Catholic. I don't believe any of that. I can't!"

"Ah. 'You shall have no other gods before me.' Don't worry about your god's henotheistic wrath. You're no worshipper of mine. I'm using you for your designs."

"My design?" Healey grabbed his head to stop it from shaking. His gaze fell immediately on the Parasol blueprints lying over the alcohol-tinted desk. "Climate influence, storm dispersal…"

Tu raised a triumphant fist. "Everything we need to defeat my brother. There is nowhere to flee to now, Tawhiri!"

The door to Healey's office burst open. It was one of the corporals, the one who made good coffee.

"Sorry, sir, but I thought, you…," he said, stumbling over the words. Before he could go on, he took several long steps across the office to the side wall of cabinets where Healey's television was. The corporal fumbled with the remote. "You really need to see this!"

The screen flicked on with a weather satellite showing the Pacific Ocean. The streaming image showed a color-highlighted buildup of an enormous cloud in the east spiraling as it grew, blues turning to greens, which then turned to reds. Then the image repeated.

"—unprecedented typhoon has just crossed the equator," a weatherman's voice said over the image. "I've never seen anything like it. I'm not even sure it's physically possible, yet here we are."

"Tawhiri," Tu whispered like a curse.

The map zoomed out further, tracing a glowing line from

the dark cloud that led straight to Jarvis Island. "Fortunately the path of this building storm is not permanently settled, though there is a military installation that has undergone recent improvements."

Healey burst from his chair and ran out of the office, down the hallway that stank of cheap carpet. His legs felt soft, causing him to lean one way and then the other.

Tu appeared in front of him. Healey's feet skidded, and he waved his arms, stopping inches before he would have slammed into the big man.

"Sober up," Tu told Healey and slapped him across the face.

Healey looked up at the huge man. Tu glared at him with dark eyes. All Healey could do was take a breath and march past him. Healey followed the flow of hallways to the center of the building, the command room.

Plastic sheets still rested over many of the computers. Colonel Bradbury was there, standing in a crowd of gawkers looking up at the big projection screen that showed the same weather map with the circling typhoon.

"It's not supposed to do that," someone said. Healey thought it was the naval meteorologist.

"What happens if it hits us?" another soldier asked.

"Nothing good," someone in civilian clothes with a huge plastic badge said.

"Complete destruction, you mean!" another civilian yelled. "We're not rated for anything over a forty-mile-an-hour wind."

"We shouldn't need anything more," the naval meteorologist replied. "Jarvis is one of the most stable places on the planet! That's why we were building out here."

"That, and the boost for equatorial launch," the first civilian added.

The crowd continued to mumble at each other.

Tu came up behind Healey and set his huge hand over Healey's shoulder. The little man looked up at him.

"This is your device. Can it stand against a storm like this?" Tu asked.

Healey realized his jaw hung open. He shut it and shook his head.

Tu sighed. "My brother resists again."

Colonel Bradbury kicked over a chair, the noise echoing off the command room walls. The crowd went silent. Everyone turned toward him. "Listen up! We've got to act. Get Admiral Irving and General Hawthorne on the phone for immediate evacuation."

"The nuke plant needs to be shut down before it gets caught in the swell," one of the civilians said.

"Do it!" Bradbury barked.

Tu nodded and looked down at Healey. "The men are scared, weak. Are you?"

Healey fidgeted. *It's all a fluke, right? Inclement weather? Routine El Nino finally shifting patterns?*

"There has to be a logical explanation for this," Healey mumbled.

"Speak up," Tu ordered.

Healey sneered up at him. "I said, 'There has to be a logical explanation for this.'"

"My brother seeks to postpone his defeat," Tu replied. "That should be logic enough."

Healey's sneer turned into a glare. His chest felt heavy. "No, the universe is built on a groundwork of laws and principles. It's not a battlefield!"

Tu let out a laugh. "How little you know!"

"I designed this!" Healey roared. "All this!"

All the eyes in the room turned toward his outburst. The little man shrank and shivered.

Tu gritted his teeth. He had to move the little man's mind. "Will you just run away?"

"It would only be a delay of a few months at most," Healey mumbled.

"The storms will come back," Tu told him. "Use your brain."

Healey shook his head. *It's practically impossible that a typhoon crossed the equator in the first place. There was simply too much warm air pushing back...*

"We can redirect it!" Healey suddenly shouted.

Tu grinned.

"What are you talking about?" Bradbury demanded. "We

need to get out of here in the next few hours."

"No, no," Healey told him. He ran to the glass walls and waved a hand over the complex laid out below them. The bold concrete towers of the power plant stood like ramparts of a castle. Beside it, the track of the coilgun ran upward with a smooth curve that led straight into the sky. Scaffolding still rested at the top, but it would work for atmospheric launches.

"All we have to do," Healey said, "is heat the air!"

"Again," Bradbury asked through pursed lips, "what are you talking about?"

Healey ran back across the room to the where the projector painted the weather map. Complex lines lay across the satellite image of Pacific Ocean and the huge gray mass barreling toward them. "The storm is following its path from being pushed by high-level currents. If we can nudge the local current with enough heat, it will redirect the storm."

Everyone in the room looked from him to the naval meteorologist, who had his chin in his hand. They looked back with wide eyes. Tu nodded.

Healey pointed at the power plant and coilgun. "The EM fields we're using are intense enough to move water as is. All we need to do is run the plant at full power and redirect the steam into the coilgun."

"But it's not finished!" one of the civilians objected.

"It doesn't have to be!" Healey cried. "It just has to get the steam high into the air."

"But running continuously… the capacitors aren't designed for that!" shouted someone who hadn't spoken yet.

Healey's throat closed up. The tech who had shouted, clutching a graphing calculator, was right. Healey looked to Tu.

The war god crossed his arms and glared at him. "Don't let them stop you."

Healey took in a breath. He marched back across the room to the civilian who stood a little away from the crowd. The others stared at him.

The tech was tall, thin, and in his twenties. Thick scruff stood out on his cheeks in patches amid the skin that didn't grow whiskers yet. He was two decades younger and six inches taller than Healey, but Healey puffed himself up to stare down the tech.

"Who do you think designed those capacitors?" Healey asked in a demanding tone.

The tech took several steps backward. His head slumped.

The rest of the crowd murmured.

"Now, listen here," Bradbury said. "I'm the ranking officer present, so anything that goes down will be on my head. What you're talking about could go Three Mile Island for all I know. It'd be safer to shut down and wait for this to blow over."

Healey turned to the colonel. He changed his tone from a shout to a whisper. "Do you want to be remembered as the man who organized an evacuation, or do you want to be the man who defeated weather itself?"

Bradbury blinked. He didn't speak.

Tu leaned over the colonel's shoulder. "Give the order. Be the hero."

Bradbury snapped out of his trance. He began calling names and barking orders. The men in the room jumped to obey them. Tu's body duplicated, sending out images of himself that ran and shouted. They reached out over the island, filling their little army with the fighting spirit.

The sky in the east grew dark.

Workers dragged together aluminum ducts from HVAC stockpiles and even pulled what had already been installed in two of the buildings. In hours, a makeshift tunnel led from the power plant's steam release to the gaping entrance of the coilgun. Healey walked among the construction, surveyed the work like Patton reviewing soldiers at attention.

When he was satisfied, Healey cried through a bullhorn, "Fire it up!"

Electricity hummed. Computers beeped warnings. Tu grinned.

A sound like wind howled from the coilgun. Sharper screeches came from leaks in the ductwork. High above, among the scaffolding at the raised end of the coilgun, a thin jet of white steam spouted. It stood stark against the growing gray wall of clouds filling the eastern horizon.

"We're seeing a lot of drag," the tech at the sensor array said, shaking his head.

Tu turned to Healey. "What is it?"

"Condensation!" Healey screamed. "I should have realized! The cold ducts… Everyone grab screwdrivers, hammers, anything! Punch holes under the ducts to let the loose water drain!"

Workers charged at the ducts. All along the line, they stabbed underneath. Boiling water shot back at them causing them to cry out in pain.

Healey shivered. They were wounded soldiers in their way. His stomach turned.

Above them, the white jet expanded to an immense blossom of white-hot steam.

"That's all we can do," Healey mumbled.

Tu appeared behind him and said, "It is."

Healey's mouth became too dry to say anything.

Tu looked down at the little man. "Keep up your guard here while I face my brother."

Tu turned away to the east and marched toward the blackening clouds. As Healey watched from alongside the duct-work, Tu shed his suit jacket and undid his tie. He grew with each step, first by a meter, then by five, then by ten. His feet sank into the ocean, which never reached above his knee as he became taller and taller.

A mask and headdress materialized on him, and a spear and shield appeared in his hands. The mask was ebony wood, dark and dense, and carved in the face of a howling man, lips in an "O" and eyes narrowed with fury. The green-grass headdress stood tall behind the mask and made Tu seem even taller. The grass swept over his shoulder and across his chest as a protective green sash. Tu raised his wooden shield, huge and rectangular with curved corners. Its entire face bore intricately carved geometric shapes and characters that seemed to snarl. Then Tu raised his spear, its shaft thin and pointed at the bottom to make it a two-ended weapon. Sharpened volcanic stone made up the main blade, and two rows sharks' teeth lined the shaft down to the grip, adding yet more blades where it could slash. These were no barbaric, outdated weapons. They were ceremonial, ancient, and powerful.

The storm surge drove the waves higher, crashing against

his legs. Tu leaned into them.

"Hear me, brother!" Tu screamed into the wind. "Face your defeat!"

Clouds twisted in the wind, taking on the shape of a scowling face and clawed hands.

Tu roared, "I am Tumatauenga, Tu of the Angry Face! Tukanguha, Tu the Fierce Fighter! Tukaitaua, Tu the Consumer of Armies! I drove you off in the beginning, brother, and I will do it again! Your days of freedom are coming to an end! You are beaten!"

Hands composed of cloud raced in the wind to tear at Tu, leaving deep cuts in the hide of his shield and the flesh of his shoulders. Tu pressed his shield against them and stabbed his spear deep into the storm.

Healey watched with sweat pouring down his brow. He wanted to look around him to see if anyone else witnessed this battle between gods, but he couldn't look away.

It's a metaphor, he told himself. *It's just a mirage for the high-temperature gas we're putting into the air.*

Yet the gods fought on, pounding at one another. The conflict went on for hours until a beam of sunlight poured through the northern end of the storm. It grew wider, like a vertical dawn. The typhoon, now a soft gray with breaking clouds, rolled southward. At times the face reappeared, twisted and weeping while the wind moaned.

On Jarvis Island, the humans cheered.

Colonel Bradbury came through the celebrating soldiers to shake Healey's hand. "Can you believe the press I'm going to get for this?"

Healey couldn't answer. He stared out to sea.

Tu marched back to the island. His form became smaller again, though he kept on his warrior garb, the mask slung back over his shoulder. Blood flowed from deep gashes along his arms and face. He grinned with teeth stained red.

"We did it," Healey whispered. "We beat the storm."

Tu tapped the little man with shaft of his spear. "I could make a disciple of you yet as I continue my campaign."

"You make it sound like you're killing nature."

"So I am."

THE WEATHER WAR

Healey shook his head and pushed the spear away. "This isn't right. That can't be right."

"It is only the beginning," Tu told him. "Soon the weather of the entire world will kneel before my warrior-humans, just as the plants and animals do."

"But what about natural biomes, and, and…"

"We conquered them." Tu snarled. "They are ours to do with as we please."

Healey broke. His face contorted. Tears mingled with the sweat. "This isn't right!"

Tu leaned over him. "It is strength."

The little man fled, away from the construction and the cheering troops, past his glamorous office, back to his bunk-room where he hid under his blankets.

Tu considered going after him, consuming him, and setting that creative human mind toward new devices. Then he turned to the celebrating humans all around him, sharing drinks and shouting curses at the retreating storm. There were plenty of other soldiers for his army not nearly as weak.

He looked out over the earth and dreamed of the warriors he would find with weapons that would kill Papa and enslave all her resources. Tu then looked up, past the blue sky now being tamed and into the shining stars that decorated Rangi's dark skin. Someday the entire universe would be conquered by his warlike creations. They would consume it all.

♉   ♉   ♉

Jeff Provine is a writer, cartoonist, editor at Okie Comics, and Professor of English at Oklahoma City Community College. He collects folklore and seeks to spread the stories through several published collections such as *A Compendium of Creeps* and leading local ghost tours. His short fiction has been included in several anthologies, including *Tales from the Underground* and *N'oublions Jamais*. In 2023, his story "Stealing Buttons" won "Most Badass Steampunk Heroine" in the University of Maryland Quantum Steampunk competition. He also writes very short stories on Twitter @jeffprovine. www.jeffprovine.com

By Karen Dales

A PALL HUNG OVER THE temple. The white votive candles flickered brightly beneath the statue of the Buddha, but their light could not eliminate the heavy presence of death. Deep resonant voices chorused from the saffron robed monks seated in double rows facing one another before the statue. The sound vibrated the air with their united breathing until it filled the hall, slipping around and between red painted columns that held crimson rafters high above.

The chant did not have the same energy it usually held. Mindful meditation was threatened by distraction from within. Normally, this would not be tolerated, but forgiveness under the circumstances was necessary, compassion over-riding expectation. Occasional glances at the empty position of the Master belied concentration slips. These, too, were overlooked by elders resigned to the sadness of their juniors.

A bell rang. A rustle of cotton and a subtle shift in position allowed the chant to die. The monks appreciated the break, to allow bald pates to lower for private thoughts, glistening dark brown eyes. Some gazed sadly at the empty raised dais at the other side of the temple, across from the votive bright Buddha.

The bell pierced the oppressive silence to indicate the initiation of new meditative chanting. Heads raised and turned to refocus. Sound pushed against the quiet, holding it back from crushing the monks with grievous sadness.

A flutter of movement added to the chanting until it revealed a middle aged monk entering the temple from a side entrance. Shuffling cotton and straw sandaled feet whispered from one end of the double row, where the youngest monk sat disrupted. His four year old eyes widened with surprise as an older boy, beside him, placed a hand on the child's forearm, snapping the boy back to his meditation.

Up the line the middle aged monk walked, occasionally causing disruptions in the chant's defence against the silence, until he bent over an elderly monk whose concentration never wavered. The chant stuttered and died, only incomprehensible whispering filled the void.

The gloom thickened, anxiety coating it, slicking it densely, bowing shoulders under its weight. Groaning, the elderly monk raised his body to stand. His gnarled hand patted the shoulder of the monk who had sat by his side. Without a word the old monk turned away from the doubled line and headed towards another open doorway, the middle aged monk following behind.

Down the stone hall he walked. His straw slippered feet shushed over grey flagstone until the manmade tunnel opened to the left, revealing a courtyard bathed in full moon light. Halting at the entrance to the garden, the monks stood silent in the sight of the one who had come to their sanctuary decades ago. Awash in blue radiance, they watched their long time guest move from one position to another along the precise dictates of one of their higher forms.

Long white hair flowed in a wind of his own making, his tall slender form clad only in the loose orange pants all the monks wore beneath their robes. The monks stood patiently despite the urgency of their message. Dark brown eyes flashed in awe. In all the years they had lived in the monastery they had never witnessed such precision and grace in the martial forms taught to the youngest among them to the daily practice of the old.

Moonlight dusted the guest's pale skin blue as he leapt, spun, kicked and punched. His movements blurring at times until the form came to a close, leaving the Guest standing still in the middle of the courtyard. For any other, heat would have radiated off of exerted flesh, sweat would create rivulets down face and body, and lungs would bellow the chest as the heart raced from exertion. Not so with the Guest. He stood there, as still as a marble statue, with only the slight breeze forming their own patterns in his long white hair.

The monks stood patiently, each hoping it would not be long before their guest would notice them. They would not interrupt the Guest, but if necessity warranted it, they would. A deep shuddering sigh escaping from the Guest relieved their growing tension and the old monk stepped onto the dew covered grass, its wetness permeating his naturally made slippers.

"It is time." The old monk's voice spread gravel across the silence.

Pale eyelids fluttered open to reveal irises of blood surrounding a darker pool. No black pupil helped to fix the stare of the Guest, only red. A pinched expression flowed over the Guest's youthful features and the old monk felt its impact upon his own innards.

The old monk remembered when the Guest arrived years ago. It had been the old monk's—then a youth—responsibility to teach the Guest their language and their ways. Despite the transformation the years had applied to the old monk, the Guest had never changed, only their friendship had grown in a triumvirate with the Master. There was no need for the Guest to voice his feelings about what he was called to do, it was written across his face and reflected in each person within the monastery.

The old monk watched the Guest close his eyes, his face belying the conflict within. When the red piercing stare returned resignation slumped muscular pale shoulders. The monk turned at the shallow nod and walked back into the cloister-garth. He did not need to see if the Guest followed and his ears did not need to hear pale bare feet upon cold stone, he could feel the presence of the Guest behind him as he turned towards the cells where all the monks slept, the younger monk taking up the rear.

Through the dimly lit halls they walked the well known paths. Not to their own rooms, but past, towards the large suite set aside for the Master of the monastery. The gilded double doors lay open, admitting a view of a bed piled high with finely crafted blankets. Propped up against silk covered pillows of yellow, the Master lay sleeping.

The old monk stepped into the room and glanced up at the tall Guest, noting the sadness in his eyes. Two monks who sat on either side of the doors stood and closed them, sealing all within the incensed confines of a room weighted down with death. The resonating boom startled the Guest. The Master did not stir. The two young monks knelt down in their positions amongst the monks that formed a row against the wall, each one in prayer, their *nian zhu* clicking and shushing through fingers.

"He's expecting you," said the old monk, his voice barely above a whisper.

The Guest frowned, staring at a spot on the stone floor in front of the bed. "I know."

"He spoke of this to you a long time ago."

"Yes." The Guest's voice sibilant.

The old monk lifted a gnarled hand and patted the Guest on his cold milk coloured arm. "We'll be here."

The Guest nodded and did not watch the old and middle aged monks sit in line, taking up their own meditation beads in prayer. Instead he stood still against the silhouette of his friend in the bed. Tentative steps brought the Guest to stand beside the supine Master. He gazed down at the one who had opened the monastery to him, providing him a refuge and a place where acceptance was norm rather than the fear and disgust he had come to expect from mortals. What was once a smooth shaven face of a middle aged man filled with love and compassion was now a shrivelled plain crevassed with age. Slack translucent grey skin outlined boney features and eyes that once sparkled in obsidian brightness now fluttered open in opaque greyness.

The heart of the Guest broke and he sat down beside the Master. "I have come."

A faint tremulous smile lifted thin grey lips that once

reached their happy pinnacle with ease. "Thank you." The Master's sussurant voice barely lifted to the Guest's preternatural hearing.

"I don't want to do this," sighed the Guest.

Sympathetic silence saddened the Master's clouded eyes.

"I want you to live." The Guest's crimson eyes searched the Master's for hope.

"But I will," replied the Master.

"You will be dead," stated the Guest. He flinched at his bluntness.

Somehow the Master shrugged a shoulder, but caught himself in a wince. The Guest's eyes went round with concern.

"I will be reborn," sighed the Master, "into a new body."

"But—"

"You have been with us a long time," said the Master. "We have accepted you and what your role is. How often did you ease those who required transition from this life into the next so that they could continue on their karmic cycle towards Nirvana? When we let you in, we let in with it the knowledge of death. Little did we know that death had no knowledge of himself. It was karma that brought us together—life and death, yin and yang. Would you deny me a peaceful transition and submit me to unnecessary pain and suffering? The world is pain and suffering. The Buddha taught us a way to help those alleviate that and work towards Nirvana. You have been given a great gift—to be an instrument to help remove suffering."

"But I suffer—"

"That is your choice." The Master closed his eyes and took a deep ragged breath.

The Guest lowered his eyes. The Master was right. It was his choice. When he glanced back at the Master he saw clouded eyes peering at him and he knew what he needed to do. "I will do as you ask."

"Thank you," whispered the Master.

*

The Guest stepped back, the taste of his friend's ancient blood on his lips. The dichotomy of pleasure and pain for his actions bound him to the spot. In a daze, he watched the old monk step forward to check on the Master, but the Guest knew it was unnecessary. Silence compressed the chamber. The monks awaited word to what their hearts told them.

The old monk straightened his back, glanced at the Guest and then nodded at the row of monks. The Master was dead.

New chanting took over and the oppressive sadness seemed to alleviate. Sombre happiness tinged the tones of their voices. The middle aged monk stood and exited through the double doors. Not long after low blazing notes from the ceremonial horns blazed through the monastery setting a flurry of activity into motion.

The Guest glanced from the remains of the Master to the old monk, halting the old man in his steps to leave the room. "What is happening?"

The old monk smiled up at the Guest. "We must prepare for the Master's return."

Confusion pulled down fine brows of white. "I don't understand. The Master is dead."

A dry weathered old hand alighted on the Guest's arm. "You do not think he will return?" The question was more statement and the Guest shook his head.

The old monk shook his head as if a student did not understand a simple lesson. "The Master will be back. He has always come back. This is not the first time. It will not be the last."

"But he is dead," stated the Guest, uncomprehendingly.

"For now, yes," replied the monk. "He has given us clues on how to find him. As it was important for you to be what you are and to alleviate his suffering from this form, so was it important for the Master to be released at this point so that we may find him in time once again."

"I understand the idea of reincarnation—"

"But you do not believe in it."

The Guest shook his head. "No."

"Then stay, wait and watch. You will see, when we have found the Master again, that our friend is not gone, but has returned to us once again, you will know."

"Know what?" asked the Guest, frowning.

"That life and death are ruled by Karma."

Karen Dales

The Guest watched as the old monk walked out of the room and then turned back to the husk that once held his friend. Yes, he would wait to discover if the old monk told the truth. He would wait to see if Karma truly ruled Death.

Karen Dales is the Managing Editor for Dark Dragon Publishing and the Award Winning Author of the Bestselling novel series, the Chosen Chronicles. She has been an author guest at FanExpo, Ad Astra, Polaris, ConCept, and many other conventions. She is a Gardnerian High Priestess who is a Seated Elder with the New Wiccan Church International and a registered wedding officiant with the province of Ontario.

Dawn of Spring

By Ralph Mack

I SLID MY LAPTOP INTO my backpack and turned off the light in my cube. With my work in the queue for automated testing, I was ready for the weekend. Liz and I would be attending a convention she and the Circle had organized to celebrate the first day of spring.

Liz and Kelly thought it up when the government announced it was yet again shifting the onset of daylight savings time. As usual, the change was due to occur early on a Sunday morning, which this year coincided with the first day of spring. Stacy, Bob, and Hank thought this was too fortuitous an opportunity to pass up, so they did some research and found a hotel. Word spread like fire from friends to lovers to what Liz called "friends and lovers yet unmet" and vendors sprang out of the woodwork, eager to offer readings and reading material, love-charms and sex-charms, herbs and oils. Melinda, the High Priestess Liz had studied under, always wise and now advanced in years, agreed to come east to chair a panel, and they soon had several well-known authors lined up to speak on their specialties, with workshops on divination, ritual design, healing, yoga, and meditation.

Liz had driven north to the hotel with Kelly in the morning and they now stood in the eye of the storm, keeping the logistics from spinning into chaos, while Stacy, Bob, and Hank ran here and there and did errands. The speed with which this convention had come together had startled me and I was more than a little scared by it all.

I had met Liz at an Emerald Rose concert. Over the first few months we dated, she introduced me to what she called her "circle of friends", inviting them by ones and twos to join us for lunch or dinner or a cup of coffee. In those conversations, I learned about the ties that bound them together, the full moons, new moons, and sabbats they celebrated by chanting naked in a circle, drinking wine, and eating cakes.

They lived in and out of each others' houses, dropping in with little more than a perfunctory knock on the door at all hours of the day or night, whenever a light was on. I always sensed there was more they weren't telling me.

The first time Liz invited me to Circle, it seemed like their eyes held a conversation I wasn't privy to, frank and approving in their glances at my body and a sense of welcome when I couldn't help glancing at theirs. It took a while before my eyes stopped darting like a frightened horse. Their prayers and offerings under the waxing moon celebrated the love growing between Liz and me.

Later, in bed, as her body lay warm against mine in the afterglow, she whispered to me, "What we share I offer for us alone so long as you wish us to carry it alone. So mote it be."

By Lammas, we were handfasted.

Since then, I learned a great deal. Liz was the High Priestess of the circle. Bob and Hank assisted Liz in training me in the ways of magic, guiding me until—at least in ceremony—I could act as her High Priest. I learned to feel and channel the flow of energy from the group and my confidence deepened as I saw our work bear fruit—gardens made verdant, tensions among neighbors turning into friendships. Along the way, I learned the difference between good and bad magic and the vital importance of knowing what you wanted to happen. I had Liz at my side, which was what I most wanted in life. Even so, I had stumbled through my second initiation in a hurry, and when I stood naked in front of the altar, High Priest of the ceremony, I felt like a terrible fraud among the people Liz loved, a mere acolyte, competent at best, my naked inadequacy exposed.

As I climbed into the Prius, the sun-gathered heat inside contrasted sharply with the chill of the March air. I set my backpack down on the floor of the passenger seat, resting against the gym bag containing my robe and all the ritual gear I used when we visited other covens. Not all groups worked skyclad. I wasn't sure what rituals would be performed this weekend, but I liked to be prepared. I eased from the company parking lot to the street and the highway on-ramp only a few feet away, hoping Liz would play it safe this weekend. She could be breathtakingly reckless.

This Ostara weekend vibrated with power. Our group had never done anything this big. Change was in the air and I knew somehow, unfathomably, it centered on me. I felt guilty not taking the day off from work to help with the logistics, but Liz insisted I go and bind the circle of my week, completing my work before stepping into the hotel to open the circle of the weekend. There was something in the way she said it, anticipation in her voice.

As I negotiated the interchange between the two major highways, my phone rang, and I pressed the button on the steering wheel to answer.

Liz sounded frazzled but joyful. "Everything's under control—well, mostly," she laughed. "A couple of reservations got mixed up and the hotel changed the vendor area after the first vendors started unpacking, but nobody's casting any hexes—yet.

"Melinda has arrived from California. She's been floating around the preparations, chatting with us as we work, listening to stories about our Circle." Liz's voice grew more serious. "She seems thrilled with the Circle, likes what we've done, but Colin, you've been summoned to a private meeting as soon as you arrive. She's got her down-to-business face on. Expect sharp words."

I was so busted. I sighed, "Thanks, Liz. I should be there in twenty minutes."

"She left strict instructions. Upon your arrival, you are to go straight up the elevator to the penthouse suite. From the moment you enter the door, speak to no one."

"Melinda trained you. She stands as mother to the Circle. If I'm found wanting…" I swallowed.

"Whatever happens in there, Colin, trust your heart. Remember, she could be wrong."

"But I suspect she hardly ever is."

"No," Liz said sadly. "Almost never."

*

I drummed my fingers nervously as the elevator ascended to the penthouse level. Doors opened to reveal a silent foyer, expansive but empty except for a skylight high above and a single potted palm. A stout pair of carved wooden doors stood in front of me. As I stepped forward, the elevator closed behind me with all the subdued finality of a crematorium. I slowed my racing heart with a meditation exercise Bob had taught me, and raised my hand to knock. Before my knuckles could strike wood, an imperious voice called "Enter!"

Timidly, I turned the handle and opened the door partway, peering in. On a raised dais at the far end of the room, a woman dressed in a blue caftan stood tall, her gray hair in a bun, her hands resting against the wooden table behind her, her expression carved in granite. Sunshine cascaded through skylights and glinted on the vessels on the table, illuminating the polished oak flooring under her bare feet. I swallowed.

"Well, are you going to peek through the doorway," she barked, "or are you going to enter like you carry a God in your breast?"

I consciously straightened, stepped in and closed the door, its solid wood at my back. "You summoned me?"

"I did," she smiled slightly, her hands relaxing, but there was steel in her eye.

Her smile vanished. "Mr. Thieroux, what are you?"

"I—I looked up at her, willing my voice not to shake. "I'm

Colin Thieroux, handfast to Elizabeth Russell. Together we are High Priest and Priestess of the Danforth Blessing Circle."

"So you claim membership in the Circle?"

"Yes." I nodded.

"You claim leadership in the Circle?"

I swallowed.

"You don't answer as readily." Steel slid from her eye to her voice. "Come up here."

I stepped across the room and onto the dais, terror wrestling with relief. I'd been found out. Whatever sentence waited for me would wait no longer.

"You stated your relationship as Elizabeth's husband before your relationship as her priest."

I swallowed again. "Yes, I dated her before I knew anything about the Circle, and we were handfasted before Bob and Hank—"

"Decided you needed to be High Priest as well," she frowned.

"Yeah," I said dully.

"So what is your relationship with Kelly?" she demanded.

"Kelly?" In blind panic, I searched for words. "Well, we're in Circle together…"

"Have you ever kissed?"

"Uh, you mean outside of ritual?"

She smiled. "Held hands?"

"No…"

Her posture softened. "Has she ever confided in you, turned to you for comfort or advice?"

"We're not that close. Kelly and Liz were lovers before I showed up, so it's kind of awkward…" I explained.

"And have the two of you ever talked about that?" She raised her eyebrows.

"You mean me and Kelly or me and Liz?"

She shook her head. This wasn't going well. "How about Bob? Are you close?"

I winced, "Of course, we kiss in ritual, and we've hugged after wine and cakes. Hank, too."

"Have you ever sat on the sofa with your arm around Bob? Asked him to hold you after a really bad day? "

"No!" I stared at her in shock.

She laughed gently. "Stacy?"

"It's hard not to hug Stacy." I relaxed a little. "It's what Stacy does. She's an out front kind of person."

She nodded. "Which goddess is Stacy especially close to? How did they get acquainted?"

"Umm... I don't know."

"And Hank? Have you ever given him a backrub?"

"I—I think Hank's gay," I stuttered. "I didn't want to start any misunderstandings..."

"You think but you're not sure, so you haven't discussed it." She slowly shook her head. "Would it bother you if he did respond like that, as long as you both knew what each of you meant?"

"I don't know," I murmured, my lips pressing together, my eyes drifting to the floor.

"So you've stepped into Elizabeth's Circle of intimate friends, taken the role of High Priest, and haven't experienced the most innocent forms of intimacy with even one of them? You haven't had a single real conversation. Can you say for certain whether you love any of them?"

My head snapped up into her glare. "Of course I do. It's just, when it comes to that kind of stuff, Liz and I are kind of exclusive..." I sighed, aware for the first time how lame that sounded.

"Yes," her voice became a bone-handled blade, "You've been so exclusive, it threatens to destroy the community Elizabeth loves and has helped to build, a community built on intimacy, a community she's entrusted you to build *with* her."

A flush rose from my neck at her words and I lowered my head and my voice under their weight. "Liz hasn't said anything about this."

"No. She's too busy trying to forestall a decision that will break her heart—whether to watch the Circle of her dearest friends dissolve, or to abandon the man she's come to love more than life itself—a decision you are slowly forcing upon her."

Staring into the woman's blazing gaze, I stared into the future: the end of a marriage, both of us still in love and miserable, or the end of the Circle, Liz wilting into the role of a dutiful wife, the fire in her eyes slowly fading away.

My voice was a dry rasp. "What should I do?"

"That depends. What do you want?" The "t" clicked as she said it.

"I want Liz to be completely happy, with me, with the circle, with life."

"I didn't ask what you wanted for *her*." She shook her head. "You can't do somebody else's wanting for them. I asked what *you* wanted."

"I—I don't understand."

She seethed with exasperation. "You're a man. You carry a God in you. You need attention, you need intimacy, and you need respect and love. You need a lot of things. What do you *want*, though? The God in you demands the dignity of choice."

"I want to hold Liz in my arms when we're as old as you are," I cried out. "I want to stand before the Circle without feeling like I'm a sham and a lie."

"What Circle?" she growled.

"The Circle of Liz's friends."

"The Circle of *your* friends?"

I paused, swallowing in the silence.

Her voice softened as she held my gaze. "Do you want to celebrate with Kelly and Liz the life they left behind for Liz to be with you? To kiss Hank and mean it, unafraid? To know Stacy well enough to become as free and open as she is? To love Bob like your dearest brother and find your soul at peace in his arms? Do you want to be truly naked, body and soul, when you dance in this circle? Do you want to support the others in being so? Do you want to dance as a priest?" Behind her eyes, I saw the fierceness of her love—for Liz, for her friends, even, impossibly, for me.

"I never really thought of being High Priest like that." I took a long, slow breath. "When you put it that way, it sounds like something I wanted all my life or maybe never dared to want, but I don't know how."

She smiled sadly. "It isn't as hard as you think, Colin. Elizabeth has known me since she was a teenager. When her father died, at seventeen, she spent the night in my bed, sobbing. My husband and I held her through the night. When my husband and high priest died, after forty years of marriage, it was I who sobbed through the night in her arms. I love Elizabeth and she loves me. Do you love me, Colin?"

I swallowed, trembling. "I suppose so."

"Then kiss me."

She stood patiently as I awkwardly stepped forward. I raised my arms to her shoulders, not knowing what to do with them. Finally I cradled my hands around the back of her head, leaned forward, and pressed my lips to hers. As they touched, her hair tumbled out of its bun and her caftan fell to the floor. I willed my lips to linger with hers and she responded, her lips exploring mine with a playful smile, her arms around my back, all welcome, but with restraint. As I stood straight, I stroked her grey hair back from her bare shoulders. My heart raced, my breathing shallow.

"Was that so hard?" she smiled. Both our eyes traveled down her form. She chuckled, "Amazing what a body comes to after so many years." She stepped out of her caftan, picked it up, and folded it, stepping past a coffee table to lay it on the sofa at the right side of the dais. "Get undressed," she said over her shoulder. "We have work to do." She turned and I saw that the table was set as an altar.

I awkwardly complied, finally sitting naked on the hardwood floor with my pants around my ankles while I removed my shoes and socks and then pants. From the floor, I looked up at her bony legs, grey muff, and sagging skin and breasts, amazed that I found myself looking forward to kissing her again.

"Get up and quit gawkin' like you've never seen a woman before." There was a twinkle in her eye as she lent me a hand to get to my feet. I set my clothes next to hers and we stood before the altar together, as she continued. "Now, you and I are going to lead the circle in a spell to support and protect the convocation this weekend. I made a few notes, but we'll need to hone it down to a ritual before the rest of the circle arrives."

"You and me? With everyone?" My eyes widened.

"Of course," a smile twitched at the corner of her mouth. "I'm the eldest high priestess of the convocation and you, against all odds, are the eldest high priest." Her eyes laughed and she glanced down. "Mmm… You got a better pair of balls on you than I gave you credit for. It's time you started growin' into 'em, don'tcha think? You ready?"

"Yes, ma'am." I grinned.

"That's better. Meanwhile, think about how you're going to bring your circle closer together this weekend."

*

After an hour of narrowing down our intentions for the conference to a few specific goals, we set about designing the ritual. I was amazed at how much Melinda knew—the number of areas that she drew on in the design. She had two Master's degrees, one in biology and another in anthropology, and she seemed to know everything imaginable about the religious rites of the Greeks, the Romans, the Celts, and the Danes, as well as the ways of nature, which she skilfully blended.

What surprised me even more were the insightful questions she asked about the world of computers, specification, and how words were used to convey ideas well enough to implement them in a program. I had heard lame parallels before between spells and programs, spoken by people who knew little about either, but Melinda opened my mind and my heart to the parallels in the human processes of ritual design and specification. "They're both about imagining and expressing what you want, defining it clearly enough that you won't be disappointed when some part of the universe gives you most of what you asked for. That's a human process, not a technical one."

We had barely finished scribing the ritual into her Book of Shadows and mine, sitting naked on a towel together on the sofa, when I became aware of someone in the doorway. I turned to see Liz standing there, lean and tall, dark hair sweeping over her shoulders, a tender, pleased expression on her elfin face. She wrinkled her nose at me, slipping out of her shoes, and ambled up behind the sofa to squeeze both our shoulders. Melinda and I nuzzled her hands and she slipped off her top.

"We're almost ready," Melinda said, and turned back to the work resting on her lap.

I followed her lead. "Have a seat. How's the conference coming?"

Liz finished stripping down and slipped onto the towel next to me, her skin soft against my one hip, Melinda's bonier leg resting against the other.

"Not bad. Most of the vendors are in and have everything they need. I delegated to Crissy Donohue—she runs 'Bring Your Own Bedknob'—to clue in any other vendors that show up while we're chanting. A speaker's flight was delayed, but she's not speaking until tomorrow afternoon, so that should work. The rest of the crew should be here shortly."

"Will we be missed?" I cocked my head at Liz, who shook hers.

"Everybody knows that we'll be up here casting this evening and have pledged their energy from wherever they are, even from LAX, apparently. I think a lot of the groups are using this as an opportunity to gather their own circles in conference rooms and hotel suites. Several solitaires that were milling around have already congregated in the ballroom to see if they can pull something together. They put up a sign telling other solitaires where to meet."

"That will be interesting," Melinda mused, setting her book on the coffee table.

"I stopped in briefly to see how they're doing, and they're actually kind of funny," Liz chuckled. "It's like a complicated and awkward first date. They're each used to doing things their own way and there's a lot of push and pull and altar envy, but so far no tempers. They could start one of the interminable arguments of the craft, but knowing they have a deadline to get chanting is helping them stay focused. I left them to it. Once we get started, I suspect the walls of this whole hotel are going to be glowing eldritch green. I hope the electronics don't all short out."

I slid an arm around Liz's back and she rested her head on my shoulder, reading from my book as I set my pen down on the coffee table. "It was touching seeing the two people I love most in the whole world working so closely together," she smiled. "I take it you will be HP and HPS tonight?"

I nodded. "It'll feel strange. I've never led a ceremony with anyone but you, but Melinda…”

Liz gave me a squeeze and nodded, looking fondly at her mentor, “I know. I long one day to be half the witch that Melinda is.”

“Nonsense, dear.” Melinda’s voice was tart. “Be one hundred percent of the witch that you are now, and you will find more witch for you to become. That’s the only way it’s ever been done.”

I squeezed Liz’s bare hip. “She’s witch enough for me. I can only imagine what she’ll be in a few years’ time.”

Melinda patted my knee. “Grow with her and you’ll both do fine, dear.”

The door opened and Stacy and Kelly trooped into the middle of the room. “The men will be up,” Stacy said in her soft, southern drawl. “They’re collecting the ritual gear from their room.” She glanced at the altar. “Oh! It’s all set up!” She bounced with excitement.

The light from the skylights had taken an orange cast that signalled the end of day. Melinda gestured toward the table and looked up at Kelly. “It’s time to light the incense and the candles, if you wouldn’t mind?”

Kelly slipped out of her sandals and unbuttoned her jeans, “Sure, glad to.” She flashed an electric smile at the three of us. Her many piercings, glinting amid the body art, fit well with her purple bobbed hair. “Will we have a problem with the smoke detectors?”

“Already dealt with,” Melinda’s lips twitched in amusement.

Stacy picked up the lighter from the altar, shifting her straight blonde hair back over her fair shoulders with the other hand, and looked around. “This is a beautiful room for a ritual. It smells like…”

“Hyssop. I got busy as soon as I arrived. The previous occupant…” Melinda sighed. “Fear and arrogance stink up a place fast.”

*

When Bob and Hank arrived several minutes later and settled in, we gathered around the altar. Night had fallen quickly. The colors of dusk settled into gray shadows and the candles cast a flickering red-yellow glow on bare skin. We danced and chanted.

> *Blessings upon this house,*
> *Dancers among us, circles in circles,*
> *Spiralling inward, drawing together.*
> *Blessings upon this house.*

As we circled the altar, I turned my attention to each of our friends. What did I know about Bob or Kelly? I knew a few fragments of their life before circle, but when had I ever sat alone with either of them, or with Hank or Stacy for that matter, and talked about our hopes and fears, what drew us into circle and kept us there, what we wanted from it, the very stuff from which magic came? Hank was probably gay, but we never talked about that. It felt like I was seeing each of them for the first time.

> *Blessings upon this house,*
> *Counter and housekeeping, hearth, keg, and larder,*
> *Parents and children, pilgrims of treasure,*
> *Blessings upon this house.*

There is so much I'd never been honest about. Stacy had a half-moon Isis tattoo above her cleavage, a simple shape, bold but understated, that I'd always admired and I'd never told her so. She probably just thought I was ogling her generous tits, which I readily admitted didn't make a bad backdrop.

> *Blessings upon this house*
> *Poolside to kitchen, boiler to penthouse,*
> *Vendor and speaker, all Danforth Blessing,*
> *Blessings upon this house.*

Conversation after conversation that I had never let happen flooded through me. Did those piercings hurt? What memories associated with each one? What did Bob's tattoos signify? There were things I hadn't even talked much about with Liz. What was the circle like before I came? What made it special? I suspected Liz and the others had carefully avoided a few of those topics, not sure how I'd respond. It was time for me to open myself to the questions and accept and embrace those answers, sorting out together in the circle what our handfasting had changed and what it didn't need to change.

Blessings upon this house,
Fruit from Persephone, Hearth Songs of Freya,
Wisdom of Artemis, guide us along.
Blessings upon this house.
SO MOTE IT BE

I almost missed my place, but Melinda gave me a sharp little pinch on the ass, which brought me to. Her roguish grin disarmed my initial glare, and I grinned back. A weight was already lifting from me. I was among friends—if I wanted to be. And suddenly, I knew that, since the day I first danced in the circle, I had wanted to be an inherent part of the lives, experiences, and memories of the people that I danced among. In their presence, I felt radiant, clean, alive.

Something frothed and bubbled inside me, splashing out into laughter as I gasped, trying to complete the words of blessing over the wine and the cakes. Melinda put an arm around me and said the words with me, her voice trembling. The last phrase dissolved into girlish giggles. I hugged her close and suddenly we were all laughing as we fed each other. Stacy was laughing so hard that wine dribbled down her chin. I reached out a finger and caught the drop as it collected, raising my finger to her lips. She licked the wine off my finger and then kissed it, her dancing eyes holding mine. Bob and Hank fed each other cakes, slowly, tenderly, eyes twinkling in the joyous game. I shared the cup with Melinda, taking turns with the last of the wine, and then I kissed her, sweetly and slowly, a hand on the curve of her neck. She reached her hands around my head, responding in kind. Our lips twitched in a smile as we took turns exploring each others' lips with our tongues, and then we pulled back, content with a boundary not crossed.

"All acts of love and pleasure are her rituals," Liz crowed.

"So mote it be," Kelly answered, as the joy coalesced into a group hug. I kissed Liz and I kissed Stacy. I turned to Hank, there was an awkward pause, and then I kissed him, too. His response was hesitant and then ecstatic as his shoulders relaxed and his arms reached around my back. I felt the brush of something below as well and I answered his frightened eyes by kissing him again, more briefly, but tenderly.

Finally, we all pulled apart to catch our breath. Liz and I were arm-in-arm. Kelly and I smiled shyly at each other. Bob looked from me to Hank, who had lost some of his characteristic edginess.

"It's like it was before," Stacy breathed, her voice barely carrying. Kelly nodded.

"So mote it be," Liz and I said in unintentional unison and looked at each other in surprise, wonder in her eyes. In answer, I kissed her.

None of us were in a hurry to dress. We draped towels over the overstuffed chairs in the room and lounged around, finishing the wine that remained in the bottle and talking about the convention until Bob finally said, "I suppose we should get back down there and get a late dinner."

"Thank you, Melinda, for hosting this," I gazed over at the older woman. "This was—very special."

"I'm glad to celebrate with you." Melinda looked at each of us. "It's exciting to see my former acolyte's circle is thriving and to meet all the friends that have gathered around her."

Kelly's eyes sparkled, "Does that make you our spiritual grandmother?"

"She doesn't kiss like a grandmother," I protested.

The whole room burst out laughing, Melanie among them. "You, sir, need to broaden your experience of grandmothers. You'd be startled at what we can do when we choose to."

"If you want to borrow him for a few hours to demonstrate…" Liz's eyes twinkled.

Melinda cocked her head, appraising me, playfully twirling a lock of gray hair around her finger and eying me up and down speculatively "Tempting, very tempting, but you're both still young and chasing thunderbolts. You haven't visited the distant regions of your passions together yet. One day, you'll be ready to settle down in the uncharted shoals of slow, relentless, sweet response, barely more than a shared pulse, but enduring beyond what you thought possible. With grandchildren of your own, you'll be exploring pleasures only grandparents have grown patient enough to know. In the meantime, remember that a slow dance is often the sweetest."

*

Dinner was a blur, frequently interrupted by vendors, speakers, and the leaders of other circles and covens stopping in to say "Hi" and to raise questions. As usual, I wasn't able to be much help, so I chewed on a roll while I watched Liz and Kelly working out the nuts and bolts of the conference and Stacy gushed positive energy with the circle leaders. About the time we were finished settling the bill, a big fellow walked into the restaurant. Hank rose and ran to him, and they met in a full hug and a kiss passionate enough to draw the attention of people at other tables. Hank pulled up an extra chair and said, "This is Gerry, the head of the circle I was in before I moved up this way."

Hank turned to face Gerry. "You here alone?"

Gerry shook his head and smiled. "We're all here."

Hank's eyes widened. "The whole circle? Jim and Hector and Luke, Forrest and—what was the new guy's name?— Toby?"

Gerry shook his head. "Hector couldn't make it. He hopes his boss will let him loose for Sunday but the rest of us are here. Jim and Toby are a couple now and were hoping to be hand-fasted at the convention, maybe something quiet on Sunday afternoon. Jim's got no family, as you know, and they don't have anybody else to invite. Toby's not close to his folks, and his dad wouldn't cut short a business trip for a marriage he opposes on principle."

Hank sighed, "Jim can never catch a break, can he?"

"Yeah, but you should see him with Toby," Gerry reflected. "Toby's so…so energetic, and Jim stabilizes him. Together, they're awesome."

Hank's voice grew serious. "How does that affect you and

Jim running circle together?"

Gerry nervously licked his lips, "I'm thinking of stepping down."

"Stepping down?!" Hank stared, aghast.

"Hank, Toby's twice the High Priest I could ever be, and he and Jim—they can take the circle places I never could."

"When is this going to happen?" asked Hank.

"Umm, I haven't actually asked Toby, but I think he'll agree. Thing is," Gerry paused, "once Toby takes over, I can't stay. People will always be coming to me for things they should go to Toby for. I've been thinking of heading north. That is," he looked at the rest of the folks at the table, "if I'm welcome."

Hank looked over, first at Liz, who was negotiating the bill with the waiter, and then to me.

I took a deep breath. "I'm sure anyone Hank vouches for will be welcome among us. Let me introduce you to my w—our high priestess, Liz."

"What's up?" Liz looked over.

"Liz, this is Gerry," Hank said. "He's thinking of moving into the area and was wondering if he would be welcome in our circle."

Liz turned to Gerry. "Who's your High Priest?"

"Actually, he's the High Priest of the circle I came from." Hank volunteered. "He's thinking of stepping down."

Gerry shot an annoyed look at Hank.

"Discord in the circle?" Liz's brow furrowed.

"No," Gerry said, "Not at all. They've grown as far as I can take them. Jim and his husband-to-be Toby can take them a lot further. I became a High Priest very early, and I need a place where I can shut up and grow for a while."

"Can you shut up and grow?" Liz's lips curved into a smile.

Gerry's eyes sparkled. "I guess I'll find out."

Liz looked at me and I nodded encouragingly.

"Then hail and well met. When will you be moving?"

"Not sure yet. Probably some time in the next month."

"They also need some space for a handfasting," I blurted. "Sunday afternoon."

"Space for how many?" Liz asked.

Gerry shrugged. "Just room for our circle and as many as

will support us."

Liz nodded. "I'll see what we can do. What's your room number, Gerry? I'll leave a message and we can coordinate early on Sunday."

"317."

Liz pulled a notebook from her purse and scribbled in it, "I'll be in touch."

As Gerry stood, Stacy drawled, "Hail and well met, Gerry."

"Yeah, hail and well met," Kelly echoed.

Smiling, Bob patted Gerry on the shoulder. "Likewise."

I went to extend my hand, but then stopped. This man was going to be one of us. Standing, I offered my arms for a hug, drawing him in as he stepped forward. "Welcome," I murmured, passing him to Liz. Soon we were all sharing hugs. Businessmen looked up from their hamburgers and cell phones in annoyance. "We'd better get going," I murmured to Liz, nodding to the other patrons, and we all walked out, me and Liz leading the way with Gerry between us.

*

"You know, I always figured you'd be the one to balk at bringing someone new in," Stacy said to me as the two of us sat at the table in the foyer with the cash box, taking people's money and registration slips.

"Gerry just felt right somehow. Besides, he and Hank have some history, and I suspect a lot more."

"You noticed that kiss, too," Stacy grinned. "Maybe there is some hope for you yet."

I shrugged, "I've been living in a sleeping bag on the porch of this circle for a while now. It's past time I moved in."

We counted money and handed out tickets in silence for a while. I quietly watched Stacy chatting with folks, giving and receiving energy so freely.

In a quiet moment, I asked "You whispered that circle tonight was like it was before. It sure felt good. What was it like to come into the circle, you know, back then? I don't even know where you first started with the Goddess."

Stacy laughed in her easy way, "I was at college in Georgia.

There was this band my friends used to drive an hour to see, and on the way home we'd go down by the river to shuck our clothes and swim in the moonlight. After a few times, somebody brought wine and cakes and we started doing a ceremony to thank the river for Her kindness. Somewhere along the way, She became real to me in a way that's hard to explain." Her slow drawl became pensive. "I realized I was made of red rivers and the whole land was made of rivers. When I listened to the waves of the ocean, my pulse answered them, and my cycles danced with the tides. I spent a summer driving around the country to swim, sometimes just to float, and the swimming became like ritual prayer."

"So how did you end up here?"

Stacy's eyes twinkled, "It was my forty-seventh state, I was out of money, it was autumn, and the ocean was freezing cold. I had to start looking for work eventually. Fortunately, I had a roommate who found me a job at the aquarium."

"Water again." I grinned.

She laughed. "I eventually got a grant to get another degree, so now I get to work with seals. How fun is that? Their minds are totally different than ours, but in water we connect."

"We should all go down to the river some time, preferably in the summer," I smiled. "You can lead us in a ritual there."

Her eyes widened and she gaped. "You'd let me do that?"

"What's there to let? You share so freely, Stacy, that's one of the things I love about you, that I'm sure we all love about you. Share your world with us and we'll swim in it with you."

"Oh, thank you!" Stacy wrapped her arms around me and kissed me.

I answered the kiss in kind and grinned back, "Blessed be. By the way, what was the forty-eighth state?"

"Maine, if you can believe it. Living only a few miles away, I never got around to swimming in Maine."

Another knot of people showed up and we got back to work.

*

I fumbled with the key card, fitting it into the slot and turning the handle. Nothing happened.

Liz leaned against me, her hair limp. "Nobody ever told me running a convention would be so much work."

I finally figured out to turn the handle after pulling the card *out* of the slot and opened the door to our room. I guess I was pretty tired, too. Flipping on the light, I said "Just kick your stuff off and go lie down. I'll manage everything else."

"You're a sweet, sweet man," she stumbled to the queen-sized bed, collapsed face down, and started battling her shoes, using the toe of one to remove the other.

I set up the suitcase on the metal rack and opened it, bringing toiletries to the top. I sat down next to her, rubbed her back, and then started unbuttoning my shirt.

She groaned and then said "What's this I hear about you and Stacy?"

I paused mid-button. "What do you mean?"

"Somebody said you and she were kissing at the registration table."

I continued unbuttoning, relieved. "Oh, yeah, she did kiss me, but it was at least partly because I'd suggested she work with us on a river ritual. She started in the craft dancing on riverbanks, so I suggested she lead us in this one. She's swum in every state of the lower forty-eight but Maine, so we'll find a river there, go skinny-dipping and then hold the ritual, bringing her full circle."

Liz groaned. "Do you have any idea what kind of logistics that'll take? Bob and I looked at doing an outdoor ritual a couple years ago. A place where we can be skyclad above the water for an hour at a time without the cops showing up, enough insect repellent to douse Napolean's army or we're going to itch in all kinds of uncomfortable places, not to mention the problem of deer ticks. The right season, the right weather. If we're talking a river, no recent drought so there's a good strong current or you'll be making a blood sacrifice to the leeches."

"Sounds like a lot of factors. I suppose I should have asked you first before I suggested it." I winced and swallowed.

"That would have made things easier," she sighed, as she squirmed her jeans down. I grabbed the hem and pulled, collecting the denim as it slid off her body.

"Actually, no." She rolled onto her elbows and held my gaze. "You both talked about this. I didn't even know about Maine. You listened, you heard her heart's desire, and as her high priest, you offered the circle to help her spiral upward. You're doing what you're supposed to do. I've just got to get used to you doing it."

"I guess we both will." I dropped my shirt on the floor and slipped out of my jeans.

"Of course, now you have to follow through and apply high magic with your rad computer skills to find the right stretch of river, the right time, the right circumstances. I'll help organize everyone when it comes to packing the cars, but the setup for this is on you. Ufff. I can't think about this tonight." She rolled onto her back and struggled with her t-shirt, half off, elbows tangled.

I quietly eased the shirt over an elbow, pulled it up over her head, inside out. Her hair cascaded over her naked shoulders and I raised her into my arms. "You are a beautiful witch, Elizabeth Russell, and I'm pleased to be your High Priest and husband."

She wrapped her arms around my neck, "And you are my high priest, Colin Thieroux, and a devastating hunk of manflesh that I intend to devour bodily in the dawn, but tonight what I want to do is sleep. On top of everything else, I've now got a handfasting to arrange space for."

I pulled back the covers, and knelt to lay them over her. "Why don't I see about that one? I don't have a whole lot of other specific duties for the convention and it would be nice if the two guys - Jim and Toby? - had an extended family in the community to lend support. I know it would mean the world to Hank - and to Gerry."

"Mmmm…" Liz sighed, closing her eyes. "Would you?"

"Mmm-hmm."

"I'll introduce you to the staff people I've been working with after breakfast. I swear if I wasn't blind tired, I'd do things with you tonight that you'd remember the rest of your life. As it is, the best I can do is kiss you goodnight." She did so, and rolled over onto her side "Tuck the K-Y in the bed by the pillows to keep it warm," she mumbled. "In the morning, there's no way I'm taking anything slow."

I finished undressing, arranged the bed, and turned out the light.

As I climbed in beside her, she giggled in the dark.

"What?" I asked.

"You're poking me in the ass."

"I'm just trying to cuddle, but it keeps…"

"Well, cuddle closer so it slides up my ass-crack and I can get some sleep." She pulled my arms around her like a shawl and rocked her hips once to center me. "God and Goddess, tonight my man's got the balls of a god and I wish I weren't too tired to fuck him righteously. Keep him warm for me until dawn. I'll take it from there." Her voice drifted into a mumble as her prayer turned into a snore. I don't remember how soon I followed her there. I only remember that I never got around to anything but enjoying the warmth of her body spooning against mine. It had been a long day.

*

On the cusp of the equinox, Liz and I shared the gray light of dawn in the oldest and youngest of spring traditions. We even managed a shower, although it took a little extra time because we took it together. Nonetheless, we successfully presented ourselves at the restaurant at seven sharp. Bob had staked out the big table for us, but there was no sign of the others.

"Where is everybody?" Liz asked, as she sat down in the booth.

"Busy already," Bob said. "Stacy's taking money from the folks that arrived in the night. Kelly's making sure the first set of speakers are all present, vertical, and coherently verbal, sober or not. Hank's probably with Gerry and his old circle. The vendor hall doesn't open until nine, so I've got another hour before I have to start rounding up the troops to keep the vendors deliriously happy. They're already pretty pleased. We've had an amazing turnout."

I slid into the booth next to Liz. "A lot more than we planned for? Are we going to run short of stuff?"

Bob shrugged, sipping his coffee. "We've made a couple of store runs, but the cash box has allowed for that. Preregistrations and last night's receipts covered what we needed for known expenses, and it's only Saturday. As long as we don't get stupid, we should do fine."

We ordered breakfast and sat in silence a while, enjoying the early morning quiet.

"Would the cost of helping set up a wedding be considered stupid?" I ventured.

"That depends on what we're paying for," Bob shrugged. "As far as the hall goes, we're already paying for the ballroom, the demo room, and most of the seminar suites for the weekend. If you start talking about catering, etc., that could easily wipe out any extra we've made and then some, but we could go around to the grocery store and pick up a few trays of cold sandwiches without breaking the bank, if that would do. As far as the other stuff—photographer, the tuxes, the cake—no way we could do that. There's no time anyway."

"As far as I know," I said, "we only have to find a space. It would be nice if we could find them some wedding guests to go with it. It'll happen on Sunday afternoon as things are starting to wrap up. How many people do you think would stick around for it?"

"If you made a full ritual of it, just about everybody. I don't think too many people have seen a pagan handfasting done like that. You know," Bob grinned, "high church. Usually it's dumbed-down for the outside guests. You don't want some drunk guy screaming, 'She's got a knife!' in the middle of everything," he snickered.

I nodded. "I'll need to go talk to Gerry's circle, find out what they want, and what they've set up."

"Sounds like you're going to make the one thing that wasn't on the program the highest point of the conference." Bob regarded me meaningfully.

I sighed. "Yeah, what do you think? Blessing or distraction?"

"A wedding can be an awful lot of work. We're still learning how to do a conference. I'd say, if they've got everything else set to go, we might pull it off. If not..." he shrugged.

The waitress arrived with our breakfast. I stared at my plate. *Here it is - the first thing I'm actually trying to organize and it might not happen at all.* I sighed and felt Liz's hand clasp itself over mine. I raised my head to her smile of encouragement. The crisp light of the morning sun flooded the restaurant and glinted off my fork. I picked it up, smiled back at Liz, and started eating.

After a few minutes communing with my eggs, I said "I'm glad you're working the logistics, Bob. You're very good at it."

Bob shrugged. "You can't manage a restaurant without being able to handle the things that come up." He speared a home fry. "A lot of that comes down to knowing what you've got and who you've got and what they're doing. There's a flow. If you pay attention and ride it, you can move with it, and it moves with you when you need it to. It's kind of like the smoke exercise."

"Smoke exercise?" I asked.

"Yeah, you light incense and watch the smoke, ride the smoke, move with the smoke in your mind, and then, without shifting focus, you give it a little mental nudge, see if it starts to move with you. It helps build your ability to connect with things magically. Clouds work, too." Bob turned his attention to his eggs.

"Huh. I never tried that one." I buttered my toast.

"It's kind of interesting. When it starts working the first few times, you get weirded out, and things fall apart, so you have to start over. As much as anything, it's about believing the magic that's in you enough to use it and accept it. By the way, these eggs aren't bad."

"So basically, you're using the same magic in the kitchen," I stated.

Bob grinned, "Near midnight on a Saturday, when the doors are locked and we're cleaning up, if the cooks and the wait staff are still friends and they aren't both ready to kill me, *that's* mighty magic, and a blessing from the gods of hearth and orchard."

I thought about my own work and smiled. *The best lines of code are the ones I was able to avoid needing to write.* "After I finish my meal, I'd better go find Gerry and see if there's anything to set up."

I tracked down Hank's old circle in the corner of the vendor room, talking to one another.

"Hi, Hank," I said, "so who's the lucky couple?"

"Oh, hi, Colin—boys, this is my High Priest, Colin. He's married to Liz." His voice rose on the last syllable of each sentence, his hand gestures more accentuated.

Good Lord and Lady, he's flaming it!

They all said "Hi" and I smiled back. Finally, a short, stocky blond guy with a moustache and chest hair pouring out of his floral shirt said, "I'm Jim, and this is Toby." The man who stepped up beside him and laid a hand on his shoulder was tall and slim, with short dark hair, dressed in a silk smoking jacket, casual slacks, and loafers.

It's like Magnum and Higgins swapped body shapes. I stifled a smirk.

Jim looked up at Toby, adoration in his eyes. Toby looked down fondly at Jim.

"Umm, so…" I paused, collecting my thoughts. "You came up here with a handfasting in mind. Did you do any preparations? Blood tests? Licensing? Catering? Tuxes? Photographer?"

"No," Toby said, "we weren't sure whether the conference would allow it. We thought we'd do the religious ceremony here, maybe collect cell phone pics, and then do the legal stuff after."

I turned to Gerry. "Did you have a ritual prepared?"

"Well, actually, no. We were so busy just getting everybody up here."

"Any family coming?"

"My dad ran off when I was little," Jim said, "and Mom's heart gave out when I was in college. Toby's got family, but—"

"I wouldn't know where to find my dad." Toby's voice was defensive. "He's on the road all the time. He used to call my mom, let her know where he is. Now he just sort of shows up between trips. They still sleep in the same bed but they don't talk much, and Dad and me, we can't talk about anything. We fight. I'd call Mom, and she'd show up. Dad wouldn't."

I cast my eyes around the room, the vendors getting ready

for the day, the attendees already shuffling to the eight AM lectures, Kelly running around making sure the speakers found the right room, equipped with water and whatever else they needed.

I turned back to Gerry. "You don't have anything ready, and it's taking most of our energy to run this conference. We could find you a room and leave you to it, but I'm feeling all kinds of uneasy about this. It feels rushed. You guys know all the magic that goes into a handfasting, braiding the love of family, friends, and circle into a knot to bind two souls together. It's an energy that Liz and I draw on."

Toby turned to Jim and clung to him. Jim, engulfed in the man's form, stroked his back.

My mind flailed around for something to make it better. "Toby, your mom - you said she'd show up if you called. Wouldn't she like to do more than show up?"

He turned in Jim's arms and sighed, "But then she'd be more aware that Dad wasn't there, that he was never there, and she'd hurt."

"Would she hurt more if you rejected her, too?"

"I'd never—" he yelped, and then his eyes widened, and a tear ran down his cheek. "Sweet Goddess…"

"And I imagine you both also have friends who aren't in circle who would want to weave their love into this event, too."

Jim and Toby both nodded solemnly.

"But your father is the lynch pin of it all."

"Good luck on that," Toby sniped.

I asked Gerry, "Have you guys ever done a circle for Toby's dad? I'll bet if you asked, the Lord and Lady wouldn't mind hogtying him, throwing him in the back of a pickup, and dumping him back home for a spell."

Toby fought back a soggy giggle.

Gerry nodded, "It's worth a try."

"Toby, I'm not trying to bring you down, but this is one of the highest rituals of pagan life. Don't run away and do this in a corner. You guys do Faerie Wicca. Before you give up, bring the magic of the Sidhe to bear, and give it a little time to see what happens."

I was startled to see that conversation in the room had

stopped and the vendors and the staff were all standing around us, tables unattended.

The crystal vendor cleared her throat. "Mom and Dad weren't happy I married another woman. They showed up at the wedding, but it took them a long time to get used to the idea. When Nikki and I were first starting the shop, Nikki lost her day job, all my money was tied up with the business, and we found we couldn't afford our apartment. We knew it was going to be all kinds of awkward, but we had to ask my folks if we could move in for a few months until we could get back on our feet. We had nowhere else to go.

"What they did surprised us. They went out and bought us a king-sized bed that filled my old bedroom, and our first night back home, they decorated the room with flowers and lit candles around the bed. They left all my stuff from when I was a kid in place. It was like they were inviting us together into the whole of my life back to its beginning. Even with all the stress we were under, that simple act of welcome was like we were newlyweds again.

"Now Nikki and my dad are good friends; they go fishing together sometimes. Mom and I go shopping, and we have dinner together on Sunday nights." Her lip quivered. "If you've got any chance of weaving your folks into this, do it. And Nikki and I will be really pissed if we aren't invited." She turned and walked back toward her table. The gathering dispersed.

Gerry surprised me by enfolding me in a bone-crushing hug. "Lord and Lady," he murmured, "the power was in front of me all this time. All I had to do was reach out and believe in what's possible. That's what a High Priest does."

Jim regarded me silently for a moment, a wall of muscle tense on his compact frame. Slowly, he stepped forward, his face stoic, not breaking our gaze. I tensed a little, not sure if he was going to hit me, but his eyes never wavered. "Until this moment," he growled, "I never realized until now how much I wanted to have a real family." His face was still stoic, but his voice was ragged. "I'm going to make sure this thing happens." He kissed me gently on the cheek. "Thank you."

I sighed with relief. "For a moment, I thought you were going to slug me."

He barked a laugh, "I'm not the one you need to worry about. Toby thought he was coming north to get married. When you head home, before you unlock your car door, you might check for explosives."

"We should go, Jim. We'll miss the lectures." Toby let Jim lead him away. Gerry nodded to me and followed.

Dear Lord and Lady, I wish I could do something to make this easier for Toby.

Hank squeezed my shoulder. "I had a good talk with Jim last night. Toby's mom, she's faced a lot of hurt. Toby feels so helpless that he tries to keep it all at arm's length, but he's hurting, too. He may hate your guts today, but you've just became one of his mom's favorite people. You did good."

I swallowed and hugged him, burying my face in his neck, my heart pounding as I was flooded with the enormity of what I had just had the gall to do. *And with somebody else's circle.* At the thought, I could barely breathe. "Thanks," I gasped.

Hank stroked my back, reassurance flowing into me, until I was breathing normally again. I straightened up, still in his arms. He bit his lip and, eyes worried, he kissed me. I wrapped a hand behind his head to continue the kiss. His body sagged with relief and then rallied with enthusiasm as the kiss lingered. Finally, we stood there, poised on a moment in the fluorescent lighting of the room, enjoying each other's faces, the warmth of our arms, the fire in our hearts, our eyes glimmering with unshed moisture.

"We should go." Hank's voice was hoarse.

I nodded, breaking away, but we left the room holding hands.

*

The morning went well. Actually, it went almost scary well. Droves of people milled around. A few circles chose to change into ritual garb within the convention, but most were in street clothes. Some walked around with gym bags. *Have robe, will travel.* There were no impromptu circles in public places and there were no heated confrontations over theological differences, but then the bar hadn't opened yet.

Bob kept a careful eye in the vendor room, observed one or two people shoplifting and quietly took down their convention badge numbers and names. I stood in for him as he disappeared periodically, often returning with pilfered items that he placed back on the tables of the grateful vendors. Having eyes everywhere at once is *hard,* and Bob was good at it. I'm not sure I was—I only managed to take down one person's name—but Bob said "Don't worry about it. These things run in waves."

Kelly would come in periodically to remind the shoppers when the next set of talks were starting. I finally caught up with her around the middle of the first afternoon session outside the panel discussion room.

"How's Melinda doing?"

"Brilliant as always," Kelly sighed happily. "Liz is blessed to have studied under her. We lucked out on a lot of the other speakers, too. A lot of substance, but within reach even for the kids starting out. Not a lot of 'fluffy magic,' but the real deal. If the groups here listen, we should have some really solid covens working in the area. I asked Melinda if she could stay afterward and do a workshop with us, but she's really busy with her circle on the west coast. We're going to try to schedule something in the summer. Of course, I'll have to pass it by Liz," she paused. "And you, of course."

I glanced up the hallway. It was empty except for the muffled drone of voices in two lectures and a lively round table discussion in the adjacent room.

I slid down the wall to sit on the floor and Kelly sat down next to me. "My arrival must have taken a lot of getting used to."

Kelly eyed me a moment and looked away, "You could say that."

I took a deep breath. "How did it play out? I mean, for you?"

"You mean for me and Liz?" Kelly sighed and stared at the wall. "Liz and I were living together. I remember it was a summer weekend, a Saturday, sitting up on our deck in our cutoffs and nothing else, enjoying the breeze. The hanging plants at our place gave a little shade and privacy. I was thinking maybe we'd slip between the sheets for a bit, when she mentioned that she'd met this guy. He didn't know much about the pagan life, but she kind of liked him and wanted us to meet him."

"Oh…" I trailed off.

"Yeah, it stung. We ended up in bed, but instead of a pleasant nuzzle on a lazy weekend afternoon, we held each other and cried our eyes out. It was kind of surreal, the breakup without the goodbye. She stayed with me off and on nights until the engagement. By then, I could see she shone ten times brighter when you were around, that what we had was good, but what you two have is better. It didn't help much. My arms still felt pretty empty."

"But you stayed with Danforth." I regarded her.

"Yeah, partly because I didn't want to leave Bob and Stacy and Hank. Liz is still my best friend, even if she's with you now. I try not to think about that part. It makes me a little crazy, and then I'm not sure how I'm supposed to kiss Liz anymore. The other part was that the circle really needed me. You were going to take a while to come up to speed, and I wasn't sure what was going to happen, if you were going to work out. I'm still not."

I grimaced and took my turn staring at the wall, "I haven't really been taking up my role. Worse, I really haven't bought into you all the way you've bought into each other. Those bonds—that's what makes a circle a circle. Melinda helped me see that. Last night was—well, it was amazing. I want our circle to be like that. I want my life with Liz to be a part of this amazing thing with you and Bob and Stacy and Hank."

"If you knew the half of it, you might not be so eager," Kelly looked at the ceiling and sighed.

"So clue me in anyway."

Kelly regarded me for a long moment before she answered. "It started one winter night after circle. I think it was Imbolc. We'd polished off one bottle of wine in circle and were enjoying a second bottle. We looked out the window and realized it was snowing—hard. Nobody wanted to bundle up and go anywhere, so we dug out sheets and blankets. We made a warm fire and curled up together in the blankets in front of the fire. We were still skyclad, and by this point we were drinking wine out of the bottle. Cuddled up in a pile of blankets with a bottle like that, everything seemed hilariously funny.

"Around the time the bottle ran out, we sort of fell asleep like a big pile of puppies. Somewhere in the night I reached for Liz and kissed her, only it wasn't Liz, it was Stacy. She kissed me back, but that woke Bob up so we both kissed Bob. Bob reached across me to kiss Hank, and before I knew it, we were all kissing and holding one another in the dark. Crawling around the hard floor was getting old, so Liz invited us to continue in our bed. One thing kind of led to another…"

I stared at her, wide-eyed. "So before I showed up, you were all going to bed together after circle?"

She shook her head and stared back at the ceiling. "Well, not the whole group, and not every time. That night kind of broke the ice, though, and we didn't mind falling through occasionally. If somebody needed company, they generally found some. If one of us wasn't ready, another would usually step forward, even if it was only for a cuddle."

"Then I came along and messed it all up," I grimaced.

"Yeah, maybe," she sighed and shrugged. "Like I said, it wasn't so often, but it was there."

I sighed, "Well, that explains a few things." I paused a while. "I'm not sure how to fix what I broke, except to be there and be willing to respond. It wouldn't be hard at all to respond to you or Stacy… or Hank, comes to that. Bob I don't know so well yet."

"I saw you and Hank coming out of the vendor room," she ventured.

"Yeah," I sighed. "It's something Liz and I have to talk over, how far we want to open ourselves to the people we love."

"Yeah, Liz and I had that same talk. Shit," Kelly's voice was a growl, "now I don't know how to kiss you either."

"Well, you could start with frequently," I grinned.

"Sounds like you're gunning for a threesome," Kelly smirked.

"It might happen," I shrugged, "but it takes attention enough to build one relationship like that. I can't imagine juggling that many. But love—there's plenty of room in both Liz and me to love."

Kelly scrambled to her feet. "You talk a good line, Colin. Stand up!" She faced me, hands extended.

I took her hands and she pulled me to my feet.

"You want frequently? It starts here. Deliver this message to Liz, verbatim." She wrapped her hands around the back of my neck and studied my face for a moment. Then she raised her lips and pressed them to mine, closing her eyes.

The pressure intensified. The stud in her tongue stroked along my lip. I opened my mouth in response, and she struck like a snake, thrusting around wildly. I chased her around with my own tongue, flicking at the stud before I entered her mouth in return. Mouths stretched wide, I received her breath and returned it. We exchanged three long, slow breaths, then our jaws relaxed, a slow dance, lips curved in pleasure. Heart pounding, my arms stroked down her back. I touched the stud in her tongue with my own as she withdrew from me. Our lips closed, pressed, and released, and we stepped apart.

"You got all that?" Her voice was husky.

I nodded, blinking, out of breath, and folded her in a long hug, which she returned. I stroked her back and murmured in her ear, "I'll make sure she knows it's from you. I'd need to get a tongue stud of my own to do it full justice, though."

A laugh like an earthquake emanated from somewhere deep inside her as she returned the murmur. "I can recommend the guy who does my piercings. Liz may have a few suggestions for how to use it."

"I can also suggest a couple of other piercings that might be interesting," a familiar voice said.

I turned to discover Liz standing in front of us, her arms crossed, eyes twinkling in amusement as curious onlookers emerged from the conference rooms. "You missed a good panel discussion. You had a message for me?"

"I'll deliver it later. But first, I've got something of my own to say." I extended an arm to Liz, who wrapped her arms around both of us. Kelly stroked Liz's back. I looked into Kelly's questioning face and then Liz's, kissing each tenderly in turn, surprised by the intensity of my own feelings, and paused. Liz and Kelly eyed each other, took a slow breath, and kissed, tentatively at first, then fervently, carrying me in their embrace.

At the end, we leaned foreheads together and I asked Kelly "Better?" She nodded. "These are our arms, Kelly. You're welcome here. You will always be welcome here."

Liz nodded in affirmation. Her lips twitched, "And if the rumor mill went into gear, Colin, with you and Stacy, and started smoking with you and Hank, it's just caught fire with the three of us. By now, they'll have decided our whole circle is poly and that's our secret of success."

"All acts of love and pleasure," Kelly chuckled. "I'm willing to leave a few of those acts for you two to pursue alone together, but I'm no longer feeling left out."

Liz kissed her between the eyes as I kissed her the line of her chin under her ear. "Never," our soft voices in unison.

"I—um—I gotta go." Kelly stepped back from the embrace. "I need to ask the speakers how their sessions ran, what we can do better. Then I'd better tell the folks in the vendor hall that the last set of lectures will be starting soon."

Liz and I watched her go, and then turned toward each other. "How long were you watching?"

"Long enough to know that was a message for me. You can deliver it in full later. I guess Kelly told you about the rest of it?"

I nodded. "Does Melinda know?"

She shook her head, "No. I never told her. It's not what circles usually do, and sage advice was the last thing I wanted. It was getting a little complicated, and I was worried it would spin out of control, but it was good while it lasted, you know?"

I drew her into my arms, my lips pressed against her forehead.

"I'm not entirely sorry it stopped," she continued, holding me tight, her eyes closed, "but I do miss it sometimes. The freedom…"

I bit my lip. "If you feel the need some night after circle, we can invite someone to stay."

"You mean that?" she raised her head, searching my face. "Even Kelly?"

I nodded, "As long as we all enjoy the warmth of our love together."

"I suppose you'll find longings of your own, too…" her

tone had a slight edge.

"It could happen. Kissing Hank did some unexpected things inside me I wouldn't mind exploring and Stacy—"

"Stacy's just incredible. You and me and Stacy, especially with Bob, too…" her eyes went far away, but when they returned, they were serious. "Do you have any idea what you're setting in motion here?"

My heart pounded. "Not really, but if this is part of what makes us who we are together, it's probably not a bad thing, and if it isn't working, we can try something else."

"The scariest thing about you, Colin Thieroux, is the reckless way you trust me." Her eyes widened. "I could lose my way."

"If you do, take me with you, Elizabeth Russell. As long as we're lost together, I'm good with that. If we find some place where we like the view, we'll build a house there and light the hearth." I held her tight.

"We need to talk about this soon, but we've got a conference to run." Liz sighed, "Besides, it would help if I went in knowing what I want. I suppose I want lots of everything, but you can't build on that." She kissed me. "I'll see you later tonight." Her hand drifted out of mine and I watched, enjoying the grace in her stride as she submerged into the bustle of the con.

*

The rest of the afternoon flew by and the big ritual that evening was a huge success. Liz and I presided, and Liz, perhaps in a fit of mischief, had asked Gerry and Hazel from a fem-Wicca coven to help us lead. Did I mention she could be terrifyingly reckless sometimes? Surprisingly, after a tense few minutes, the balance of energies started to work. Hazel's yang blended smoothly with Gerry's yin as the priest and priestess roles reversed in our acolytes. Wine and cakes and blessing then flowed on to the banquet, where we all stuffed ourselves silly.

My job after the banquet was to keep an eye on the bar and make sure things stayed peaceable. I was surprised to see that Gerry and Hazel's covens had collectively commandeered one corner and were relaxing, laughing, and passing the wine around, comfortable being together, but it generally set the mood for the whole place, so there wasn't much for me to do. Mostly, I sat at a corner of the bar where I could nurse my one drink and watch the room. I did notice that Jim and Toby were absent, but they might have needed some time alone.

An older man in a business suit two seats down from me shook his head. "Used to be when you saw a bunch of guys and girls together, when there was touching going on, it was the guys touching the girls."

I shrugged, "Things change."

"Yeah," the guy gave a gruff laugh. "My son would fit in with that crowd."

"Your son's gay?" I asked.

"When I was their age, we had another word for it, but that's what he tells me."

I shrugged. "I'm sure he's heard that word. It probably didn't do anything for him."

"You aren't one of those…" he waved his hand, limp-wristed.

I tensed, "No, but I have friends who are."

He grunted and we stared in our glasses.

"How do you talk to someone like that?" he sighed.

I took a sip while I searched for an answer. Finally I said, "Depends what you want to say."

He stared at the bottles along the back of the bar. "What if I don't know?"

I shrugged again, "Then tell him that."

"I want to say a whole bunch of shit that doesn't fit together." He swirled the ice in his glass.

"You can tell him that, too." I nodded. "Maybe you pour the whole thing out on the table together, you can work together on it, like a jigsaw puzzle."

"He'll just get pissed at me." The man frowned.

"And you aren't pissed at him?"

He looked over at me. "Yeah, you've got a point. We end up shouting at each other."

"You don't want to be pissed, but you are anyway."

"Something like that." He nodded.

I held his gaze. "So you've got something in common. You're both pissed. You're probably both disappointed in each other. Maybe scared to death. Doesn't have to stay that way."

His eyes narrowed. "You a preacher or something?"

I stifled a smile. "Something like that. The big thing is—don't turn away. Handcuff yourselves to the table if you have to, but don't shut him out. He's your son."

"Hmm," he paused. "The last I spoke to him, he was talking about getting married."

I nodded, "You gonna be there to give him away?"

The man laughed, "Father of the bride?"

"Something like that." I shrugged and sipped my drink. "Just depends if you want to be part of his life afterward."

"I wouldn't mind being a part of his life now." He took a long draw from his glass.

I smiled sadly. "Be sure to tell him that. He may not know."

He stared at me. "What denomination are you, anyway?"

I chuckled, "I'm a witch."

The man sighed, "He's into that stuff, too." He set his drink aside. "Name's Gordon, by the way."

"Colin."

We shook hands, then sat some more. I nursed my drink while Gordon got a refill. A group, still in robes, was making a racket down the other end of the bar, but it was a happy racket, so I let it be. Jim came in alone, saw me, and headed toward the bar.

"How's it going?" Jim took the seat between me and Gordon.

"Not too bad. Jim, this is Gordon."

"Jim," Gordon nodded.

After Jim ordered, I asked him, "You know, Jim, I never asked you what you did for work."

"Huh? Oh, I own Jim's Pool and Spa."

"It pay?" Gordon asked.

"Not bad. It keeps the wolf from the door. How 'bout you?"

"I sell telephone systems," Gordon said, sitting straighter.

"You like it?" Jim asked.

"Yeah, or at least I did. I get to visit with people, listen, find out what they want, sell them something that'll do all that and more. Keep 'em happy and they buy more. Everybody wins."

Jim nodded. "The key thing is the product." He emphasized every word.

Gordon leaned in, "You got that right. You can't sell a product if there's nothing to buy. If it turns to crap, you're going to have to work hard on that relationship or you can kiss that customer goodbye."

"Yeah, we had a run of hot tubs that were like that my first year." Jim shook his head. "After a few months, they kept developing cracks. Turns out the company never tested them out anywhere but southern California and the temperature gradients up north did bad things to the material. Nearly ran me out of business. I spent a full year winning back customers but we made good on every last one of them, and now they're some of my most loyal folks."

"Yeah, that's what it takes." Gordon gestured with his drink. "I've rescued a few of those situations. Some salesmen just don't pay attention. You use outside contractors for installation?"

Jim shook his head. "I tried that, but I finally decided it made more sense to train our own people and put them in ourselves. If something goes wrong, we're the ones who are going to have to be there anyway."

"Not so different from telephones, only we don't have much choice." Gordon grimaced, "Some of the things they pull to save a buck…"

"Yeah, tell me about it," Jim said with feeling. "And they bring their 'shortcuts' with 'em wherever they go. You gotta be careful who you hire."

"So you out here on a sale, Gordon?" I asked.

"No," Gordon sighed. "Company's calling me back to headquarters. Wants me to train a bunch of young guys how it's done. Oversee them for a year before I go out again. At least that's what they say. I got a bad feeling once those guys are on their feet, they'll offer me early retirement before they send me anywhere." Gordon took another swallow.

"And that's where the 'at least I did' comes from." I added.

Gordon raised his glass ironically, "Here's to progress. I've seen it happen before. Not where I work, but you know, you hear things."

"That's why I like owning my own place," Jim said. "At least that way, I can ensure it's got a soul."

Gordon sighed, "It's easy to say that when times are good."

"I'd lose it all before I started pulling dirty tricks like some of those contractors," Jim's voice was fierce. "Besides, the gods' would come down on me like a ton of bricks if I did. I made oaths and the gods don't forget."

Gordon grunted, "I guess religion keeps you honest."

"So where do you live? California?" Jim asked.

"Not that far south of here, actually. Maybe a two-hour drive? My flight came in barely in time for rush hour. I looked at three or four hours in traffic and I figured, what the hell. One last night on the road and the company will pay for it." He looked dismally into his now empty glass, "maybe the last time. Truth is, I've spent so much of my life in hotels, they feel more like home than home. There's a rhythm to them. At home, everything just kind of stays put."

"You married?" I asked.

"I suppose so. Past few years, I've almost been afraid to call from the road and have her tell me she's leaving. I figure if we don't talk, at least she can't say goodbye." He smiled ruefully. "If I were married to someone like me, it would have been over long ago. Of course, I make sure she never lacks anything, but I know that doesn't count for much. Still, I show up and she's still there, I got something to be thankful for."

Jim looked at me with dawning understanding as Gordon continued, "Now I'll be home for a while, so I guess I'll lose that, too."

I shifted in my seat, "Oh, I don't know. Why don't you go on a sales call instead?"

Gordon and Jim both looked at me puzzled.

"You're giving sales training." I turned to face Gordon across Jim. "Treat me like I'm one of your students. What's the most important skill in sales?"

"Listening." Gordon warmed to his subject. "Listening for what the customer is looking for. Then work like hell to make sure they find it in your product."

"What's the first thing you do on a sales call?" I continued.

"Figure out everything you already know about the customer. Get it in your head that half of it is probably wrong."

"Good start. Then what?"

"Well, you call ahead for an appointment at a time that's convenient for the customer, when they'll have plenty of time to talk to you."

Jim watched the two of us like a spectator at a tennis match.

"And when you get there?"

"You ask some questions and you listen to the answers. If you hear a lot of crap about your product, you don't argue. I mean, they're mad for a reason. So, you note down the kind of things the customer isn't getting from the product, things you can work on, then you research it."

I nodded. "Okay. What do you do next?"

"Well, you decide some things you can offer them right away, things that'll keep them from getting on the phone to the competition, and you suggest some things you can do longer term. Oh, and if possible, you do it all over food. People are always less upset over a plate of cacciatore." He leaned back.

I spread my hands. "So, tomorrow, prepare for going home like you were going on-premises for a sales call. Your customer is familiar with the product, worked pretty closely with it, if your son is any evidence, and you can't fault the customer's loyalty. Sounds to me like this is one you've got to win back from the edge, though. In-house, you could work the relation-ship for, oh, several years or so, while you work on the service and support side of things. It isn't like it's anything you don't know how to do. Hell, you've trained your whole life for this one sale. Next to this one, that training gig at the company's going to be a side job and, like Jim says, there's a certain satisfaction in working for yourself."

Gordon stared at me and Jim for several long moments, and then his face transformed into a reflective smile. "Bartender, buy the reverend whatever he wants. Put it on my room charge." He handed Jim a business card. "You got one?"

Jim pulled a card out of his pocket and handed it to Gordon. Gordon looked at it, "Hey that's not far from me." He looked into space. "A hot tub or a spa might not be a bad sweetener down the line, sized for two." He grinned at Jim, tapping his card. "Not right away, but, hey, we might be doing business soon."

Gordon slipped out of his seat. "I'd better be turning in. Tomorrow's going to be a busy day, and I've gotta be up early writing notes. Nice meeting you both." He shook both our hands and turned toward the exit.

"Don't forget to believe in the product," I said to his retreating back.

"I'm writing the advertising copy already," he called over his shoulder as he moved, " 'One bonehead, high mileage but a true classic, proven durable. In consideration for long customer loyalty, all upgrades and maintenance are free.' Hey, I'm the deal of the century." He strode away, chuckling.

Jim waited until Gordon was gone and then tapped the card, "That's Toby's dad."

I grinned. "Yep. I figured that out. The gods have been busy tonight, haven't they?"

"They sure came through fast." Jim shook his head. "Hazel and Gerry mixed that particular supplication into tonight's ceremony. Figured all the energy would give it a boost."

"I suspect a few of the Goddesses were already working together on this. They don't like to see their daughter unhappy. Sometimes we draw down the moon when it's already in descent. They've definitely already got him tied up and into the bed of the pickup, and his boss supplied the rope. All that remains is to see what happens when he lands on the doorstep."

"Toby doesn't know he's here. You think I should tell him?"

I sighed. "That's up to you, but it might be more interesting to wait and see what happens. It'll take a lot to make sure Toby doesn't blow everything with the first words out of his mouth, but at least this way, he won't spend all night preparing the grenades he's going to lob. I'm sure you two have much better things to do, like thanking the gods for their bounty."

Jim grinned, "Point taken."

*

By the time I crawled up to our room, it was after midnight. Liz was still up, sitting in one of the chairs, staring at the bed, naked to the waist.

"I had a visit from Kelly tonight," she stated.

"Yeah…" I ventured tentatively.

"She asked if I put you up to what happened this afternoon so I could be with her again."

"Oh." My voice fell.

"In a few short minutes, you sure managed to stir up a whole lot of old business. She wanted to go to bed with me before you got back." She swallowed.

"I screwed up, didn't I?" I sighed, sinking to the edge of the bed.

Liz shook her head, "Don't throw yourself under the bus yet, Colin. Kelly's realized that she was staying in the group to be ready to catch me and the group when you fail. She's pretty sure now that you're not going to fail, that you and I may very well be the constant center, like she and I were, so she doesn't know what to do."

"She's welcome to try things until something works." I looked up at her hopefully.

"I think that's what she was doing tonight." Liz sighed. "Actually, I think you got her unstuck. She won't be coming to circle for a while, not until she's found someone she can go home with."

I stared at the floor. "I kept hearing that yearning in people's voices for the way things were. I wanted to bring back the old magic."

Liz got up and sat next to me on the bed, her arm around me. "Colin, when you came, you brought magic with you, new magic, focus magic. I think, since we brought you in, Stacy and Bob have been spending nights together, off and on. When Gerry comes in, Hank is going to be over the moon, and they're likely to share an apartment. Kelly had the most to lose and she's finally ready to move on. We're growing into a circle of couples—if we let it happen."

"So that winter and the following year…?"

"…was a good season to have enjoyed together, but times change, Colin." Liz paused. "I thought about you joining me and Kelly in bed tonight to see what happens. I realized I'd be jealous, but I couldn't figure out who I was jealous of. I wanted you both, but I wanted each of you for myself, Kelly for what we had, and you for what we have. The thought of you and Kelly making love in my arms, I just—couldn't."

She sighed. "With Kelly and Bob, it was a beautiful riot. Kelly and I had made love and my whole body was tingling. We were all slick with sweat and I had both of them in the V of my legs. My face was buried in their hair, bathing in their scents, arms cradling them both as they clung to each other, all bruising kisses and bites, and then they started, pounding away, shifting their hips to carry me into their rhythm. It blended into all that afterglow, it was wonderful, and it will always be my favorite memory of those days. But that was with Kelly and Bob, not with you. Sharing was okay then. Now—I want you, only you, and all of you."

I wrapped her in my arms and we kissed.

I stroked her cheek, "So did you…"

Liz laughed sadly, "Once I knew she was saying goodbye, we tried, starting in this chair, but by the time we got our tops off, we could both tell it wasn't going to work. We knew where to find and give each other pleasure. We could have done it but the fire was gone. It would have been hollow, and we didn't want hollowness to be our last memory of each other as lovers. She did, however, stay long enough to leave you a message."

I looked up. "I hope it doesn't involve bleeding or a sharp pain in the groin."

Liz laughed and kissed me on the nose, "No, the message was intended to offer a catalog of activities that would improve immensely with a variety of piercings."

I grinned, "I'll be sure to read it carefully, then."

Liz's face grew serious. "Only after you've delivered her message to me—and any messages of your own."

I pulled her into my arms and we stretched out on the bed, our lips locked in a long kiss. She slowly unbuttoned my shirt and then she tucked her head under my chin with her ear against my heartbeat as we unbuttoned each other's jeans, pacing ourselves, letting the sweet tension build.

*

When Liz and I came down for breakfast, Gordon was at a corner table with a yellow pad, probably enumerating everything he knew about his wife, Toby's mom, and everything he could offer her. Occasionally his lip would tremble and he'd have another sip of coffee. As I headed to the nine o'clock session, I saw him standing outside the lobby doors, head down, cell phone at his ear, his breath puffing in the morning air, occasionally taking a swipe at his eyes.

I found Toby standing next to me, stock still, staring. "That's—"

I gave him a hug. "Yeah. It is."

Toby jutted his chin, his voice gathering steam. "Was he spying on me? I should give him a piece of my mind."

I shook my head. "It'd be a shame if you did that. It would spoil the moment."

"What moment?" Toby demanded. "What's he doing here?"

"At the moment, he's talking to your mom. Correction. He's listening."

"I don't get it." Confused, Toby shook his head.

I smiled gently. "No, you don't. You want to do yourself and your parents a big favor?"

"Uh, sure."

I kept my voice even. "Don't assume you know everything, and be patient with your resentments. Your dad is trying to do something very difficult."

"What's he selling this time?" Toby smirked.

"Himself. To your mom. If she'll buy. And to you, if you'll let him. But in your case, he doesn't know the market and he's scared shitless."

Toby rolled his eyes. "I show up with Jim and he'll be hollering at the top of his lungs for us to get out."

I smiled. "Don't be too sure of that. He likes Jim."

"He met Jim?" Toby stared at me.

"They shared a drink last night at the bar, talked about business, exchanged cards. He might even buy a hot tub down the line."

"For what?" His voice rose.

"For him and your mom."

Toby stared out the door as his father closed the phone and walked to his car. "Huh."

I squeezed his shoulder. "Leave your dad room to grow, Toby. Today could be the dawn of spring—if you don't trample the garden."

Toby stood watching his father drive away. "If Dad'll speak to me and Jim like we aren't circus freaks, you and Liz are marrying us."

"Would you settle for being *his* circus freaks, at least at first?"

"Yeah," Toby's voice grew soft, "I'll settle for being his anything."

*

Stacy sat at the table in the foyer with the cashbox, counting the piles of bills, while Bob recorded the counts and did the totals. Liz and Kelly and I smiled and thanked what seemed like hundreds of people for coming to the convention, with a "Blessed Be" and a hug for each one. Stacy had told me we had twelve full circles and maybe fifty solitaires. From where we stood, I could see Gerry's circle and Hazel's by the lobby door, saying their goodbyes.

Gerry turned and came toward us. "So, I'll be going soon. I think I may be staying with my circle a little longer than I thought. Jim and Toby are going to need some time to get settled before they take over. They aren't saying anything, except that something's happening with Toby's family, and they want a little time with that first. They asked if I would be put out if you two led their handfasting ritual. I wanted to let you know in person that I'm very good with that, and thank you. It's time I grew into this priesthood thing."

I gave him a hug, "Yeah, me, too. Blessed be, Gerry, and stay in touch. Our circles may have a chance to do some work together from time to time. We throw one heck of a Yule party, and let Hazel's crew know they're invited, too."

He grinned, "Yeah, I'll do that. The guys are talking about working together with them on a ceremony the night before this year's Pride March. We'll make sure you get an invite."

"You'll still be up to visit?" Hank's voice carried an edge.

"Any weekend we don't have circle," Gerry nodded, his eyes warm.

Hank swallowed and mumbled, "You'll always have somewhere you can stay."

"That's kind of why I'm visiting," Gerry's voice was muted, but his eyes were steady. "As long as I'm welcome."

Hank wrapped Gerry in a fierce hug and kissed him. "Always and forever," he breathed.

As Gerry walked away, Liz squeezed my shoulder. "Faery Wicca boy scouts and Who-needs-a-god-when-we've-got-a-perfectly-good-goddess feminazis partying together? That's supposed to be impossible in nature, you know."

I shrugged, "Yin and Yang find harmony however they're proportioned, if they aren't crowding each other out."

Liz put her arm around me, laid her head on my shoulder, and sighed, "Who is this hunky priest, and what did he do with my husband?"

"I think I'm growing out of me," I sighed contentedly.

Melinda came around the corner, dragging her suitcase behind her, purse clutched in her hand. "Well, I'm off. I want to get to the airport in plenty of time. It's been a good visit, Liz. You've all done very well. And you" she turned to me, "I've been hearing very good things about you, as well as scandalous things. Are they true?"

"Probably. Which ones?" I beamed.

She laughed. "The trick is to concern yourself with what you're doing, and let your reputation take care of itself. Even a bad reputation makes people curious, and that's not such a bad thing."

"Thanks to you, this weekend, I think I've made a pretty good start." I squeezed both her hands.

Kelly smirked. "He's one hell of a kisser, too."

Everyone laughed.

"Just remember what I told you about grandmothers," Melinda admonished.

"Oh, believe me, we're already working on that matter," Liz said.

I looked at Liz in surprise.

She shrugged, "In the heat of heading up here, I kind of forgot to pack my pills. And then, well, you turned into this sexy priest…"

"So we could have…"

"Yeah," she grinned, "it kind of adds a new dimension to it all, doesn't it? Maybe it's the season, but if it's okay with you, I think I'll forget where I put those pills for a while."

I stared at her, dazed. I think I may have had a foolish grin on my face. The only functioning corner of my psyche bobbed my head up and down as I surveyed the beautiful woman who had just told me she was ready to be the mother of my children.

"Well, I'll leave you kids to it," Melinda chuckled. "If you're ever near San Diego, you know where to find me."

"I may be headed out there," Kelly blurted out.

We all turned and looked at her.

"Half of my work is remote with the San Diego office anyway, and my boss has been hinting to me about the virtues of southern California all winter. I think the Goddess has been pushing me to take the transfer, but I've been resisting." She swallowed. "It's a little like being born. You want to stay where you are, but when it's time, it's time. This morning, I scheduled a phone meeting with Kathy, my boss, for tomorrow after-noon."

Melinda pulled a card out of her purse. "Give me a call when you arrive. You'll have a circle waiting. Gotta run, kids!"

Kelly took the card and said, "Thanks. Blessed be…" to Melinda's back as she walked away. She exchanged a startled glance with Liz and mouthed "Wow".

"You know we're going to give you one hell of a send-off," Bob's eyes twinkled.

"Count on it," Stacy added.

I nodded.

"It's going to be a par-ty!" Hank grinned.

"And you two," Kelly turned to Liz and me, looking at us evenly, her eyes moist, but her heart steady behind them. "Thank you both for everything." She reached an arm around each of our necks and kissed first Liz and then me, her lips tender and lingering. "I'm ready for a new start. Make me an auntie, and I'll be on the next plane. If the Goddess blesses me,

Ralph Mack

I'll arrive with company, but I may give that whole thing a rest for a bit. I don't know. I haven't been on a date for a long, long time, but the idea doesn't sound unattractive anymore." She gave us a small smile. "I should give the conference rooms one last check before I go."

"Why don't we go do that together," Stacy said. "I've been stuck behind this cash box the whole weekend."

Kelly nodded and the two women walked down the hall, Kelly's arm over Stacy's shoulders, Stacy stroking Kelly's back.

I watched them go. "Looks like we'll be a tad down in numbers."

"I wouldn't count on that," Bob said. "There are a lot of solitaires in our area that have had a good look at us working together and are starting to think about the advantages of being part of a good circle. Our next full moon could be very crowded."

"Of course, half of them will leave when they find out they don't get to play tonsil-hockey with the hunky priest," Hank chuckled.

"Am I getting that kind of reputation among the women?" I groaned.

Hank gave me a saucy grin, "I wasn't talking about the women, sweet cheeks."

I laughed, "Come here, you!" and wrapped Hank in a hug, kissing the top of his head. Bob and Liz piled in and we stayed there for a while, enjoying each other's warmth.

A warm, southern drawl washed over us. "Now, see what happens, Kelly? We turn our backs and what do they do?"

Liz and Bob opened arms and gestured Stacy and Kelly into the middle with me and Hank.

I sighed, at home and complete, Colin Thieroux, High Priest of Danforth Blessing Circle, called by God and Goddess to serve the men and women I love, and how I love them all.

Ralph Mack writes and codes at his home in New Hampshire, with his wife, who knits, beads, and quilts, and his son, who cooks our meals, supervised by a gray cat with white paws, who mostly naps.

About the Editor

Karen Dales is an award winning, best selling author of *The Chosen Chronicles*, and is the Managing Editor for Dark Dragon Publishing. Her short fiction has been published in several anthologies. She has been an author guest at Fan Expo, Ad Astra, Polaris, and many other literary conventions.

She lives in Toronto, Ontario, Canada with her husband and son as human servants to five cats.

You can find her works at www.karendales.com or www.darkdragonpublishing.com

If you have enjoyed this anthology, please remember that reader reviews are beneficial to authors and editors. Please consider posting a review. A few kind words goes a long way.

CANADIAN DREADFUL

An Anthology

Edited by David Tocher

Available in paperback and ebook.

"CANADIAN DREADFUL showcases some of Canada's best voices in horror fiction. This anthology is a harrowing tour of the northern landscape that will leave you both dazzled and terrified."
~David Morrell, New York Times Best-Selling Author

In the pages of this anthology, you will not find the Canada you are accustomed to, nor a Canada that the world has grown to know and love. Between the covers, you will discover a dark landscape that will challenge your perspective. From sea to shining sea, stories of a darker Canada will arise, and within them all a kernel of truth. Stories of sacrifice, cannibalism, ghosts, and mystical forests, the authors will plunge you into the country that is Canadian Dreadful

www.amazon.com/Canadian-Dreadful-Anthology-David-Tocher/dp/1928104150/

THE CHOSEN CHRONICLES:

Changeling
Angel of Death
Shadow of Death
Thanatos

By
Karen Dales
www.karendales.com

"Dark… compelling… that will keep readers turning the pages
well past bedtime."
Kelley Armstrong,
New York Times Best Selling Author

"A dark and gripping tale by a true mistress of supernatural
fiction. Karen Dales brings fresh blood to the vampire genre."
Michelle Rowen,
National Best Selling Author.

"For readers who adore textured layers in their literary tapestries,
rich in colourful emotions, Karen Dales is one writer of vampire
fiction they'll want to read."
Nancy Kilpatrick,
Author: Power of the Blood
Editor: Evolve: Vampire Stories of the New Undead

"A fresh and intriguing new look at the
vampire mythos."
Violet Malan
The Novels of Dhulyn and Parno

Available in paperback and ebook
everywhere where books are sold.

www.amazon.com/Karen-Dales/e/B004TG6U1Y

Abandoned and left to die, alone in the forest, the Angel's life is transformed, evoking demons that demand more than he can give.

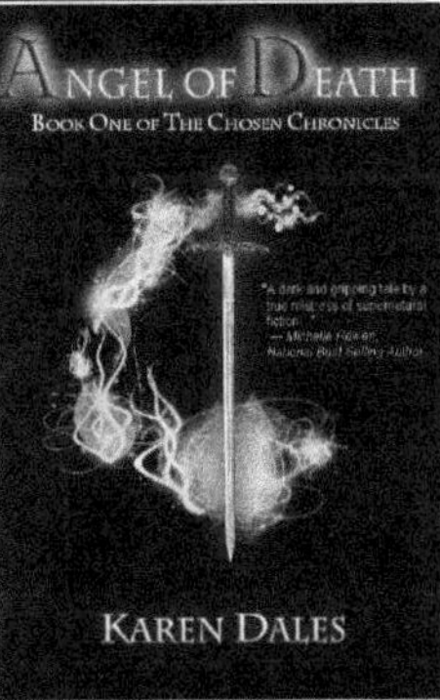

The Vampires of London are being murdered and only the Angel of Death can save them. Plagued by demons from his past, the Angel walks a fine line. Can he discover the culprits without the discovery of what he truly is and the destruction of one he loves.

Haunted by nightmares of his past misdeeds and failings, the Angel wants nothing more than to be left alone. It is across the Atlantic, in a foreign country, that he takes up the mantle once more as a protector in a land where those who would see him dead have flourished.

The Angel embarks upon a journey to the past to discover the truth about himself and his connection with the white faced demons. Through the quest, the Angel discovers a threat that endangers to topple his beliefs about himself and change the Chosen forever.

BOOKS

To see a full list of our amazing books,

please check our website:

www. darkdragonpublishing.com/books.html

All Books Available At The Following Retailers:

Amazon.ca
Amazon.com
Amazon.co.uk
Amazon.com.au
Barnes and Noble
Books A Million
Book Depository
Smashwords
Powell's Books